An Unplanned Encounter

Two Lives Forever Changed

JONATHAN R. HUSBAND

An Unplanned Encounter: Two Lives Forever Changed is a work of fiction; names,
characters, and the assembly of incidents are the products of the author's imagination
and while often based on true events, are used fictitiously in this novel. Any resemblance
to actual happenings and persons, living or dead, is entirely coincidental

ISBN: 978-1-4834-0807-1 (sc)
ISBN: 978-1-4834-0809-5 (hc)
ISBN: 978-1-4834-0808-8 (e)

Library of Congress Control Number: 2014901945

Lulu Publishing Services rev. date: 03/05/2014

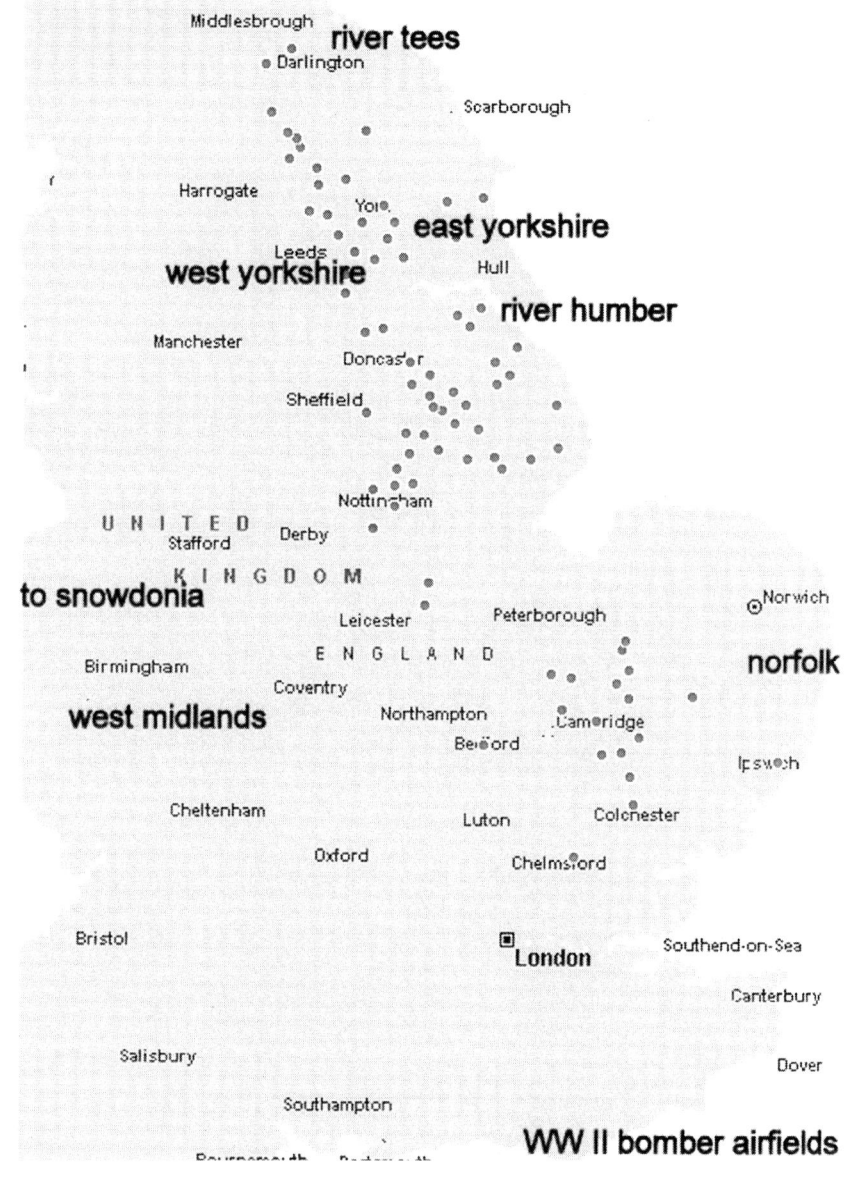

Middlesbrough
river tees
Darlington
Scarborough
Harrogate
York
east yorkshire
Leeds
west yorkshire
Hull
Manchester
river humber
Doncaster
Sheffield
Nottingham
Derby
UNITED
Stafford
to snowdonia
KINGDOM
Leicester
Peterborough
Norwich
ENGLAND
Birmingham
norfolk
Coventry
west midlands
Northampton
Cambridge
Bedford
Ipswich
Cheltenham
Luton
Colchester
Oxford
Chelmsford
Bristol
London
Southend-on-Sea
Canterbury
Salisbury
Dover
Southampton
Bournemouth
Portsmouth
WW II bomber airfields

To the memories of my Yorkshire-born mother, Florence Maud, and my Scottish-born wife, Mary Lynne, both of whom left this world within fifteen months of each other, beginning December 12, 2008.

I am also enormously grateful to several other women in my life who made this book possible. The encouragement given to me by my daughter, Louisa, and my daughter-in-law, Amber, are of particular note, as are the reviews and information provided to me by my loving half-sisters living in England, representing both sides of my family, Jane and Gill.

Special thanks go to Frances Gordon of Larkspur Library, Larkspur, California, and to Nancy Reich of Novato, California, who provided me with many improvements to my early manuscript. A special thank-you must surely be awarded to Linda Jay Geldens of Kentfield, California, a copyeditor possessing extraordinary talents when it came to reviewing my manuscript.

Also I will remain forever indebted to Elizabeth Peters of Kent, England, who during 2009 and 2010 helped me track down my missing father's family.

There remain too many others to name, both men and women, who have personally accompanied me through my life and who have helped me flourish and achieve my potential after a very uncertain start to my existence.

"A fascinating story, rich in historical detail and based on true events. Highly recommended for fans of historical fiction."

—Frances Gordon, Librarian, Larkspur, California

"A really moving and engrossing story. I didn't want to put the book down. The World War II background, while set in England, brought back memories of my childhood growing up in California."

—Dr Doris Jansen, writer and photographer, Novato, California.

"Plan to 'encounter' this book. The characters live with you long after the last page is turned, leaving you looking forward to Jonathan Husband's second novel."

—Donna F. Bookin, JD, assistant professor, School of Social and Behavioral Sciences, Mercy College, New York.

"As one who has lived in both England and Northern California, I found the descriptions of wartime Yorkshire and hippie San Francisco particularly compelling. From a medical perspective, the unregulated use of insulin with its predictable complications and the lack of paternity testing illustrate how far medical practice has advanced in recent years. A recommended read."

—William Mentzer, MD, professor emeritus of pediatrics, School of Medicine, UC–San Francisco

CHAPTER 1

THE ROYAL AIR Force air commodore sat at the wheel of his black Vauxhall 10 automobile as it cut through the dim morning light. The vehicle was seemingly eager to reach the eastern coastline of England and to travel on to Germany. The sun strained at the morning horizon as the car and driver traveled slowly eastward.

It was 5:30 a.m. in late July 1943. The air commodore was on an important mission to visit the last bomber airfield under construction in East Yorkshire; it was due to open well before Britain and its allies launched the invasion of Europe that would defeat Germany and bring World War II in Europe to an end.

The outline of the Yorkshire Wolds in Northern England lay ahead as the car and its driver made deliberate progress. To the left and the right was a flat landscape, the Vale of York, a rich agricultural area bounded by the Howardian Hills and Wolds to the east, the Pennines to the west, the Vale of Mowbray to the north, and the remnants of a former ice age, the Escrick moraine, to the south. This was a countryside in transformation.

Ever since the British Royal Air Force Expansion Plan of 1935, there had been continuous building of new military airfields in Britain. By the time World War II began on September 3, 1939, one hundred new airfields had been built or were in the process of being built in Britain. Bomber Command had access to thirty-three permanent airfields at the start of the war. By the closing months, it had access to more than sixty airfields, many of which had been built or were being built in Yorkshire or the county immediately to the south, Lincolnshire.

1

The 1935 Expansion Plan had anticipated a new war with Germany and emphasized the need to construct more airfields. To defend itself against an enemy with thirty-five fighter squadrons, England was to fight back with seventy bomber squadrons. The Air Ministry Aerodrome Board was established to select and inspect potential sites that were reasonably flat, free from obstructions, and between fifty to six hundred feet above sea level.

A requirement of each new bomber airfield was that its bombers should be close enough to be able to reach Berlin in a latitudinal straight line. This made the eastern English counties of Yorkshire and Lincolnshire the obvious locations for the construction of these new airfields. If a location was considered suitable, the land was requisitioned under the Emergency Powers Act of 1939. As a result of the plan and the selection criteria, by 1943 the lands around Yorkshire had become known as the aircraft carrier of England, fighting a war that was just waiting to be won.

The air commodore was on temporary assignment to the headquarters of the Royal Air Force Number Four Air Group, based near York, in the north of England. Number Four Air Group was part of the national Bomber Command that was organized into several groups to support the mission of winning command of the skies and then exploiting this command to win the war.

At the time, Britain regarded aerial bombardment of the enemy as a legitimate weapon of war, although it understood that this activity should be directed only at military targets. After the British retreat from Dunkirk in June 1940, Britain and its allies had no other way of hitting back at Germany other than by bombing it. The construction and increase in the number of airfields in England had taken on a much greater urgency.

Separate from Bomber Command was a Royal Air Force Fighter Command deploying Spitfires and Hurricanes to defend Britain against a German aerial attack. Also, a Coastal Command was responsible for reconnaissance, and a Ferry Command was responsible for all aspects of military logistical support, including the ferrying of aircraft from factories to operational units, general supply and medical evacuation services, the dropping of paratroopers, and, at the end of the war, the repatriation of prisoners. In 1943 the Ferry Command had been renamed the Royal Air Force Transport Command. During the war it ferried over nine thousand aircraft across the North Atlantic from US and Canadian factories.

Number Four Air Group had been given responsibility for a number of bomber airfields situated in the east and south of Yorkshire. The group had been reorganized in March 1943 to concentrate its responsibilities on approximately ten bomber airfields and a dozen bomber squadrons located in this part of Yorkshire. Construction at some of these airfields was still in progress.

The air commodore had been appointed to ensure that all new airfields as well as stations undergoing repair in Number Four Air Group became fully operational according to the group's timetable. Number Four Air Group had been flying since September 1939 when it had dispatched ten planes to drop leaflets in the Ruhr area of Germany, over Hamburg and Bremen. Its first land bombing mission had taken place in March 1940. Subsequently the group had grown significantly in terms of numbers of aircraft, and it had started to convert its armament from Armstrong Whitworth Whitley bombers to the Vickers Wellington medium and the Handley Page Halifax heavy bombers. It needed expanded facilities to improve its effectiveness.

That day, the air commodore intended to visit the one remaining airfield in Number Four Air Group that was not yet operational. As

3

a substation, it was grouped with three other substations under the administrative control of a parent airfield located a few miles away. The airfield was scheduled to open by year-end 1943, but there were rumors that its completion date might be delayed. There was a great deal of pressure to complete construction on time.

A nearby Royal Air Force bomber squadron was waiting to move to this new station so that its current facilities could be released to the French Air Force. However, there was no flexibility to move squadrons outside of the group's territory. Nationally, the Royal Canadian Air Force had already formed a new group under the coordination of Royal Air Force Bomber Command and was appropriating facilities elsewhere in Britain.

The United States Army Air Force (USAAF), known as the US Eighth Air Force in Northern Europe, was also being allocated airfield bases and newly constructed advanced landing grounds in preparation for the planned invasion of Europe. The USAAF had begun flying in August 1942 with limited aircraft power but had rapidly grown and was able to carry out its first raid on Germany during January 1943.

The air commodore was also contending with more local issues. Some Number Four Air Group airfields had been bombed by the Luftwaffe during the early months of the war, which reduced their capability to launch new attacks against Germany. This happened in late 1940 at an airfield only a few miles away from where the air commodore was now going. On that night in August, over 150 bomb hits were recorded with significant damage to hangars and other buildings. Twelve aircraft were destroyed, and a number of air force personnel were killed.

There had also been design problems with some airfields. For example, one bomber station had been built too close to a river. Its operations were hampered and made dangerous by almost nightly river-hugging mists that overflowed across the airfield. Efforts to switch to bomber pilot training had proven too dangerous, and now the facility was being transferred to Fighter Command.

As the air commodore's Vauxhall 10 automobile continued its journey, the persistent throb of its tiny engine announced its coming, as did the horizontal strips of light that were thrust from the slit masks covering its headlights. The side indicators were no longer emitting the color of orange peel, and the tail lamps were dimmed in response to the rules of the blackout. Fear of invasion had led to the implementation of blackout standards in September 1939, and while this fear had lessened in recent months as Germany focused on its Russian front, air raid patrol wardens and eagle-eyed neighbors were quick to report transgressions.

The Vauxhall came from a plant that was no longer manufacturing automobiles; production in the Luton factory, just north of London, had been switched to Churchill tanks in 1940. Fortunately, reliability had been engineered into this last generation of prewar vehicles. The hand-cranked engine was easy to start, the clutch purred immediately on engagement, and the gearshift was easy to pass through on flat country roads.

A bottle of whisky lay on the backseat, a gift for someone that the air commodore had yet to meet. The twenty-mile-an-hour speed limit, introduced in 1940 for safety and economic reasons, gave peace of mind that the bottle was unlikely to fall onto the floor during the trip. The air commodore daydreamed as he drove.

He reflected on the rumors that abounded about the preparation for the Allied invasion. No one said anything, but everyone believed that they knew everything about what was to come. The role of the Royal Air Force Bomber Command during the months before the invasion was considered essential for the invasion's success. Bomber Command needed to fly the maximum number of bombing raids to destroy the German military and support installations. It was now capable nationally of flying on average over one thousand aircraft daily, whereas at the start of the war this number was below three hundred. With the additional support of Canadian, Polish, Dutch, Belgian, Czech, Norwegian, Australian, New Zealand, and French squadrons, Bomber Command had grown into a formidable force. Delays in opening new airfields and repairing existing airfields were unacceptable to the higher-ups because they interfered with Bomber Command's flying capability and its reputation for success.

As a result of this increased emphasis on bombing strategy, airfield construction seemed to be taking place everywhere across the country. Often workmen had little idea of what they were doing and relied on local knowledge to understand the geography, soil, and drainage. The very farmers who only weeks earlier had received government letters requisitioning their land and buildings were now working the tractors and horses to tear down hedges and remove debris.

Farm buildings were bulldozed, and the rubble was used to level the land. Large trees were cut down and cleared by using only cross saws, and roots and trunks were splintered with explosives. Empathy for the environment had been replaced with energy for winning the war. Once the land had been cleared and the ponds dug out, it was time for the heavy equipment. The cranes, scrapers, concrete makers, and bulldozers arrived. It had become standard to construct three paved runways for each bomber airfield.

The importance of Britain's capability to conduct bombing raids had been recognized in late 1941, when the Air Ministry had switched its bombing priorities. Area bombing had been given first priority, replacing target bombing. Bomber Command was asked to attack German cities for their intrinsic industrial and psychological value on nights when conditions prevented the identification of the primary military target. The formal policy behind this change was published in February 1942, and a directive was issued targeting fifty-eight major German industrial cities. The words of Churchill conveyed the importance of this strategy: "The fighters are our salvation, but the bombers alone provide the means of victory."

The air commodore's daydreaming was abruptly ended when something dark and low flashed through the lines of light at the front of the Vauxhall but was gone before the air commodore could touch the brake pedal. It was a barn owl, known for its eerie, silent flight. Its heart-shaped pale cream-colored face, with two piercing black eyes, startled the driver back to reality.

The air commodore was driving along narrow lanes whose hedges reached toward each other across both sides of a single track road. The car also passed the occasional farm, its silhouette sharp across the sunrise. Signs of early-morning activity were welcomed noisily by cattle on their way to milking and by free-range hens that once more were experiencing the theft of their overnight egg production. Windows were darkened by blackout curtains; early-morning mist hid the grass, and the stillness of the air magnified the sound of sheep bleating in the nearby fields.

The driver had no idea of the places he was traveling through. He knew only the direction of the route to be taken. Most road signs were missing because of the invasion scare during the summer of 1940, and those that remained were typically tampered with by local villagers to point in the wrong direction. The occasional dark outline of a church would mark the site of an approaching village.

Typically clustered around common land, the names of these hamlets bore witness to past invaders from continental Europe. Included were the Romans, Anglo-Saxons, Vikings, Danes, and Normans. There was reason to wonder about the success of these past civilizations and their effect on the land—such as the Scandinavians, who left the name *howe* for hill, *borough* for stronghold, *thwaite* for clearing, *by* for village, and *thorpe* for a village of lesser importance. Mixed among these names were the earlier Anglo-Saxon words, such as *ton* or *tun* for farm, *ham* for homestead, and *beck* for stream. The word *Wold*, meaning forest or wooded country, is also Anglo-Saxon. By 1943 few trees were left, thanks to sheep grazing on the Wolds during previous centuries.

Once upon a time, Ancient Britons lived here in thatched huts, surrounded by earth defenses. Even the Normans had left their mark, with names such as *caster* for fort and *foss* for river. Although these names were everywhere, they were hidden when village signs were removed earlier during the war.

Nearby towns and villages with such names as Howe near Thirsk, Boroughbridge, Brackenthwaite, Selby, Allerthorpe, Malton, Yapham, Skirpenbeck, Easingwold, Tadcaster, and Wilberfoss would only emerge from their present anonymity once the war was over.

Soon the air commodore found himself driving northeast toward his destination. The sun by now was above the horizon. That change of direction relieved him of having to face the summertime glare. The car was climbing up a slight incline on a hill made of boulder clay left behind by a long-departed glacier. Eventually the climb flattened out, and both car and driver found themselves perched on the crest of a hill that looked down onto a very flat landscape.

In the distance, the outline of a village could be seen. Its lone church stood upright and silent. The ringing of church bells had been banned in mid-1940, with the directive that the bells should only be rung to call out the Home Guard as a signal that enemy troops were invading the country. During the summer of 1940 Britain stood alone, prepared to defend itself against the likelihood of German invasion. An exception to this rule had been made a few months earlier when, in November 1942, Britain celebrated the victory of the British Eighth Army at El Alamein.

Winston Churchill believed that this battle was the turning point in the war and ordered church bells to ring across Britain. As he later said, "Before Alamein, we never had a victory; after Alamein, we never had a defeat."

Between the Vauxhall automobile and the village lay the driver's destination. In front of him were the signs of an emerging airfield; construction had begun only months earlier. Already the layout of the three concrete runways and perimeter track was visible. Some of the dispersal pans to be used for scattering the bombers across the airfield to minimize damage from enemy attacks could also be seen.

Most of the buildings were taking shape. Nearest were the skeletons of two prefabricated hangars, and in the far distance bomb storage bunkers were being constructed. The layout for sleeping quarters and common eating areas and the construction of the control tower could also be seen. The driver sighed in relief and smiled. Progress, good progress, was being made.

The air commodore was visiting to talk to the planning director, a youthful-looking man called Jock McGregor, and his technical adviser, an American of Belgian extraction named Michael Fromm. The car and driver quickly descended the hill and arrived at the construction gate.

"Are you expecting me?" asked the air commodore.

"Certainly, sir," was the guard's speedy reply. "Please park in the paved area of the car park, and Mr. McGregor will meet you outside the contractors' canteen."

The air commodore parked the vehicle, collected the bottle of whisky from the backseat, and made his way up to the base of the control tower close to the canteen.

CHAPTER 2

I WAS DRIVING ON the same day in July 1943 to the same airfield that was to be visited by the air commodore. My name is Mary Louise. My journey had started earlier that same morning, because I live in West Yorkshire, almost seventy miles away. There were three purposes for my journey by car that morning. The first was to see my parents, who live close to the airfield under construction. They had moved to their new home two years earlier after losing their farmland because of the construction of another airfield some miles away. To add new sources of income, they had decided to take in lodgers from among the people who were assigned to build the nearby airfield.

My second purpose was to meet with the assistant canteen manager at the airfield to discuss the implications of recent rumors that the canteen would need to be kept operational weeks longer than planned. A few weeks earlier I had been appointed as manager for this canteen, in addition to the several much larger canteens that I managed in West Yorkshire.

The third purpose was to go dancing with my older sister and her boyfriend, a local farmer. Dancing was my most favorite pastime. I was excited at the thought of returning to the dance floor that night near my parents' home, yet felt tired and drained because of my work. The war also made me apprehensive, and distracted me and so many others from enjoying the good things in life. You never knew when something bad might happen, either to you or to a loved one.

I currently lived away from home, to be close to my West Yorkshire work. However, I was rationed sufficient petrol during the war to visit my parents at least twice a month. My father had bought me a car when I had first moved to West Yorkshire. Here I was, in the early-morning darkness, driving the twisting narrow roads as I headed eastward toward my destination. Earlier in the morning the air raid sirens had sounded, signaling the likelihood of an imminent attack by the Luftwaffe. All forms of lighting, including car headlights, had to be turned off whenever that alarm sounded. So only the sidelights on my car were in use.

Fortunately, so early in the morning I was unlikely to encounter much traffic, or livestock being brought in from the fields, moving in the opposite direction to me. At one point I heard a plane overhead. It was a clear, starry night so I could see its outline. I still could not identify the different types of aircraft from either their profile or their engine noise. I assumed it was a Luftwaffe bomber returning to Germany. It was flying in the same direction that I was driving; most Royal Air Force bombers arrived back in their stations by around two o'clock in the morning. It was already four o'clock in the morning.

In January 1943 I had turned twenty. I was slim, slightly over five feet tall, and was frequently told that I was very good-looking and physically attractive. I wore my shoulder-length brunette hair curled upward; I permed it myself. My eyes were light blue and usually twinkled; I had a pear-shaped face and a delicate mouth with an almost permanent smile. I also knew that I was strong-willed, very determined, and enjoyed forming new friendships. These combined characteristics had helped me enjoy a very successful career during the past six years. I had left school when I was just fourteen.

During my school years I walked and bicycled to school in the local village about two miles away; in my spare time, I worked on the farm. When I left school, I first found work as live-in home help for family friends who lived in the nearby city. However, once the war broke out in 1939, my career took an unexpected turn.

My father had been dispossessed of most of his land because of the construction of a nearby Royal Air Force airfield. He was more fortunate than two neighboring farmers, though. Not only had they lost all of their land, but they also watched as their homes were bulldozed to rubble.

The financial consequences of land requisition at this time were severe. The compensation paid by the government was based on the land's rental value, was determined by the government, and ignored the remaining land that then often became useless because of lack of access or loss of utilities; worst of all, receipt of compensation payments could be delayed months, if not years. In our case, living off what could be grown on the remaining land and selling what we could not eat in the local market was insufficient to support a family of five. I was the middle daughter of three; my older sister was two years my senior and my other sister was four years younger than I.

When the buses of workmen started to arrive from across Yorkshire to build the airfield, my father came up with a creative idea to supplement our land-sourced income. He realized that the workmen needed to be fed during the workday. Although they were billeted in local homes, most of the initial two hundred men were not provided with lunch by their hosts. My father's idea was simple: Put a henhouse on wheels and convert it into a snack bar. The henhouse would be positioned close to the construction site and would offer homemade tea, coffee, soup, sandwiches, and lemonade prepared each day in the farmhouse. Café Louise was created and became an instant success.

For workmen working far from the henhouse, food delivery came by pony. Each morning my older sister or I would ride the pony over to the opposite side of the airfield, and offer "drinkings," as they were called, at a fixed price. My sister was a little taller than I and had the typically sturdy frame of a farmer's daughter. We had both been told we were attractive; we had to put up with the whistles and the usual sexist jokes shouted at us by the workmen. The word "drinkings" was traditional Yorkshire dialect for morning snacks taken out to the fields for farm workers. When we arrived at the work location, we would be greeted with "thank you, gaffer"; gaffer was the dialect term for boss. That made both my sister and me feel important.

As the number of workmen increased, the construction firm offered us the use of a Nissen hut to allow us to expand our services. I would oversee the food preparation and organize my sisters and other ladies from the village to operate this new café. It was only when the air crews started to arrive that my restaurant business came to an end. The Navy, Army, and Air Force Institute, known as the NAAFI, took over the operation of the canteen, and we had to close.

Fortunately, the reputation of Café Louise had spread to other parts of the county, so I was almost immediately offered new work. I was asked to manage a large food services installation at a wartime training institute about thirty miles to the west. It served over three thousand workers daily, working a three-shift system. The institute trained men and women to become army and air force mechanics, and instructed women who had been called up for service in factory work. My management appointment was soon expanded to include canteen facilities for a nearby underground factory manufacturing parts for Lancaster bombers, and for a munitions plant. By the age of nineteen, I was responsible for operating canteens feeding over seven thousand people daily.

I continued my drive eastward. There was no time to stop. My appointment at the airfield was at ten o'clock that morning. I wanted to leave sufficient time to catch some sleep before I went out dancing that evening. I hoped that either my sister or her boyfriend would have found me a dancing partner. The war had robbed me of all my regular dancing partners. The best dancer I knew, who I also considered to be my boyfriend, had been posted to Africa as a tank mechanic, and he was not likely to return until the war was over. Other partners were either fighting in Europe, had become prisoners of war, or I had not heard from them for some time.

Prewar dancing partners in civilian clothes had been replaced by new faces dressed in full uniform. Most never knew if this would be their last dance. With preparations for the invasion, many strangers were around with unusual accents. Dances were easy to find. Church halls and schools, even in the smallest villages, would regularly organize social events to give the people waiting to fight something lighthearted to do.

I arrived at my parents' home around six thirty that morning. It was remarkable how quiet everything sounded after the din of canteen work. I heard the brittle crunching of gravel as I pulled into the driveway. It was already light, and the bright sun was stuck in a watery, pale sky. I grabbed my suitcase and went into the house. Mother was busy preparing breakfast.

My elder sister, in her Land Girl uniform, sat at the breakfast table, and was close to finishing her breakfast. This morning she was dressed in a fawn cotton blouse, brown corduroy breeches, a green jersey, long woolen socks, and rubber boots. She wore a tie around her waist and a knotted headscarf on her head. She was about my height but a little plumper than me, and rounder in the face.

She had joined the Women's Land Army shortly after my parents moved to this new house; she was one of nearly eighty thousand women nationally who had signed up to work on farms in place of the men who had gone off to fight. It was hard, dirty work, involving long hours. Her preference was to be told what to do rather than to use her own initiative, just the opposite of me. She was unbelievably kind and loving.

"Where is Dad?" I asked. "And my other sister—is she still asleep?"

Not turning from the stove, my mother replied, "Dad is already in the garden hoeing the vegetables. You know how single-minded he is, and he loves to be outdoors. Your younger sister has a job now that she has finished school. She is working at the airfield and is already down there, serving tables in the canteen. We can do with the extra money that she earns. She went off with some bread that I just baked to share with the workmen."

Nodding, I continued, "I'll take a quick wash upstairs, unpack in my bedroom, and then I must go down to the airfield. I have a ten o'clock appointment with Joan Sykes, my assistant manager."

My mother mumbled something and turned to face me, a plate of hot food in her right hand. She was a few inches smaller than her three daughters, so it was easy to see what she was holding.

"Here, eat this," she said, "and then go upstairs and prepare; you have plenty of time. You need to say good-bye to your sister. She is on her way to work at her boyfriend's father's farm."

"Can I drive you up to the farm?" I asked my sister.

"No, thanks," she replied. "I'll use my bicycle. I need to lose a little weight, so cycling will be good so long as I don't fall off the bike. I fell off a fortnight ago when I ran over a rut in the road; I came home with a boot full of blood. Because of my breeches and long socks, I didn't see the gash in my knee and the blood running down my leg until I removed my boots. I'm recovered now, so let me cycle."

I looked at my sister and smiled. Turning back toward my mother, I took the plate with its three rashers of bacon, two poached eggs, a piece of fried bread, and an assortment of mushrooms picked locally early the previous morning. I sat down, ate, and drank two cups of tea. When I had finished, after my sister had departed, I picked up the empty plate and returned it to my mother.

"Thank you, mother," I said, "I need you to come and work in my canteens. Your food is incredible. Tell Dad that I am home and that I will see him around noon today. Is the lodger upstairs, or has he gone to work?"

"He left for the airfield at daybreak, as he usually does," replied my mother. "You should meet him sometime. He is a very nice person, and I am pleased he stays with us. He is so quiet and tidy that I hardly know that he is living with us. He is considered very important at the airfield and has lots of qualifications. He is also rather handsome and pays his rent on time."

My mother was clearly proud of her lodger.

She continued, "I also met his wife a few weeks ago. She traveled all the way here from the West Midlands by train with her two-year-old son to see her husband. She was pregnant. I think her baby will have arrived by now. Apparently she was an important opera singer before she married. Anyway, there is no one upstairs at the moment, and I don't expect the lodger back here before about five thirty this afternoon."

I thanked my mother for the information and went upstairs to my bedroom.

My room had been shifted to the former servants' quarters because I rarely slept at home. It was accessed by a separate set of back stairs that led directly from the kitchen. A bedroom at the top of the stairs on the right-hand side was used by the lodger, and opposite was the toilet and the bathroom. My room was at the end of the corridor at the front of the house. In the good old days, this is where the farmhands had lived. Now it had become home to me and to the lodger.

I didn't know the lodger too well, although I sometimes saw him working at the airfield. I had to admit that he was good-looking, probably in his late twenties, but I had never paid him much attention.

After all, he was married, and I had a regular boyfriend currently posted to North Africa.

The only attention he paid to me was on one occasion at the airfield. He was with another senior engineer who worked for him. They had both stared at me one day when I was working inside the main canteen. They spoke to each other and then his friend gave me a wolf whistle. I felt a little embarrassed with this happening in front of the people who worked for me, so I ignored the attention.

On the way to my bedroom I passed Mr. McGregor's room. The door was open, and I peeped inside. Nothing was out of place. The bed had been made carefully, his shoes were in a tight line alongside his bed, all his clothes had found a home either in the wardrobe or the chest of drawers, and even his personal belongings and radio on the side table were neatly organized. I could understand why my mother regarded him as the ideal lodger.

I went to my room and unpacked, visited the toilet, and next went to the bathroom, where I washed my hands and face. I then went back downstairs and outside to the car, to drive down the hill to meet with Joan. I knew I would be a little early, but Joan would have been on shift since about five in the morning.

CHAPTER 3

THIRTY-YEAR-OLD JOCK MCGREGOR had a high opinion of himself because of his abilities as a civil engineer. He had been appointed the planning director for Number Four Air Group of Bomber Command to design and construct a new airfield in East Yorkshire. Construction had begun at the start of 1943.

Jock was slim, considered very attractive by most people, and was just short of six feet tall; he had an engaging smile; sometimes he could be the nicest person you would wish to meet; at other times, he was the opposite. He was strongly self-disciplined and expected others to be well-organized, punctual, decisive, and obedient to his instructions. If they were not, his annoyance would show through very quickly.

This morning he was waiting for the imminent arrival of the Number Four Group air commodore to give him an update on the status of construction of the new airfield. He was anxious, because some of the news he had to relay would likely not be well-received.

Jock's family roots lay in the blue-collar communities of the West Midlands. His father, who had moved to the Midlands from Clackmannanshire, Scotland, immediately following the General Strike of 1926, often talked about his days in "Tilly," working in the coal mines. Back in April 1926, the mine owners had started to lock out their workers in a dispute over longer working hours for less pay. The strike of May 1926 had lasted nine days but was called off by the labor organizations without any concessions being obtained from the employers.

Rather than go back down into the mines for less pay, Jock's father had chosen to join the ranks of the unemployed and move. Jock was twelve when they left Scotland, and he still remembered the everlasting train journey south to the West Midlands, where his father had found a job at a nearby motorcycle assembly plant. It was a time of great innovation in the road transportation industry, and despite the Great Depression, he was able to stay employed during the 1930s. The number of vehicles, including motorcycles, on the roads in Britain during this period doubled. Many of his father's colleagues back in Scotland, who had stayed down in the mines, found themselves unemployed, destitute, and dependent on the services of soup kitchens.

Jock was clever and artistic. He had attended the local boys grammar school. He decided not to go to university, but rather to combine work and study to become a civil engineer. He worked during the day and studied in the evenings. He was granted one day a week Day Release to attend classes at the local technical institute and quickly found himself working for city development offices, designing residential housing, roads, bridges, and other facilities as instructed.

By accident he had found an occupation that uniquely blended his intelligence and social skills with his passion for creativity and design. Early in his career he had become a student member of the British Institute of Civil Engineers. This membership had offered him a pathway to formal qualifications and visibility among others in his chosen profession. With the outbreak of war, he found himself excused from conscription because of his engineering background. This placed him on a list of reserved occupations that were considered essential to the war effort. While his male colleagues ages eighteen to forty-one who were not working in reserved occupations were liable to be called up to the services at any time, Jock was asked to support the war effort by staying in England. At first he continued his career in civil engineering working for local city authorities. But during 1942 he was asked to transfer from his city development office and manage the planning and building of Royal Air Force airfields in Yorkshire.

He was assigned to East Yorkshire to oversee the construction of a new Number Four Air Group airfield. Although he was not assigned to the battlefront, his life was not without physical risk; there was always the possibility of a visit from the Luftwaffe to any of these bomber airfields. Indeed, even before Jock started his new assignment, the Luftwaffe had been ordered by the Nazis to eliminate the Royal Air Force as a fighting force. Starting during late 1940 there was a concentrated effort by the Luftwaffe to bomb and strafe British airfields nationwide, and some of them near to where Jock now worked had been targeted. Fortunately the Luftwaffe's lack of long-range fighter aircraft to accompany the bombers had forced it to focus its strategy more on the south of England than on the north. Whenever it did visit the north of England, the Luftwaffe encountered a highly effective British daytime fighter defense. Ultimately this drove a change in bombing strategy on Germany's part.

The Luftwaffe shifted its priorities to large-scale night attacks against industrial targets. This had translated to a greater Luftwaffe presence in Yorkshire at the time that Jock moved to East Yorkshire, as heavy bombing raids now took place on the nearby Yorkshire cities of Hull, Sheffield, and Middleborough. Even local towns were not immune.

Just over a year earlier, York had been targeted in an apparent reprisal for the Royal Air Force bombing of the ancient German town of Lubeck. In late April 1942, York had received a visit from an estimated seventy-four Luftwaffe aircraft that dropped an estimated ninety-five tons of high explosives plus incendiaries on the city. Seventy-four civilians were killed. British night fighters intercepted many of the raiders, but this increased the risk that a damaged German bomber would choose to crash on a nearby airfield. The attacks on York continued periodically until the end of the year.

The nearby city of Hull, the most frequently bombed city in Britain, received regular visits from the Luftwaffe throughout the war; here the risk was that a vagrant damaged bomber would find its way across the Wolds and inflict reprisals on military installations in the Vale of York. Nights when the clouds hung low and the mist and fog rolled over the countryside to disrupt the Luftwaffe were nights when sleep came easiest.

Jock now found himself nearing the end of his first year of planning and overseeing the construction of his assigned airfield, located about one hundred miles away from where his wife and children lived in the West Midlands. He considered himself to be very fortunate. He had found lodgings nearby in an old farmhouse. The landlady considered him to be the "bee's knees." He understood this phrase to be a strong compliment. It was also his good fortune that he had ended up living in a home occupied by three very attractive young daughters, aged sixteen, twenty, and twenty two, whose father kept a paternal eye on them.

Their father was also a casualty of war. He had been a farmer about twenty miles away when war broke out. His farmland had been requisitioned for the building of a fighter airfield. Having settled on his new farm, he quickly lost two thirds of this land to the creation of this latest airfield. Reluctantly he had sold the remaining land to a nearby farmer and had divided the old farmhouse in to two, selling one half to a lady villager who wanted to leave farming after the death of her husband. He had kept some of the farm buildings and the walled garden so that he could busy himself with gardening chores each day.

The airfield was only a ten-minute cycle ride downhill. This ride was usually exhilarating in the early morning for Jock, except for those winter days with snow or heavy fog. The payback came in the evening when the journey home was largely uphill. Jock would usually cycle the first third and then walk his bicycle home for the remainder of the way.

This early morning in July 1943 celebrated the return of the sun after several days of absence. It had been absent without leave for nearly a week. Deteriorating weather had caused persistent drizzle from a gray sky that periodically obscured the deep sided dry valleys that dissected the Wolds, and would simultaneously appear to slice off the tops of the surrounding hills. The clouds would rise and fall, forever denying the sun even a brief appearance. This weather also made it difficult for the Luftwaffe to find its targets, so there had been less bombing during the last few days.

Jock had just returned from visiting his bride of five years in the West Midlands. She had delivered him a daughter whom he dearly adored. The visit had also given him the opportunity to meet his son again, for only the fourth time in the nearly two years since he was born. There had been objections at the airfield to his visit home, but he strongly believed that family obligations were greater than his responsibilities to the Royal Air Force.

Now he was waiting for the arrival of the air commodore, who was on his way to assess construction progress, and probably read Jock the riot act for abandoning the airfield in favor of his family. Jock intended to stand his ground. Work was progressing well. His assistant from America, Michael Fromm, would join him for the meeting and explain why the delay in constructing the runways had occurred, and thereby hopefully give him an alibi for his absence. Michael knew everything there was to know about laying concrete and the composition and thickness needed to accommodate the ever-increasing weight of the bomber aircraft. He also possessed that wonderful American twang that caused most Europeans to automatically believe everything that he said. He could get to the point very quickly and seemed decisive

22

and confident in expressing his own opinions. He was not the British stereotypical American who was viewed as brash, loud, rude, and uneducated. He would be a useful ally to have present during the imminent meeting with the air commodore. Jock really liked Michael, and he thought Michael liked him.

CHAPTER 4

IN JULY 1943, Michael Fromm, an American from California, had reached twenty-one years of age, had originally lived in Sacramento, and a year earlier had volunteered to help the Royal Air Force Airfield Construction Branch design and construct safe and reliable runways in England to accommodate the largest and heaviest bomber aircraft. He had been asked to move to East Yorkshire to assist with the building of a new bomber airfield. Michael was a specialist engineer in the use of concrete.

Currently he was a direct report to the planning director, Jock McGregor, whose civil engineering abilities Michael respected. Michael was of average height, possessed a mop of blond hair, and displayed exceptional good looks. His face wore more of a grin than a smile. His personality, on the other hand, was reserved, verging on shy, and sometimes he was almost silent when around his colleagues. Some attributed this to his not understanding the dialects of the people with whom he was working. He did admit that he often found it impossible to comprehend the Yorkshire dialect. So he often used a strategy of silence to lessen the likelihood of verbal embarrassment.

He was a very polite and caring person but was of an age where the opposite sex consumed a lot of his time and attention. He combined his good looks, shyness, and American accent into a package that often had the English girls wanting to date him out of curiosity.

He also experienced problems of comprehension with Jock McGregor's accent. Although Jock could speak clear English when he wanted to, coming from the West Midlands, Jock often lapsed into his "black country" dialect. This speech was impossible for Michael to understand. It combined rarely used Middle English grammar with its inflectional endings on words and at the end of sentences, its own vocabulary, a strange twang when spoken, and its use of slang phrases. For example, on those occasions when Jock accused Michael of lying or telling a fib, he would use the word "carradiddle" for lie. Jock would also talk about "all raind the Wreken" when referring to the long way round having been taken to reach somewhere on the airfield or in the local community.

Michael respected Jock's intelligence and professionalism but felt that Jock sometimes used his smartness to embarrass or ridicule his colleagues and subordinates. He was sometimes almost too public with his criticism of others. But Michael would quickly overcome any personal annoyance he felt as a result of his treatment by Jock.

Michael was also affectionately known as "the Yank" among his British colleagues.

His father had been a refugee from Belgium during the First World War. He had fought in the Belgian army alongside the British after Antwerp fell to the Germans in October 1914. Belgian neutrality had been threatened earlier that year by Germany insisting on a safe passage for its soldiers through Belgium to invade France from the north. Belgium had resisted the demand, arguing that a German invasion would be a violation of international law, and it threatened to respond using all means available to it. As war broke out, the Belgians fought more stubbornly and courageously than anticipated by Germany, and delayed the advance of the German army toward northern France. Its resistance also gave Britain the excuse it needed to declare war on Germany.

It was to be a bitter war, with some of the harshest treatment reserved for the Belgians. As Germany occupied their territory, rumors grew of atrocities committed against the local population. Included were the burning of houses, the killing of old men, deportation of adults to Germany to work in the factories, and even allegations that Germans were slicing off the thumbs of small boys so that they would be of no future military use. Eventually Fromm Sr. decided to flee to Holland to avoid likely internment by the Germans. He was one of several thousand military personnel who disguised themselves as civilians. On arrival, he and his travel companions were housed in a variety of restored barracks, brickyards, tent villages, churches, and private houses. Hygiene was poor, and overcrowding was standard. He found work as a farmhand.

Daytime consisted of hard labor; nighttime was a state of boredom. The local Dutch remained suspicious of the intentions of their uninvited guests. Eventually Fromm Sr. concluded that he must move to England, where he hoped he could make a more direct contribution to the war effort. He arrived in early spring 1916, on a passenger cargo ship that docked at the port of North Shields, close to the city of Newcastle in the north of England. He quickly found work at a nearby munitions factory.

Despite the warm welcome on the dockside, he soon discovered that the Belgian and English communities were suspicious of each other and were kept apart; he also learnt that work in the factories was enforced under strict military standards. He was housed in a self-contained village that permitted only Belgian residents. Belgian law applied in the village, and it was guarded by Belgian policemen. He considered his work to be of value but his living conditions intolerable. So he began a search for new opportunities.

The United States was on the brink of joining the war and needed to build up its armed forces. Its ships were being attacked by Germany, but it was almost completely unprepared to participate in the war. Consequently the country was open to accepting volunteers as well as relying on the draft and conscription. Volunteering as a trained soldier, and particularly one who could speak English, French, Flemish, and

German, Fromm Sr. was a perfect fit for the United States Army. His German had been learnt at school, whereas his other three languages were either learnt at home or self-taught.

By volunteering, he hoped he would qualify after the war for fast-track US residency. As the war came to an end, the Fromm family was given approval to emigrate to the United States and decided to settle in Wisconsin, which already had a substantial Belgian population. Many of these people were descendants of farmers and farm laborers who had moved to the United States in the mid-nineteenth century due to land shortages and the potato blight in Belgium.

However, after a short period of farm laboring, Fromm Sr. decided to seek his fortune in California, and chose to move to Sacramento. He was fortunate enough to find employment at a newly opened local air force base, and after the required number of weeks of training, he became a qualified aircraft mechanic. His work provided occasional support for the army air force, but much of his time was given to servicing aircraft belonging to the California aerial forestry patrol.

Socially, he quickly fell in love and married his first sweetheart. She and her family had emigrated from Germany in early 1914 to avoid religious persecution. Initially her family had established its home in Cincinnati but moved west to California because of local anti-German sentiment that surfaced during the war. Her parents took exception to allegations that they were "hyphenated Americans," and should not be trusted. In early 1922 Fromm Sr. and his wife welcomed the arrival of Fromm Jr. Only this one child was possible due to subsequent medical difficulties experienced by Fromm Sr.'s wife. Consequently, as the only child, Michael was given all the encouragement and funds he needed to obtain a comprehensive education and to start a meaningful career.

By accident, he had fallen into concrete, not literally, but because of attending night classes at a nearby state college that introduced him to construction engineering. A growing component of this profession required technical knowledge of the strengths and characteristics of concrete. As buildings grew taller and aircraft became heavier, there was an emerging new science focused on concrete technologies and new construction techniques. Paved runways replacing earlier grass landing strips had become essential for increasingly heavier bomber aircraft that needed all-weather operational capability. Early-age cracking and early-age volume changes to concrete used for runways jeopardized the safety of aircraft operations. Designing surfaces that would provide maximum friction for wheel-braking and minimum risk of hydroplaning, along with sufficient load-bearing capacity for increasingly heavy bombers, was essential. There could be no single solution. Ground conditions varied between airfields, and these were the key determinants of a suitable runway.

Michael had volunteered through the British Air Ministry to provide the Royal Air Force with advice on runway construction. His services were quickly accepted. As a result, he now found himself living in East Yorkshire and working on the construction of one of the last bomber airfields to be opened during World War II. Unlike his planning director, Michael had decided not to take up village living but had moved to the nearest town and found accommodation at a local inn. This posting inn, dating back to Tudor times, was warm and welcoming and was less than a fifteen-minute car ride from the airfield.

Initially he had traveled to work by taxi. However he had been unnerved by an incident a few miles away. One evening a taxi, with its lights on, had been mistaken, presumably, for a fighter plane, and had been strafed by a Luftwaffe bomber that was returning to Germany. He had immediately gone out to the local dealer for British Small Arms' motorbikes and purchased a 1940 BSA M 23 Silver Star.

But he hadn't brought sufficient funds with him from America, so he had used hire purchase, or what the British termed as the "never-never" to complete the purchase. In only another fifteen months his "never" would end with the payment of the final installment, and the bike would belong to him. The chromium tank and matte silver panels that he polished daily gave him a sense of importance and pride as he straddled this piece of machinery. He smiled whenever he thought about how a gun manufacturer established during the time of the Crimean War a hundred years earlier, to manufacture rifles by machinery, could evolve into a successful bicycle maker, and then end up making its fortune producing motorbikes.

This particular morning the bike seemed eager to attack the country roads and return Michael to his workplace. He knew that Jock McGregor would be aware of his imminent arrival about two miles from the airfield because of the roar of the BSA engine. Reaching the brow of the hill and looking toward the partly completed control tower, he could make out his boss's profile; he was waiting for him, talking to another man whom Michael was unable to identify.

CHAPTER 5

By THE TIME Michael Fromm had padlocked his motorbike and reached the control tower, the two men had disappeared. The sweet smell of sizzling bacon coming from the adjacent canteen told him where they were. Scraping the mud off his heavy boots, he entered the canteen and saw Jock McGregor and the stranger seated at the far end of a long wooden table. Local village girls who were no longer at school were busy taking orders and disappearing into the kitchen.

"Come over here," shouted Jock. "We've already ordered you breakfast. Let me introduce you to the air commodore from Number Four Air Group headquarters. Air commodore, please meet our 'Yank,' otherwise known as Mr. Michael Fromm." Jock then returned to eating his favorite meal of fried eggs and french fries.

The air commodore nodded toward Michael, who reached out and shook hands with him. The air commodore was in his late fifties, over six feet tall, slim, stern-looking, and wore rounded spectacles that perched on the end of his nose. Unlike everyone else in the canteen that morning, he was the only one in uniform. He wore his Royal Air Force uniform to signal his importance and his presence on official duty.

"My pleasure, sir," said Michael.

"Sit down," said Jock. "Your breakfast will be here shortly. Let's finish eating, and then we can give the air commodore an update on our construction progress. He tells me he drove here by car this morning, but next time he wants to fly into the airfield using his Tiger Moth airplane. I've promised him that we will do everything possible to make that happen."

taxiway is nearing completion, and work on installing defense pillboxes will start in September."

At this point, the trio was interrupted by the arrival of a new pot of tea and a replacement jug of milk. After topping up their mugs of tea, Jock resumed his monologue.

"The building of offsite accommodation is proving a little more difficult than we had expected. We need to house several hundred people away from the airfield. Most of this housing is being built a short distance away close to the village. Some of the villagers are objecting to the sites we have selected because they are too close to their homes and use some of their land.

"Additionally, no one likes the architecture of the Nissen huts that we plan to construct. The villagers claim that, with cement floors and prefabricated half cylinders of corrugated steel, these facilities will be cold, draughty, and unfit for people to live in. Unfortunately, given the land and materials we have available to us, this is the best we can do. We have meetings arranged in the village to explain what we are doing and why we are doing it. We are hopeful that the villagers will eventually accept our reasons."

At this point, it was clear even to Jock that the air commodore was becoming irritated and impatient.

"Look, you two, you don't seem to understand. We are on the brink of the final phase of this war, and the more bombs we can drop on the Germans, the sooner this war will be over. What matters are the runways. We have the planes and pilots, but they need runways to do their work. Stop the rambling and tell me about the status of these. This airfield is supposed to be built to Class A specifications that were established last year by the Air Ministry. It needs to have its three runways operational soon. What is going on?"

Jock looked at Michael, and Michael returned the look, one of despair tainted with a little fear.

"Michael, you explain," said Jock.

Michael took out his pack of Lucky Strikes. He selected a cigarette for himself and then offered the remaining cigarettes to the other two. Both declined. However, Jock accessed his pack of strong unfiltered Wills Woodbine from his inside pocket, popped one into his right hand, and then shared the lighted match as both he and Michael lit up before resuming the conversation. Both were regular smokers.

"Well, the problem is this, sir," started Michael as he lit his cigarette. "As you know, as the war has proceeded, the bombers we are using have become much heavier. We have had to adjust the originally planned layout for the runways to extend the main runway to two thousand yards and the two subsidiary ones to thirteen hundred and fourteen hundred yards to meet the new standards adopted by Bomber Command. We have also been told that the paved runways need a stress tolerance of at least two thousand pounds per square inch to allow for the heaviest Halifaxes to land and take off in all weather conditions.

"The other problem here is the geology of the location. As we excavated, we found boulder clay and large tracts of sand and gravel. Not only did a glacier once leave a moraine here, but it also contained large underground streams that deposited masses of gravel and sand. Gravel and clay do not compact at the same rate, so it's not a simple matter of laying hardcore and pouring concrete. We need to scrape away about three feet of topsoil, remix the sand, clay, and gravel, and then redeposit it. After that, we have to put in place the hardcore base and then pour concrete that is at least nine inches thick and fifty yards wide. Once that has been laid, we will coat the runways with asphalt.

"We also have had to build more dispersal pans or hardstands than we expected in order to park the aircraft when they are not in use. Unfortunately, this will all take more time than we had predicted, probably another eight months or so from today, to lay the foundation and to complete the three runways. We estimate next April as the earliest date to have the airfield operational."

Michael stopped talking at this point and watched the air commodore process the information that he had just been given.

"Look," the commodore said sharply, "this is not the news that I want to hear. I understand the difficulties you are experiencing, but I lose confidence with your explanations when I hear that you, Jock, are wasting time visiting family, and see that you, Michael, are giving more attention to the Land Girls than you are to the airfield. If the contractors need more men and equipment to finish the job more quickly, tell me. If you encounter problems, don't wait for me to visit; send me messages with suggested solutions.

"Regrettably, I have no alternative but to accept your explanations and report them back to headquarters; but I am very unhappy with the situation. I will give headquarters a revised estimate that the airfield will be operational sometime during April 1944. Both of you need to apply more energy and commitment to getting this job completed on time. Do not treat this assignment as if it is a countryside vacation. Do you understand?"

Both understood very clearly, although neither of them said anything in reply. Jock's offer to escort the air commodore to his car was rejected.

"One last thing," the air commodore said. "While I hesitate to leave behind this bottle of whisky for you two after all I have heard this morning, it may motivate you to work harder to complete this airfield."

He handed Jock the bottle of whisky and said, "Drink it slowly, and each time you take a sip, think carefully of the words I have spoken."

With that, the air commodore stood up, gazed around the room, and walked across the canteen to the open door. Jock and Michael followed, watching him recover his automobile, hand-crank the engine, drive past the gate guard, and disappear over the top of the hill, on his way back to headquarters. Michael went out of the canteen to consult with the runway construction superintendent.

Jock left the canteen and walked over to his office, feeling thankful that the air commodore had left but annoyed and upset over the content of the conversation. Jock was over a hundred miles away from his wife and two small children, and he had just been notified that there would be no more family visits until after the airfield was completed. With two small children, his wife could not visit him.

He strongly believed that no one did better engineering work than he and that he was being unfairly disciplined because of circumstances over which he had no control. He also was convinced that he was smarter and better informed than the air commodore; only rank allowed the AC to treat Jock that way. That this altercation had occurred in front of a subordinate was doubly unfortunate. He decided to take home the bottle of whisky to help him drown his anger.

CHAPTER 6

I LEFT MY PARENTS' home and arrived at the airfield canteen about an hour earlier than my appointment time with Joan Sykes. This gave me time to check the staff schedule for August and to review the inventory folder of food orders for the stockroom. When I arrived at the canteen, Joan was busy behind the serving counter. I told her what I was doing and that we would meet in the canteen office in about forty-five minutes. She agreed that that would be convenient.

Joan's appearance and personality were ideal for what she did. She was a portly, homely woman of average height with a round, florid face. She had lived in the village for all of her life and knew everyone. Joan was always calm, listened when people had complaints, and was trusted to make wise decisions.

I knew her from church; I attended the village church whenever I was at home on a Sunday. She was a regular churchgoer and always led the carol singers on Christmas Eve when they went singing from house to house in the village. She was hard-working and well-organized. When I arrived at the canteen, she had her staff preparing sandwiches for the workmen's lunch. Today's selection would be cheese, sardines, beetroot, cucumber, and corned beef.

Joan was already seated in the office when I arrived forty-five minutes later. She welcomed me with a big smile.

"So how was the journey; any bombs fall on you recently?"

I assured her that my journey had been uneventful and that the place where I lived received far fewer visits from the Luftwaffe than most other major cities in Yorkshire. That didn't mean that there was no bombing, but the inland location where I lived was far away from any major river, which made it difficult for the Luftwaffe to follow the topography and drop bombs on us.

"So have you heard?" Joan asked.

"What?" I replied.

"We had the top brass here earlier this morning. The planning director had to tell the air commodore that our opening date is being delayed maybe three to four months later than the original plan, because of problems with the runways."

"No, I haven't heard," was my reply. "Did anything happen to the director? Is the RAF replacing him?" I asked, knowing that he was my mother's lodger and an important source of her income.

"He's fine except for a slightly damaged ego. He went to his home in the West Midlands a few days ago, without permission, to see his family. He has been told that he cannot visit his family again until the airfield is completed. That may take another eight to nine months."

Joan stopped to take a question from one of the serving girls, who wanted to know if there was any news regarding the construction of Nissen huts in the village. Her mum was mad that one was to be built at the village's lane end. This would be an eyesore for everyone coming into and leaving the village. She had told her daughter that she would stop her from working at the airfield unless these plans were changed. Joan could give her no assurances.

"That's our biggest problem around here," Joan asserted. "Not only will some of the ladies not show up when the air raid sirens go off, but some are threatening to stop working here altogether because of the Royal Air Force's insistence on building in the village. Our other problem is this operating delay. Apparently it is caused by difficulties in completing the runways. Now that we are to be a base for heavy bombers, we need to excavate more before we can lay the runways; we also have to increase the amount of concrete we intended to use, and the runways must be longer than originally planned.

"In addition, we need to staff the canteen for this extended period. I have spoken with the NAAFI. They will not come in earlier and take over responsibility for managing the canteen until the flight squadron moves in."

I nodded my understanding. This would cause a serious staffing problem, made more difficult because more and more people were moving away from the village to support the war effort. I would need to give more of my time to this airfield to make certain that it continued to serve the workmen appropriately. I might have to visit neighboring villages to see if I could recruit staff to come and work in our village. Finding people through contacts with other village churches was usually the best way to recruit additional staff.

I thanked Joan for the update and said I would visit her one more time before I returned to West Yorkshire. We discussed the results of my review of operations. Everything looked good. She assured me that there was sufficient food in storage and that daily attention was being given to hygiene and safety. As I left, Joan thanked me for my mother's supply of bread, potatoes, apples, and other fruit to the canteen, which allowed her to offer a broader menu selection to the workmen.

I drove home feeling tired, wondering if I should move back home from West Yorkshire to dedicate more time to this airfield. Running four canteens many miles apart was beginning to stress me out. Even more important was that less and less of my time could be spent on the dance floor; that was annoying and frustrating, because I was being kept away from my favorite pleasure.

Returning to my parents' home, I discovered that my father was still in the garden, and my mother was in one of the outhouses washing the family clothes. I wasn't hungry, so I went up the narrow, twisting stairs leading from the kitchen toward my bedroom, entered my bedroom, quickly got undressed, fell into bed, and was asleep in a few moments.

It must have been about 6:30 p.m. when I awoke. My elder sister was standing at the bottom of the stairs, shouting.

"Mary Louise, Trevor's here, and he has brought his cousin Roger with him. We are going to have some tea, and we will be leaving for the Fox and Fig Pub at about seven thirty. You might want to get up now."

"Okay," I shouted back. "Don't leave without me."

Her reply was quick. "We can't; you are doing the driving."

With that, I lifted myself out of bed, went over to the wardrobe to choose my dress for the evening, laid it on the bed, and went down the corridor to the bathroom. I felt grimy and smelly after all the travel and work that day. I decided to take a bath. I lay in the bathtub, pampering myself with warm water but using as little soap and water as possible. I knew I needed to get ready quickly or suffer the wrath of my sister for being late. Her relationship with her boyfriend had become more serious, and I had heard my parents talk about whether they would use the church or the chapel for the wedding.

I climbed out of the bath, wrapped the towel around me, and headed back toward my bedroom. I heard the lodger shout in my direction. I hadn't realized he was home.

"Is that you, Mary Louise? I saw you down at the airfield today. You are doing a first-rate job for us; come over here. I have a bottle of whisky; let me toast you and thank you for your work."

"I can't," I replied. "I just took a bath and have nothing on but a towel. Maybe at some other time. But thank you for the invitation anyway, Mr. McGregor."

"There won't be another time. This whisky will be gone by the end of today, and I don't expect to receive any replacement bottles. Don't worry about wearing your towel; it won't fall off. Come and enjoy a quick drink."

With that, the lodger opened his bedroom door as I passed by on the way to my bedroom, and said invitingly, "Come inside; don't be so pompous."

I hesitated. He took my hand and led me into his room while I clutched at my towel. He was in his shirtsleeves. At the foot of his bed was the bottle of whisky on a low table, where a second glass was already waiting. The bottle was a little over half full. It stood next to the ashtray, in which sat a part-smoked Woodbine waiting to be relit at some future time.

He passed me a glass, poured it full to the brim, then clinked his glass with mine and resumed drinking. On one side of the table was a letter he had written; from the address, I assumed it was to his wife. Although a small couch was opposite the table, we stood as we drank.

"Thank you," I said after I had emptied my glass. "It's unusual to have the opportunity to drink alcohol of this quality these days. I must be going, though, or I will be late for my dance."

He looked across at me, smiled, and reached out to take my hand again. I thought he was going to lead me back to the door and say good night. Instead, he suddenly pulled me toward him and crushingly kissed me on the lips. At this point I let go of my towel as I tried to push him away. Then I felt myself being lifted up and placed on his bed.

I was not sure what was happening. He fell on top of me, and I felt him fumbling with his clothes. Then suddenly he was deep inside me. The shock; I had never been sexually attracted toward him although I knew that he was good looking. Should I physically resist his unplanned assault and shout for help? If I did, what might he do to me; I had no idea of his motives. Worse, if I screamed, my family would become involved. My sister's boyfriend was only a few yards away downstairs, and he

41

had brought his cousin Roger, who I had never met before. Everything would become public; the whole village would know quickly. How might people react? Would they blame me, given Jock's importance and seniority at the airfield? I was increasingly confused and frightened into doing nothing.

I lay there underneath Jock as the silent victim of his assault and his continuing thrusting movements. I submitted without any act of cooperation. As the thrusting continued, I began to get ready to physically resist, but suddenly it was all over. As soon as he was satisfied, he kissed me several times on the forehead and then once on the lips. I looked up at him. He took my hand and lifted me off the bed.

"Thank you for that," he said. "I hope you will forgive me; I think it's the whisky that caused it. You really are very attractive. Thank you for not resisting. Don't say anything to your parents; they are just as likely to blame you as to blame me. You remind me of my wife."

What should I do? I was trembling and continued to be in a state of shock. I felt embarrassed, ashamed, and somehow considered that I was responsible for what had just happened. I went back to my bedroom. I sat on my bed for a few moments. The thought of involving my parents terrified me. How stupid I was for wandering around upstairs dressed only in a bath towel. I knew my mother regarded the lodger as the bee's knees. Not only was he seen as very important, but he was a critical source of family income. Saying nothing probably was the best answer. But my sister and her boyfriend expected me to go dancing this evening. What if I suddenly changed my mind? This would require an explanation. My partner Roger was already waiting for me downstairs.

I decided to go to the bathroom to wash myself. Taking a shower was not an option. World War II bathrooms in England typically did not possess a shower. Running water for a bath risked creating suspicion because I had only just taken a bath. Earlier in the war the king of

Great Britain had announced that his palace baths would be limited to five inches of water and would only be taken weekly. Like many English households, this standard had been adopted by my parents, who expected each of their daughters to comply with these rules. It was inconceivable that I could take two baths within hours of each other. So after washing myself at the sink, I returned to my bedroom.

I really didn't want to go out that evening; dancing was the last thing I wanted to do. But the circumstances compelled me to act otherwise. I started to tell myself that the assault was unimportant, that it soon would be forgotten, and that life must go on as before. The state of denial that I sought to establish helped me to calm down and regain my self-control. I slowly dressed and went downstairs to meet my date for the evening. He welcomed me, and we left the house to go dancing with my sister and her boyfriend for the evening. No-one downstairs had any idea of what had just happened upstairs. I then experienced the most stressful evening of my life.

From the beginning, I wished the evening would be over and that I could go home and sleep. In the pub it was impossible to concentrate and participate in the conversation. I felt as if I was in a different world. I kept telling myself that the assault didn't happen, that it was all a dream. Then my thoughts would turn to fear over what Jock had done to me; the next moment I was flooded with feelings of guilt and shame. I had been taken into his room wearing only a towel. I hadn't resisted or run away when he grabbed me. These conflicted feelings stopped me from saying anything to my sister. It would be impossible to justify what had happened. I felt unclean when I danced with my partner; I felt threatened by his touch. I couldn't stop thinking about what had just happened to me. It kept recycling through my memory.

It was a great relief when the dance was over, and I was home alone in my bedroom. I again washed thoroughly and went to bed. I hid below my sheets but still found it difficult to fall asleep. The memories from earlier that evening kept returning to disturb my mind.

The following morning it was difficult getting up. I wanted to lie in bed until the memories from the previous night had gone away. They wouldn't. During the coming days I worked hard to forget the experience so that I could regain my positive attitude and return to my regular lifestyle.

CHAPTER 7

THE REST OF the 1943 Yorkshire summer passed quietly, other than an incident involving me that occurred toward the middle of September.

I returned to West Yorkshire at the end of July but made arrangements to stop working there, and moved back to live with my parents by the middle of August. I explained to my superiors in West Yorkshire that this was necessary because of my new family responsibilities. My older sister was getting married, and I now needed to live permanently with my parents to look after them. Additionally, I had to spend more time at the local airfield because the canteen there would probably have to remain open several months longer than had originally been planned because of problems with the runways. Permission to transfer was given, albeit reluctantly. Similarly, my landlady in West Yorkshire was saddened when I told her of my decision to move home to live with my parents.

The weather stayed hot and slightly humid.

As the war progressed, more bombers were leaving Yorkshire for Germany than were arriving from Germany. Rumor had it that Germany was giving up on its bombing strategy and instead planned to use pilotless aircraft, or as some people called them, "flying bombs."

Efforts by Bomber Command to disrupt this plan were already under way. Hundreds of bombers had been sent to a small island off the coast in the Baltic Sea to bomb what was believed to be a research center for the making of these weapons. There were also flights south across Germany to bomb armament and munitions factories. A Messerschmitt factory had been bombed, along with a large ball bearing plant. Some of the bombing was more controversial. The campaign that had been named Operation Gomorrah had started at the end of July 1943 and continued into the first few days of August. It involved several days of nearly continuous bombing over Hamburg, with British pilots conducting the night raids and the Americans the daytime visits. The industrial damage inflicted was severe, but so was the consequence on people. Some twenty-one thousand women, thirteen thousand men, and eight thousand children lost their lives. The war was turning brutal once again.

Back living with my parents, each weekday and Saturday I would spend several hours at the airfield canteen making sure that it operated without problems. I had recruited additional staff and had prepared schedules that would keep the canteen operating until the end of April 1944. My younger sister continued her employment there, and I had to be careful to avoid the perception of showing favoritism in her direction. My older sister had announced her engagement and was planning to marry later in the year. My mother was busy organizing the wedding, and my father continued to work in the garden.

I had not spoken to anyone about my encounter with Jock McGregor. On occasion, I would see him down at the airfield. He sometimes waved at me, but he kept a distance and rarely spoke to me, even to say good morning. In the evenings he would usually return to my parents' home but go straight to his room upstairs and stay there.

Some evenings he was out in the village giving presentations to the villagers to explain the reasons behind the accommodation zoning plans. The community appreciated his willingness to meet, but as the building began, inertia set in. There was more interest in enjoying the brief period of summer sunshine and preparing for the crop harvest than there was in complaining about the location of a Nissen hut in the village, or criticizing its color.

On Friday evenings, Michael Fromm would call at my parents' home, and he and Jock would go off to the pub in the next village. Usually Michael was able to borrow a vehicle from the airfield motor pool. He was beginning to feel more comfortable with the English and was finding more to do as more and more Americans arrived to help with the war effort. At one point at the airfield he briefly tried to talk to me. Jock came over and told him to worry about his Land Girls and to leave me alone.

It seemed that Jock and Michael were developing a close relationship as a result of these weekly pub meetings. Although nothing was said to me, it seemed that the two were working more closely together to complete construction of the airfield, and that they respected the knowledge that each brought to the project to ensure its ultimate success. This mutual respect was transforming their relationship into a personal friendship.

Work on the runways was progressing very well. The contractor had brought in more scrapers and bulldozers, and an additional twenty men had been assigned to the project.

Harvesting on the farms had begun. The reaper-binders had been dusted off, oiled, and moved into the sunshine in readiness to start work. Horse-drawn or with tractor, they were beginning to arrive in the wheat fields. The hot summer weather had turned the wheat golden and dry. Young and old, the villagers were gathering in the fields to celebrate the harvest. Not only was this the time for reaping wheat, but food was also becoming plentiful in the hedgerows.

Picking blackberries, elderberries, rose hips and crab apples was enjoyed by children, both boys and girls. The elderly men operated the harvesting machines and replaced the coils of twine or string. The women followed behind, gathering the sheaves of wheat and building stooks with six or eight sheaves to complete the drying process.

Arranging the stook from east to west to catch the prevailing winds usually distinguished the professional helper from the amateur. It would be a few days later when the farmer would return to gather the dry sheaves of wheat and store them in a dry place until the arrival of the annual visit of the threshing machine. Drinkings would be brought to the fields, and workers would rest when rest was needed.

There was also a new source of protein. As each wheat field gave up its grain, the reaper granted freedom to the rabbits and the occasional hare that had found refuge among the tall stems of corn. This freedom was usually short-lived. The farmer's gun was rarely inaccurate, and dinner was frequently rabbit stew.

At times Michael Fromm would visit the harvest fields. His purpose usually was to catch up with a Land Girl to arrange a date for that evening or that week. He particularly liked the girls who had moved to the farms from towns in the south of England. These were the ones whose accent he understood the easiest. If his invitation had been successful, you would hear him leave, his motorbike making a gentle, purring noise; if he had been rejected, his disappointment would be communicated in the harshness of the bike's acceleration. Stories concerning Michael's love experiences were frequent topics of conversation in the airfield canteen, and everyone seemed to know about his successes and failures. But because of his kind demeanor, he was liked by everyone.

At the beginning of September 1943, the village church announced that once again, in a few days' time, the ladies who volunteered to help with the church Harvest Festival would be taken on a two-day walking trip to the mountains of Snowdonia in North Wales. This had been an annual event before the war, but was canceled in 1940 and 1941 because of the risk of a German invasion. For most of the village ladies, it was the only opportunity they had to get away from home each year.

I had already volunteered to help the church, since I now regularly attended Sunday services because I was living at home. So I was one of the first to sign up. The trip would include one day of travel, one night away from home, and a full day of hiking.

It would be a long journey to the town of Llanberis in North Wales, which stood close to the mountains and lakes of Snowdonia. Llanberis was positioned at the head of a pass occupied by two lakes that over time had cut a way through the mountain range. The area was noted for its beauty and rugged scenery. The town of Llanberis was more than 130 miles away from our small village and would take several hours to reach by bus. Each person on the tour would stay overnight in cottages provided by the local Llanberis church.

Exactly what we would do once we arrived in Llanberis depended on the weather. The mountains could cloud over very quickly. The hope was that we would include a visit to Dolbadarn Castle at the head of the Llanberis Pass. The castle dated back to about 1230, and had been built by Llewellyn the Great to help fight the English. It had been captured by Edward the First in 1283 and, starting two years later, parts of it were dismantled to be used to build Caernarfon Castle, a few miles away.

We then planned to follow the Llanberis Path up to the summit of Snowdon, the centerpiece of Snowdonia. At approximately thirty-five hundred feet, Snowdon is the highest mountain in England and Wales. This was the longest route to ascend the mountain, but it was also the most gradual to climb. The trip would be about ten miles there and back, and would take about five hours.

The Snowdonia Mountain Railway ran nearby, but we had been told that the train was no longer accepting passengers because of the war. If we decided to climb the mountain, we would each have to walk back down. We were told that the slate quarries that we would pass on the way gave work to people living in the surrounding area. Slate quarrying was a harsh job, especially in winter.

It was also mentioned that during the previous year's visit, some members of the group had been told that in one of the quarries there is an underground labyrinth of chambers that was constructed to store and protect the art collections from the National Gallery and the Tate in London. These collections had been relocated to North Wales for the remainder of the war because of the bombings in London and the southeast of England that began during August 1940.

We met on the village green near my parents' home early that September morning. Most of us carried a rectangular light tan leather suitcase containing our nighttime clothes and hiking attire. The bus arrived a few minutes late. It was delayed because of stopping in other villages to collect passengers who were accompanying us on the tour. All in all, about two dozen people were participating in this year's event.

The bus and its driver had kindly been donated by the local garage owner. He operated a fleet of green Leyland Tigers; we would travel to North Wales in one. The fact that the bus was green made us feel a lot safer. It was less easy to be seen by German bombers during the night than if it was cream-colored, and during the day it could pull over onto the grassy verges and be less conspicuous if the Luftwaffe was present. Wartime black was another preferred color, but it didn't offer the same daytime safety.

I climbed aboard the bus and chose to sit next to Joan Sykes. Joan had persuaded her sister to supervise the canteen while we were both gone.

The engine of the bus roared its approval of the journey, and we were on our way to Snowdonia.

Joan started the conversation.

"So who is the latest boyfriend?" she asked. "I hear you go dancing most weeks. What's the name of the lucky man?"

I looked at her, feeling just a little annoyed.

"He is in North Africa right now with his tank regiment. Or at least I think he is. Maybe he is in Italy. I am not sure. I haven't heard from him for months. Even when I do, the letters are censored so that you learn very little. But at least I know he is alive."

"Do you miss him?"

"Yes," I said. "But the war will end; I am willing to wait."

"Meantime, are you practicing with anyone else?" She smiled and looked at me straight in the eyes.

"No," I replied. "I am too busy at work. And when I go dancing, my sister's boyfriend usually brings along a male chaperone. I dance with a few other people, but having a male escort gives me an excuse to stay out of new relationships. It's fun, though, and I like meeting new people."

I tried to change the subject. "What about your family?"

"Not much to say, really. My youngest has just started school, and my husband is busy on the farm. We miss our eldest son, but we do hear from him. He is down at some secret place near London."

There seemed to be lots to talk about. We chatted about our futures once the airfield was built and the war was over, and laughed about some of the people we knew at the airfield. Michael Fromm attracted a lot of our attention, in part because he was an American, and in part because of his clumsiness with his girl relationships. Joan didn't mention anything about Jock McGregor, and I chose not to speak his name.

We also talked about fashion, the latest dance music, and where we preferred to hike in the Wolds. We discussed the church vicar, but needed to whisper since his wife sat at the front of the bus. We also remarked about some of the damage we passed, inflicted on England by the Luftwaffe.

At one point I asked Joan who she was staying with during our trip. Joan gave me the name, but it was in Welsh, so I couldn't even say the name, never mind spell it. This person was someone Joan had stayed with previously.

"But this will be a difficult and sad visit," Joan said.

"Why?" I asked.

"She has just lost her twenty-year-old son. He was in the air force with Bomber Command at an airfield just down the road from us in East Yorkshire. Back in April, his Halifax failed to return from Germany. He was in one of nine bombers that didn't return that night. No one believes he or any of his colleagues survived."

Joan asked me about my work in West Yorkshire. Did I miss it? Was it a good experience? I replied that I did miss it but more because of the friendships than the task of managing the canteens.

I went on to talk about some of the people that I had met.

"We occasionally had to train colored people. They were very friendly, nice people, and often their English was better than ours. They had come from the West Indies in the Caribbean, and were all volunteers. Most were taking on factory work for the first time in their lives. A few months ago, a group of eighty colored people came in to become machine operators, trained to use lathes, cutters, grinders and the like. It was sixteen weeks of training, and none of them missed a day."

"Did you ever hear from any of them after they were trained?" asked Joan, curious, since she had never met a colored person.

"Oh yes, often. Some would return for additional training, and others would have friends still at the institute."

"Did they ever tell you anything about where they were from?"

"Occasionally. Some came from islands such as Jamaica, Trinidad, and the Bahamas, and others came from Guyana and British Honduras. Yorkshire was a whole new world to them. Both women and men had volunteered to come here to serve a common cause—to beat the Germans. They thought that the Germans would bomb their homes in the West Indies if Britain lost. This was because the Germans would need to use their islands to attack the United States.

"They would talk about the people they knew serving with the Royal Air Force, the army, and even the merchant navy. It was fun hearing their stories about mixing with the English. The two cultures seemed to adjust well to each other. It was not unusual to find mixed dances with coloreds and whites dancing together. Attending chapel, singing in church choirs, playing cricket, competing at the ping-pong table, and learning to use ration books to shop kept the two groups mingled.

"Some would talk about how different it was in America than in England. For example, a woman whose husband had become a Spitfire pilot told me that airplanes in the Caribbean islands are all piloted by white people. Her husband could never use his new flying skills back in the West Indies."

At this point in our conversation, the bus pulled off the road and stopped. We could use the toilets at a school that was closed for classroom repairs. Everyone seemed cheery, and the weather remained dry.

Once on the road again, we began to see off to our right the coastline of North Wales. We knew that our destination was not far ahead. With everyone feeling a little tired, we finally arrived at Llanberis. We were shown where we would sleep that night and told to meet in the village square at eight o'clock the following morning. If possible, the bus would leave for home about three o'clock that same afternoon.

The Welsh weather chose to be kind. The following morning was sunny, with virtually no clouds. In the distance, Snowdon smiled down on us. We had been told to expect rain later and to carry our rainwear. However, it was not likely to be one of those days when the mountain hides behind an overcoat of cloud.

Most everyone was on time. Only Florence, the church organist, was missing. She had sent down a message that she would not join the group but would be at the bus at three o'clock. She and the friend she had stayed with overnight were going to spend the day exchanging recipes. Florence planned to cook Yorkshire pudding and would share her cooking secrets with her Welsh friend. She would explain the need for the correct temperature of the oven, the right balance of milk and water, and the need to add a tablespoon of very cold water to the batter just before pouring it into the heated tins to be placed in the hot oven.

In return, her friend would show her how to make leek soup. The importance of having the leek sweat for the appropriate period of time and the advantage of adding a little Stilton cheese would be demonstrated. There was sufficient lard, flour, eggs, and vegetables available at this time of year to make the recipe exchange possible.

The rest of us departed for the walk. After a brief tour of the castle, we headed for the hiking trail and began our ascent of Snowdon. Initially it was fairly easy, but the walking became more difficult toward the summit. The views of the sea and surrounding countryside were breathtaking. So was the view across the valley to the slate quarries. We repeatedly passed under the adjacent railway line and walked by a number of old cottages.

Toward the end of the trail it became windy and much cooler. I began to feel nauseous. I thought it was the altitude, or maybe the fish fingers that I had eaten the night before. I belched a little and then felt a little sick. By the time I reached the summit, I was throwing up. I was the only one who was ill, and everyone seemed concerned for my welfare. I was helped down the mountain, and by the time we descended and reached the bus, I felt much better. I wasn't sure what was happening to me.

Joan sat beside me on the way home. Periodically I felt nauseous and on two occasions tried to vomit. The homeward trip seemed to never end. We passed close to Liverpool and saw some of the destruction caused by the German bombs.

By the time we reached Yorkshire, it was dark. We could hear bombers and fighter planes overhead, but because there were no alarms sounding, we assumed that all the aircraft were ours. It was about midnight by the time we reached our village. Joan walked me home and carried my suitcase. I went straight to bed and slept. The morning arrived quickly, but I didn't feel any better. Joan called at the house on her way to the airfield. She told my mother what had happened and suggested that she may want to call the doctor. I tried to be sick in the kitchen sink.

The doctor arrived shortly thereafter and sat me down at the table. He asked me a series of questions, with my mother listening to the answers. He then checked my pulse and tongue. When he had finished, he leaned over, held my hand, and said, "Do you realize what is happening to you? You are pregnant."

The blood instantly left my face. I heard my mother gulp for air. The doctor spoke to us both about the importance of rest and receiving regular medical checkups. He then packed his bags, stood up, and left. My mother's eyes hooked onto mine; I tried to look at the floor and the walls. After the doctor had left, my mother said to me sternly, "You and I need to talk, young lady, and your father needs to be involved."

She called my father in from the garden. Memories were returning to me of that event six or so weeks ago. What should I tell my mother? How would she react? Would she believe me? What would happen to Jock McGregor? I waited for my father to arrive.

CHAPTER 8

I HAD BEGUN TO cry.

My father came in from the garden, carrying his trowel. "What in the world is going on, child? Why are you crying?"

Together, my parents could appear very threatening and intimidating. My mother was small and petite but wore her hair tight to her thin face; she could display a glaring harshness behind her round-rimmed spectacles. My father was slightly taller, with thinning gray hair; he had filled out with age. His reaction to stressful situations was to become stiff and growl and scowl when something didn't please him.

My mother explained to my father that the doctor had just driven off, leaving the family with some awful news.

"Your daughter is pregnant."

My father almost fainted from shock.

"We need to go and sit in the front room," said my mother. "We should talk there. Let me make some tea, and then you, Mary Louise, had better be prepared to give us a full explanation of what is going on. I don't know what you have done, and with whom, but I do know that this will bring terrible shame on our family. The entire village likely knows about your sickness in Snowdonia yesterday, and people will soon find out that you are pregnant. I can't imagine what you have been up to, to do this to yourself."

Ten minutes later we were in the front room; I was seated on a sofa, and my two parents sat in separate armchairs. The room looked out across the village green. I could see children playing.

The tea was hot. I took three spoonfuls of sugar.

"So, Mary Louise, what in God's world has happened? Who is the father? Do you know? Do we know him? Is this some little devil you have brought back to us from West Yorkshire? How on earth could you be pregnant?"

I was trembling and sobbed quietly into my handkerchief. My feeling of sickness had been replaced by fear. I was terrified for my future. Only my father offered me a little comfort. He seemed concerned as he looked at me from across the room with a softened scowl and signs of sadness.

I started to explain. "It shouldn't have happened. I am in love with my boyfriend in Africa. When I was grabbed and assaulted that evening, I thought nothing of it. The experience was unpleasant, but I thought by ignoring the incident, it would go away. It all happened in a few minutes, here, upstairs, a few weeks ago. I was scared to tell you because you think so highly of him, the lodger who lives upstairs. I think it was all an accident. He grabbed me when I came out of the bathroom. He had been drinking and said he was sorry afterward. There is no other reason for this to be happening to me."

I then proceeded to describe in detail what took place that evening. It hurt me to talk about it. I thought I would never have to describe those events to anyone, especially not to my parents.

Both my mother and my father were speechless.

"You mean the lodger is the one?" said my father. "That seems impossible. You let this happen, but you didn't tell us? I can't believe that you were so silly. You were near his bedroom wearing only a towel!"

"But it's true, father," I said, tears running down my cheeks. "That's the honest truth. He told me not to tell anyone. And I haven't been with anyone else. I don't know what to do. Maybe I should go back to West Yorkshire and stay there, if that's the best for the family?"

"You can't run away!" shouted my mother. "We are going to have to talk to various people and decide what to do with the baby. At least you don't have to think about an abortion. That's an offense anyway, and you could get sent away to jail for life. Everyone in the village is likely to know about your condition, so you would be called a murderer if no baby is born."

Father stepped in.

"This is terrible news, but we need to think carefully. We must talk to the man you say did this to you before we do much more. Does he know?" my father asked.

"No, he has no idea," I replied. "He has his own family in the West Midlands; you know that already. So I don't think he will be willing to marry me, and I don't think I want to marry him."

"Don't rush to conclusions," said Father. "I will drive down to the airfield and bring him back. You, daughter, had better go upstairs and wait until I return."

Mother nodded. She collected the teacups and went back to the kitchen. I went upstairs and waited—confused, fearful, not knowing what would happen next.

It was less than thirty minutes before I heard the car return. I looked out of the bedroom window and saw both my father and Jock McGregor get out of the car. They were not talking to each other. Jock followed my father to the back door. Jock looked relaxed; my father looked tense. A few moments later, I was called downstairs.

I returned to the front room. There were now three pairs of accusatory eyes looking at me. I sat on the sofa next to Jock. My father described to Jock what I had told him and said, "Is this true?"

Jock hesitated. He looked at everything and everyone except me. He started by saying, "It's true that your daughter and me had an encounter a few weeks ago, but what you describe isn't exactly what I remember. She was in my bedroom wearing nothing but a towel. She seemed as though she wanted to spend time with me. We cuddled, and she didn't resist. When we lay on the bed, she didn't tell me to stop. She didn't say anything, so I thought it was consensual. She seemed to be enjoying our time together. She didn't complain when she left."

"No, I was not liking it!" I blurted out. "And you were the one who pulled me into the room, and you told me not to talk to anyone. Now I'm pregnant!"

"I know I told you to be quiet. I didn't want you to get into trouble," was his reply. "I'm sorry for what happened, but I only have your word that this baby is mine. You go dancing and meet lots of other men, and you are really very pretty. Are you sure that I am the father?"

I couldn't stop crying. How could he say this to me? My father came over and hugged me. My mother sat there, her fingers twitching with irritation, her face still looking very angry.

"Whether it was him or someone else, we need to do something," said my mother. "The whole village will be talking about this in a few days."

Jock McGregor was beginning to look uneasy. "Look." he said, "if you want, I will pay for Mary Louise to go away until the baby is born. She has been very good to us at the airfield, and I am willing to help. I can help support her. It's also a way of thanking you for being such a nice landlady." He looked at my mother.

My mother muttered her thanks and my father gave him a look of bewilderment. Jock continued, "I don't think we should talk to other people at this stage. Maybe you should tell your other daughters, but I don't see a need to tell the rest of the village. There are always rumors. I would prefer that nothing be said down at the airfield, at least not about me. I probably should move out of this house, but I need some time to make arrangements."

My parents did not know what to say. I felt angry since I was being blamed for everything.

There was a pause in the conversation. Jock broke the silence by suggesting that he needed to get back to the airfield and that we could resume the conversation in the evening, if that was necessary. My parents didn't object. My father accompanied him back to the car and drove him back to the airfield.

I went upstairs to bed, having taken all that I could stand. I was beginning to feel nauseous again. If I had to throw up, I would rather do it privately in my own bathroom than in front of my parents.

Suddenly my life had shattered into a million pieces. All the things I had planned to do in the future likely could no longer happen.

Who did I need to tell before they discovered my condition for themselves? What about the baby? I didn't know if I wanted the responsibility of looking after a child. There was so much to think about. I sobbed myself to sleep with all these thoughts rushing through my head.

During the coming days, my parents seemed subdued. They treated me respectfully, but their smiles and laughter had disappeared. They told my eldest sister and her boyfriend what had happened but decided not to tell my younger sister. There was not much speculation in the village that we heard of, although several neighbors did enquire about my illness in Snowdonia. My mother told them that I had been working too hard and was suffering from stress and exhaustion. Joan Sykes came round with some flowers. She was given the same story but clearly did not believe it to be the truth.

Several weeks later I decided to tell Joan. I had continued to work at the airfield because of the speculation that would result if I stopped working there. I remained at the canteen until the first week of November 1943. During that time I saw Jock McGregor on several occasions, but we never talked. Our infrequent conversations only took place in my parents' home.

I needed Joan to take charge of the canteen once I stopped working. She accepted my invitation, and then she asked me if I was going to report the incident. I said no; my parents had told me that was unwise. If we reported it to the Royal Air Force, the RAF would have to conduct a public inquiry, and if we told the police, they were so understaffed that they would be unable to do anything. It would be my word against Jock's. The matter would be viewed as trivial, and that would only make matters worse.

During this time at the airfield, no one appeared to know anything about the incident. Jock McGregor apparently had said nothing, not even to Michael Fromm, his assistant. He did start discussions with his superiors to change his place of work. He claimed that working from an airfield already in operation would help him better understand the consequences on Bomber Command's operations of his final construction decisions. His superiors apparently agreed with him. He asked Michael Fromm to be his deputy at the airfield when he was not on-site, and started a search for new digs. He traded his bicycle for a car while I pondered my future and that of my baby.

CHAPTER 9

MY MOTHER TOOK charge of the home situation. Our relationship took on a very formal tone as she decided what was best for me. One evening when I returned home from the airfield she announced, "You need to go away from here. We can't have you on parade in the village with 'a bun in the oven.' I will make the arrangements."

"Where are you sending me to?" I asked.

"I don't know yet, but I am working on it," was her terse reply.

I did not know at the time that she had visited the local post office and sent a telegram to her sister who lived in the North East of Yorkshire, very close to the sea. She had been careful to stress to the post office that the telegram must not look like those used during the war to notify the recipients that a relative had been killed in battle. The telegraph boys on their small motorbikes were nicknamed the "Angels of Death," and she didn't want to upset her sister. Even the appearance of a telegraph boy was likely to create anxiety and speculation. Yet she wanted to communicate quickly. The Royal Mail was still functioning, but with fewer postmen and a large censorship staff, mail delivery was slow and unreliable.

My mother was the youngest of thirteen children and therefore was not very close to most of her siblings. She thought that the sister she selected would be ideal because, before the war, she had operated a bed and breakfast for holiday makers who were visiting the coast near her home.

She said very little in the telegram, just asked her sister to call the village red telephone box at a certain time on a certain day. Then she would be sure to be passing the box at that time. Neither my parents nor my mother's sister had a home phone, so we had come to rely on the "red box." These boxes had appeared in most of the local villages during the late 1930s, with their A and B buttons. Press A, and you lost your money but hopefully you were connected to the other party and could start your conversation; press B and you got your money back but no conversation.

One evening in late October when I returned home, my mother announced, "You are going to stay with your aunt."

"Which one?" I asked.

"The one who lives near the seaside. You should count yourself lucky that my sister has agreed to put you up until the baby arrives. I have agreed to pay her five guineas a month, and Jock McGregor has told me that he will give me the money. So next Saturday, you and he will drive up to my sister's."

Five guineas was equivalent to five pounds and five shillings. Rents and the cost of professional services at that time were still often expressed in guineas rather than pounds.

It seemed that I had no say in this arrangement. With the average weekly wage approximately seven pounds, the rent appeared high. It was significantly more than I had paid in West Yorkshire.

"What do I need to pack?" I asked.

"Everything," was her quick reply. "I don't want you coming back to the village while you are in this state." She frowned as she stared at the growing bump on my tummy.

"If necessary, Jock can visit you and bring you additional clothes when you need them. You will need some maternity clothes. Also, think about what you will need for the baby when it arrives. We don't have anything here, and we can't afford to buy you clothes, cots, prams, and the like. Right now, you had better go upstairs and start packing!"

The day after the British Guy Fawkes Day on November 5, Jock and I set out for the home of my mother's sister. It would be a journey of about forty miles. All the celebrations associated with Guy Fawkes had been banned in the village and elsewhere since 1939. The lighting of bonfires and the explosions of decorative fireworks were invitations to the German Luftwaffe to bomb us; also, those activities consumed vital war materials.

It was sad to reflect that Guy Fawkes Day had survived its annual celebration for hundreds of years since 1606, but now it was canceled. The celebration was to commemorate the failure of Guy Fawkes and a group of Catholic revolutionaries who tried unsuccessfully to overthrow the Protestant King James I.

It was ironic that Guy Fawkes had been born only a few miles away from where I, pregnant, now sat in Jock McGregor's car.

My aunt lived on the coast between the River Humber to the south and the River Tees to the north. It was these rivers that the Luftwaffe would follow inland to find their bombing targets. The risk of being bombed at my new home was lessened because of its distance away from both these rivers. Jock did the driving. I had been told to leave my car at home. My parents didn't want me driving around the Yorkshire countryside in my current condition.

Jock and I didn't talk much during the journey, although at one point he surprised me by asking, "Do you expect me to marry you? I will if you want."

I looked at him in disbelief.

"Why would you want to marry me when you are already married and have two children at home? If your offer is supposed to be an act of kindness, it's not the type of kindness I need from you. You have fundamentally changed the rest of my life. I am carrying your baby, yet I don't feel attracted to you. I want you to help me bring up the baby, show it some love and affection, and provide it with financial support. But I don't need you to marry me. Personally, I need nothing from you. There is no need to offer to marry me just because you feel guilty over what you did to me. Frankly, I don't particularly like you."

Jock appeared clearly annoyed by my rebuttal.

"If I am truly the father I would have expected you to want to marry me. I am offering to consider marriage, but I am not promising you that I will marry you. I have many things to consider, like my career and the effect on my two young children in the West Midlands. If you don't like me, it is probably best that we end this conversation right now. You say that I am the father, yet your opinion of me suggests otherwise. Because of my successful career, I wonder if you are just after my money."

I felt anger well up in me, and it was all I could do to stop myself from physically attacking him.

"If you truly care about your baby, I would expect you to explain to your wife what happened, explain that it was a mistake, if it was, and ask for her forgiveness. If she still wants to stay married to you that would be fine with me, but at least that way you can have a relationship with this baby and help it enjoy the best life possible. My parents want me to have the child adopted. This way I can keep the baby, and you can help me look after it."

Jock's reaction was to end the conversation.

"I don't know what I want to do" he replied. "I need time to think about matters. Who knows how and when this war will end. If you don't need me to marry you, then I will not rush into any quick decision. My life has been successful so far, and I don't want your child spoiling my future successes."

We both stayed silent for the rest of the journey. It was cloudy, and when we reached our destination, there was a bitter cold wind blowing off the North Sea. We were civil toward each other on arrival, but there was a strain in our relationship. Jock quickly departed once he and I had met my aunt, and she had shown me my bedroom.

My aunt's home stood on the top of a cliff overlooking the sea. The house was an old farm cottage made of gray sandstone. A small hamlet was about half a mile away, and beyond that, a huge hall built of the same gray sandstone as her home. During my stay I learnt that this hall had stood there for nearly two hundred years. It was rumored that George III had been incarcerated there during the early 1800s. The owner of the hall had treated the king for his insanity. But no one knew for sure. As I looked out of my bedroom window that evening at the windswept and desolate landscape, I thought how this was more of a place that made you mad rather than cured you of madness.

In the days that followed, I came to know well the weather that blew in from the North Sea. There were many days of nothing but horizontal rain and snow. The damp chilled me to the bone, and it felt as if the rain would turn to ice on your skin if you didn't move indoors quickly enough. Mist was the worst because it would roll in and stick to everything. I worried that I would fall over the cliff's edge because of the fog-induced blindness. All was silent except for the waves crashing on the rocks below and the occasional screech of seagulls.

In my aunt's house I felt like a prisoner in a jail cell. My aunt was kind and fed me well, but there was nothing to do. The only entertainment was the British Broadcasting Corporation's Home Service. We received the BBC programs through an old battery-operated valve radio that crackled and faded in and out as I would listen. There were hours of dance music. *It's That Man Again* was one of my favorite shows. There was also the singer Vera Lynn, *The Week in Westminster*, and the *Children's Hour*. I read a lot and began to think about what I should do when the baby arrived. The war seemed a million miles away.

I did occasionally manage to leave the house. My aunt would drive to the local town every Thursday and Saturday. She would invite me to go with her, and most times I would accept. Thursdays were always interesting. My aunt's garden was not exposed to the wind. She was able to grow gooseberries and black currants, and she also owned three damson plum trees. She collected the fruit and made delicious jam. On Thursdays we would carry as many jars as we could, find an open table in the local town market, and remain there until we had sold every last jar.

On one occasion she drove farther south than normal to see a friend. I was supposed to be the niece that was to be seen but not heard. So I was made to sit there while she told her friend about me and my pregnancy, and they talked about people and things that meant nothing to me. At one point the coal fire was so hot, and I was very sleepy. I was fortunate that my aunt stopped me from falling into the fire at the very last minute.

On the way home we passed another airfield under construction. I asked whether it was for fighters or bombers.

"Neither," said my aunt. "Or, should I say, both. This is supposed to be a FIDO."

"A what?" I asked. "What is a FIDO?"

"Well, I am no expert," replied my aunt, "but it's going to be an airfield where damaged British and Allied planes can land if they can't make it back home to their base airfield. There is supposed to be a very wide runway and two rows of burning oil on either side of the runway to help pilots land. As well as creating a hole in the fog, the pilots can see the flames from a distance."

I wondered who was managing this airfield's canteens.

Christmas came and went. There were no gifts and only a handful of old decorations for celebrating the season. At least we had Christmas dinner. My aunt had prepared a Christmas pudding back in February. She also went out to exchange five bottles of jam for a goose that was supplied by a local farmer. My stomach grew with the baby as well as from the food.

It was another knock at the door and the arrival of a telegram that was to end this phase of my life. The telegram read, "Man stopped paying rent; will collect Mary Louise Saturday 3:00 p.m. Thank you."

The following Saturday, at the beginning of January 1944, my father arrived at the house at around two forty-five in the afternoon. He had made an early start because it was a dull, rainy day, and on the Wolds, the rain was falling as snow. After a quick cup of tea served by my aunt, he carried my bags to the car, made sure that I was comfortably seated, and then cranked the engine to start the car. As we drove homeward, the evening turned dark but the weather cleared, which allowed us to make good progress. My father asked me how I felt; I told him I was well and looking forward to being at home. Thereafter we didn't talk very much.

At one point he broke the silence and said, "Your mother has found you a new job. It's a few miles away, but it should give you something to do for the next few weeks."

"What is it, Dad? Tell me more."

I was curious to know what my mother had been up to.

"Well, it's an office job," he said. "You will be sitting down, so that's a good thing. You can have your car back and drive to work. It will give you an income and will help you buy things for the baby."

"How did she find the job?" I asked.

"She was helped by one of her cousins. The cousin knows what's going on with you and offered to assist by using his work contacts. You can leave home early in the morning when it's dark, and you should return home in the evening after dark. Hopefully, that way, no one in the village will see you."

I knew our house offered several avenues to privacy. It was surrounded by a ten-foot brick wall that no one could see over. Additionally, the wooden gates at the end of the drive were ten feet high. Nobody would see me until I pulled out of the driveway, and by then I would be in the car on my way to work.

"Oh," I said and fell silent. A feeling of guilt swept over me as I thought about my condition, its origins, and the obvious suffering I had caused my parents.

We completed the journey without further conversation, arriving home late in the evening. The weather remained damp but soon turned cold and icy. I kissed my mother on arrival and went straight to bed.

CHAPTER 10

I AWOKE A LITTLE after daybreak the following morning with a continuing sense of sadness and shame over what was happening to me. I felt isolated and alone. The overcast, rain-laden, dark gray sky outside my parents' home had not departed during the night. It hung outside, waiting to deliver its watery embrace to anyone who entered its world. I went downstairs to the kitchen, the warmest place in the house. My father would light the coal-fired cooker even before he dressed in the morning. Its warmth seemed to soften my fears for the future and hardened my resolve to take charge of the challenges that were being put before me.

Coal was available during the war, delivered regularly by the coalman, with his horse and cart. It was not rationed at this time, but we were only allowed two-thirds of what we used before the war. A couple of paraffin or kerosene heaters were in the old stable, but they were only used for emergencies. There was no electric heating; coal, and the occasional wood, was all we had in the house for heating. Sometimes it meant early nights to sleep so that we could hide in the warmth of our beds.

When I arrived in the kitchen, my mother was sitting at the table, drinking tea and eating toast. The jar of red currant jam beside the toast was almost empty. After our morning greetings, I asked, "Where is Father?"

"Upstairs, putting on his shirt and tie. We are about to go to church. Don't you expect to come with us. In your state, I don't think the church will welcome you. I don't want you to be seen by my friends."

This rejection did not surprise me. The condemnation in her tone of voice did. Little had changed since I had left to stay with my aunt. Mother continued, "Eat some breakfast while we are gone. When we get back, there are lots of things to talk about. We need to speak to you about having your child adopted."

"Adoption?" I said. "I am the mother, and I should make that decision."

"We will talk about that later," asserted my mother sternly as she cleared away the breakfast table. "It's not just what you want. What you have done affects the whole family. We have a say in this matter as well. Your sister will be calling to see you this morning, and she agrees with us. She and her husband have talked about adopting the baby, but they want their own children, and we have told them that they shouldn't adopt your child."

My father arrived in the kitchen, and my parents left for the morning service at church. As they departed, my younger sister darted from her bedroom to join my parents.

I had completed my unpacking, eaten my porridge, dressed, and cleared away the kitchen dishes by the time my older sister arrived. I was very pleased to see her and had missed her. More importantly, I had missed her wedding because of the baby. Ava, as she was called, was now living with her new husband on a remote thirty-acre farm a few miles away. She was pleased to see me.

We talked about married life. She asked me about my condition and what it felt like to carry a baby and asked if I had enjoyed living with my aunt.

Aware of changes at the airfield, she told me that the construction was almost complete but that the bad weather was causing last-minute delays. Aircraft were scheduled to start arriving at the beginning of March, along with ground crews, mechanics, and NAAFI girls. The staff for the airfield was being housed in the Nissen huts that had been erected in the village.

She then surprised me by asking, "Have you heard that Jock McGregor has been promoted by Bomber Command?"

"I hope not," I replied. "What has happened?"

My sister told me of a long conversation that she had had with Joan Sykes. Joan and she had met on December 26, 1943, at a Boxing Day party. Apparently, Number Four Air Group, which was in charge of our airfield, had other stations that needed repairs and maintenance to support the number of bombing raids that the group was expected to conduct. The group needed someone to oversee construction across all stations, and Jock McGregor had been given the job. He was now under extreme pressure to perform.

In December 1943 the national head of Bomber Command had claimed that the British bomber squadrons would bring about the collapse of Germany by the end of April 1944, and that invasion of Europe would not be necessary. While many airmen believed that this was impossible, there was a campaign to make sure that every available plane was able to fly. It was Jock's responsibility to provide the facilities for this to happen.

My sister paused for a moment to see if I had questions. Before I could ask anything, she switched on her more serious face and continued, "Mother is really very, very angry with you. She blames you for all that has happened. She says it is shameful what you did and that the shadow of shame falls on all of us. She wants you to have the baby adopted. She wants its new family to live as many miles away from here as possible. She will not permit the baby to live in her home. She has talked to all of us about this. She is really very upset."

I told my sister that I didn't think I wanted to give up the child. I had not asked to become pregnant, but now that I was, I accepted my responsibilities toward the child.

When my parents and younger sister arrived home, we first sat down and ate lunch. The leftovers of the joint of ham prepared earlier in the week were taken from the meat safe in the larder and placed on the lunch table. Mother quickly boiled some potatoes, cabbage, and carrots. The meat safe kept the meat cool, protected it from flying insects, and allowed the air to circulate so that the meat did not sweat. A metal frame that was painted a cream color surrounded wire gauze on all four sides of the safe. It was not possible to buy ice for cooling purposes, and refrigeration was not available.

Once lunch was over, we moved to the front room, where the coal fire was already burning. My father was already there, seated in his favorite armchair. My younger sister was sent upstairs. The contrast between my surroundings and my situation seemed enormous. Here I was, in a warm, care-giving house about to receive a cold, unsympathetic set of instructions from my family because I was pregnant.

My mother opened the conversation. "I believe your father has told you that I have found you a job. You start tomorrow morning at eight o'clock."

She gave me the address and continued, "It's a few miles to drive each day, but you can use your car. It's a government office, and the work is clerical. Your supervisor is a woman called Nan Dawson. She is expecting to see you in the morning. I hear there is a lot of overtime, so the wages should be good."

I thanked my mother. It would be a welcome change to find myself busy and surrounded by other people.

"There are some other things I need to tell you about," she added. "First, so long as we allow you to live here, I do not want you going beyond the driveway; I am deeply ashamed of what you have done. I don't want the village to see you in your condition. You also need to change your doctor. You can find a new one to visit nearer to your workplace. I don't want the district doctor coming to this house and causing the neighbors to speculate about what's going on."

I nodded my understanding. I wondered how I might find a new doctor.

"Mary Louise," she said with great seriousness. I knew that her use of my full name meant something very important was about to be said.

"Your father and I have spent a lot of time discussing what should happen to the baby. We don't believe that you should keep it. It will destroy your life as well as bring shame to all of us. Your child is illegitimate, a bastard, who will be born out of wedlock. You need to have it adopted."

I felt humiliated, cornered, attacked by my own blood. I swallowed my tears.

"What do you mean, adoption?" I asked. "I'm not ready to give up my unborn like a sack of potatoes or a bushel of corn. I need time to think. I believe I will love my baby."

My mother continued, "Your father and I have spoken with lawyers. The decisions our parents might have made in the same circumstances are no longer available to us. Sending unwelcome children to baby farms, such as what happened to Oliver Twist, is no longer allowed. In the olden days we had a right to do whatever we liked with our children. Today, we can't even give a child to a relative without going through this new legal process."

At this point my father broke his silence by adding, "Your mother's eldest brother volunteered to take your baby. But now that he knows he has to register the adoption, meet all sorts of conditions, and be subject to auditing by the local authority, he has withdrawn the offer."

But I didn't want to give up my child anyway.

"Mum, Dad, I really don't want my baby taken away from me. At least give me some time to think. If I do decide to adopt, what would I have to do? Wouldn't its father have to give permission?"

"That man has no say in the matter," said my mother. "Since you are unmarried, the child legally will have no father. No father will be named on the birth certificate. You should start to worry about the child's welfare and not be blinded by your own selfishness. We need to try and find someone rich who can give the child some social status and a good start in life. That's much better than you keeping the child or putting it in a government care home. By all accounts these homes are overflowing with unwanted children because of the war. There is talk about sending some of those children overseas for adoption. An adoption by a willing, qualified family is the right answer for you."

We continued to discuss and argue for at least another thirty minutes.

Finally my mother said, "Go and think about it and decide. If you keep the baby, you will not be welcome in this house. We could choose to have you sent to a hostel for unmarried mothers, but we don't want to have to do that. Alternatively, we could have you go off and pretend to be a war widow with the child, but that would be a lie, and people would find out. Also, I don't know where you would go, and you wouldn't be able to look after your child and work at the same time.

"That's why we believe that having the baby adopted by a family is the correct answer. But you will have to decide soon. Under the new law you have to have the child adopted within fourteen days of birth, you have to use an authorized adoption agency, and once it is adopted, you cannot claim back the child."

With that, my mother hurriedly left the room. My father picked up a book and started to read. My sister excused herself, went outside to her car, and drove home to her husband. I was left to anguish over what I had just heard.

I remained unconvinced that the baby should be adopted. It was clear, though, that if I kept the baby, I would no longer be welcome in my parents' home.

Later that evening, after the family had taken tea, I excused myself and went to bed early. After the stresses of the day, I needed a good night's sleep before starting my new job the following morning.

CHAPTER 11

I ROSE EARLY WHILE it was still dark outside. I would not be late to work on my first day. I could feel the baby's presence inside me, with the occasional kick to my stomach wall. My parents were still asleep. Only my younger sister appeared before I left. She was on her way to the airfield. Since leaving school, she had worked at the canteen every day. I prepared my lunch, an egg sandwich and a flask of tea. Dessert would be an apple. I checked my looks and lipstick in the mirror, went to my car, and drove off into the dark. It was raining "cats and dogs," as they say. It had been raining like this on and off for the past week, permitting only a few dry intervals, usually in the afternoon and early evening.

I left home early, yet arrived at work late. My route took me over a bridge that crossed a normally slow-moving, meandering river on its way to the North Sea via the Humber Estuary. Throughout the past few days the river had been collecting rain and the melting snow that had earlier blanketed the North Yorkshire moors. The river was in serious flood stage as the excess water breached its banks. Several feet of water blocked my path to the bridge.

Fortunately, I knew the geography of the roads in this part of the countryside. I was able to find an alternate route, but it took me the long way round to reach my destination. Consequently, I arrived at my new workplace thirty minutes late.

My new office was located on the third floor in an old stone and brick building that was cold and damp. There seemed to be very little heating in any of the offices. I later discovered the benefit of wearing an overcoat and neck scarf to work. Occasionally gloves were also needed, although they interfered with my work.

When I arrived on the third floor, I tracked down my supervisor, Nan Dawson, and gave her the employment information she needed for her records. She asked me for my name, address, age (now twenty-one), tax details, and names of my next of kin. She accompanied me to my desk, instructed me about the forms and standard letters that I would be using, wished me well, and left. During the day she came over several times to be sure that I understood what I was doing and to answer questions. Nan was easy to talk to, with an engaging sense of humor.

She lived nearby in a two-up/two-down terraced house. The front door opened directly into the living room. Her kitchen opened onto the walled back garden, which included the outdoor toilet or lavatory. Her husband had worked on the railways but had been made redundant several years earlier when he injured his back at work. So she had become the breadwinner. They had planned for children, but Nan, who by now was in her late fifties, remained childless. She was slim, about six feet tall, with light brown hair curled off her face. She would usually walk to work but occasionally used the bus that followed the tracks of the trams that had ceased to operate a few years earlier.

I quickly grew to like Nan. She cared for her staff. She stopped at my desk late one evening to remark on the amount of overtime I was working. My tummy was pushing its way from beneath my overcoat. She asked me about my circumstances. I told her. She agreed that what I did with the baby at birth was the most important decision I had to make. She sympathized with the views of my parents but believed that, whatever happened, I must feel that I had done the right thing for the child. My decision should be governed by the needs of the baby and not by some selfish wish of mine or my parents.

She asked about the baby's father. I told her about Jock McGregor, what an important person he was, and how my mother idolized him. Nan reacted angrily when I told her that Jock was no longer providing financial support. While technically the baby might not have its father's last name, Nan believed this did not excuse him from financially supporting the child. She also expressed concern that I was driving too far when I was about to enter my third trimester. She asked to have lunch with me later in the week, and I agreed.

We ate at one of the civic restaurants opened during the war to feed members of the public who otherwise would not have had access to hot food because of war damage to their homes. The choice on the menu was limited, but the price was well below the five shillings maximum that any restaurant was permitted to charge for a meal at that time. As we ate, I asked Nan about finding a doctor nearby to help with my pregnancy. She suggested that I use her family doctor and also kindly offered to arrange an appointment. I thanked her.

She then asked me what I had bought for the baby, and I told her nothing so far. She was a little alarmed at that because of the late stage of my pregnancy.

"Let me help," she said. "We can go shopping together during our lunch breaks."

I said that would be nice. She also asked about maternity clothes because she could see that my tummy was winning the battle against my overcoat. I told her I had none.

Nan commented that she would ask her neighbor, who had given birth to a boy six months earlier, if she had maternity clothes that she no longer needed. Nan's willingness to help me seemed to be limitless.

The next topic on her agenda was Jock McGregor. Was he good-looking, how old was he, where did he live, was he already married, how did the pregnancy occur, and why had he stopped giving me money? I could answer all her questions except the last. That did not satisfy Nan.

"Legally, he may not be registered as your child's father, but that doesn't excuse him from his financial responsibilities. If the baby is not adopted, you will need financial support."

She went on to suggest that I obtain legal advice before it was too late. That might cost me a few pounds but could prove to be money well-spent in the long term. I said I knew someone at the law offices that my mother used, and I would contact one of them.

"You should keep a list of everything you buy and receipts for all the expensive items," she suggested. "That way, the courts will know what the baby cost you."

I told her I thought that was a good idea, and I would start a list as soon as we started shopping.

She had one more surprise for me. Her next words were another example of her abundant kindness.

"I worry that you are about to start your third trimester, and you're driving these long distances to work every day. Anything could happen to you when you are miles from anywhere. I could never forgive myself if something dreadful happened to you and the baby. Why don't you move in with me and my husband? We have a spare bedroom. That way it will be much easier for us to go shopping together, as well as you continuing to work."

I was stunned by the offer. With my parents I had learnt not to be tongue-tied. But with Nan it was difficult not to be. When I went home and told my mother, she was delighted. She thought Nan had my best interests at heart. She also praised the arrangement because it would keep me out of the village and away from prying eyes.

I accepted Nan's offer and moved in with her the following Monday in late January 1944. I stayed with her a little over two months, only moving back to live with my parents when the doctor told me to stop working. During my stay with Nan, she did everything to help me prepare for my baby's arrival, including accompanying me on my doctor's visits and sitting with me during the meeting with the legal people. The lawyer told me that the baby's father did have some financial obligations to support the child and that I should file a claim with the local court. I did.

Our greatest fun together was when we went shopping. I moved slowly because of my condition, but Nan was patient with me. We bought lots of things, and I recorded the price of each item. Of particular pride were the following purchases:

Cot and mattress: 2 pounds, 19 shillings, 9 pence
Pram: 8 pounds, 6 shillings, 6 pence
Nappies/diapers: 1 pound, 16 shillings, 0 pence
Baby dresses: 1 pound, 9 shillings, 9 pence
Name tags: 6 shillings, 0 pence

I also spent some of my wages on maternity clothes and received maternity nightwear as gifts from Nan's neighbor. My savings were disappearing fast. The doctor needed to be paid for each of my visits, and the fee charged by the solicitor was not insubstantial. My list of expenses soon totaled in excess of seventy pounds.

There were evening occasions when Nan and I would stay in town after work. One night we treated ourselves to the movies and saw Humphrey Bogart in the war film *Sahara*. Another evening it seemed that the whole town had been invaded by military people. Fog was blanketing most of Europe, and bombing raids had been called off for the evening. So everyone had come to town to "razzle," or have fun. The streets were drenched with blue-hued uniforms worn by British, American, French, Canadian, and Polish servicemen and servicewomen. Children moved among the groups, asking for gum and sweets.

Even French airmen had learnt the local dialect to use to ward off an over-persistent child. "Al teel tha mam 'o thee if tha don't gow." Translated, this meant, "I will tell your mother about your bad behavior if you don't go away."

When I left Nan in late March 1944 to return to my parents' house, Nan once again displayed her extreme generosity, telling me, "After the baby has arrived, you should know that you and your baby are welcome to move in at any time, and live here with me and my husband. If your family doesn't want you, we do."

Once home, I decided that I would write just before the baby arrived to my aunt, with whom I had lived during my pregnancy, and to the family that I had stayed with in West Yorkshire when I worked there. I was also trying to build up sufficient courage to write a letter to send to North Africa or wherever my boyfriend's tank regiment might happen to be at the moment.

I hung around my parents' house most of the time for the next few weeks and occasionally visited the garden to help my father. Only my older sister came to see me. The baby's movements were becoming more obvious. I found myself a more frequent visitor to the lavatory; I continued to put on weight.

My father would always be anxious when I was in the garden with him. My shortness of breath and occasional reports of early contractions had him scrambling to leave the car positioned with its engine pointing down the driveway, and the petrol tank holding as much petrol as the ration book would allow. The occasional Halifax bomber would fly overhead. My younger sister told me that the squadron had moved into the completed airfield and was preparing to start bombing operations. And so I waited for my child to arrive.

As the end of the third trimester moved closer, I became increasingly certain that I should keep the baby. It was hard to imagine giving up my child, and I worried that I would not find a suitable family for adoption. Also, I would have to act sooner than I wanted to because of the new regulations. There were many illegitimate babies out there. Why should I think that mine would receive special treatment? There was absolutely no assurance that I would find a kind, rich family.

I knew my decision would determine my future, but I had no idea what would happen as a consequence. There was the consolation that I knew I could move back in with Nan if I needed to. Maybe under those circumstances, I could pretend to be a war widow and avoid the stigma of being an unmarried mother. There also remained the last-resort choices of placing my child in a government home or both of us checking in to a "mother-and-baby" hostel. The last idea made me frightened when I thought of what I had read about the conditions in these hostels.

Earlier in the year, while I was working, I had made arrangements to be admitted to a nursing home close to my place of work when the time came. At the same time, the solicitor whom I had spoken to contacted me to tell me that he would initiate legal proceedings against Jock within the next few weeks. I received an update from my younger sister that the first bombing raids from the airfield would likely take place toward the end of May 1944.

It was one of those warm, sunny spring days when my baby decided to arrive. I was in the garden during the evening, helping my father weed the strawberries. The weeds had flourished, thanks to recent April and early May showers. I suddenly felt persistent severe contractions and told my father. He did not hesitate. He and I quickly got in the car, and we were immediately on our way through the narrow country lanes to the hospital.

Within an hour, I was in the nursing home. Two hours later, I delivered a son. As the child cried, I could hear a gramophone record playing in the background. It was an Italian tenor accompanied by a violinist playing "Ave Maria," a song that was to become my favorite for the rest of my life. Surely the words behind the music were a message from God: "Blessed art thou amongst women and blessed is the fruit of your womb."

I felt joyful, relieved that my baby was healthy, and happy that at last he had arrived. During the months that I knew I was pregnant my feelings were all over the place. Early on I experienced the negative emotions of rage, repulsion, feeling violated, shame, and anger. My focus was on Jock and his violation of me and my body. The knowledge that I could not have an abortion made me doubly angry. My life had been destroyed, and my support system of friends and family had largely disintegrated.

Yet, as the baby grew inside me, I felt a growing bond with its presence. This was my child. We were in partnership. Together we would fight the stigma of illegitimacy and the loneliness of lost friends, and would stand up together against whatever challenges the world would put before us. I felt an emerging pride and joy that I was bringing another life into this world. I would give it my dedicated love and support. I knew there were emotional and physical demands ahead of me, but at least Nan Dawson and my older sister would reinforce my courage and determination. I could not hate the child growing in me. I was giving it life. I could not turn around and abandon it the moment it arrived.

I listened to my baby cry; I smiled; I wept with joy. I would be strong and determined, both as a mother and opportunist, as I sought to raise my son in an image that would make me proud. If it was required, I would sacrifice my own well-being for his. My faith had helped me through these difficult weeks. Although I had been banned from attending church by my parents, they could not ban my God from being present in my mind. I felt a closeness with him. Only he and I truly knew what happened that evening with Jock. He gave me the strength to accept and survive the consequences of my pregnancy. I believed that he would remain with me always and be the guardian of my joy and suffering as I raised my baby son. I would stay with him for the remainder of my life, and he would always be there to console me in my times of despair and adversity.

My sense of contentment continued as I lay there with my baby.

My older sister visited the nursing home the following day and sat with my father by my bedside. The only other visitor I received was Nan Dawson.

I felt relaxed. I had already decided to call the baby John, if it was a boy.

"Why John?" inquired my father.

"Because of John Bull," I replied.

John Bull had been the national mascot of England for some time. I had seen him on posters during the war, looking out at those passing by, wearing his Union Jack waistcoat with his English bulldog by his side.

"He represents the character of England and our resolve never to accept defeat and the reason why we will win the war. I want my son to be like him."

My father nodded but stayed quiet.

The comfort of my stay in the nursing home had come to an end. First, I had to return to my parents' home, and then possibly move in with Nan, depending on the mood of my family. My parents and sisters were kind to me and seemed to enjoy my baby as much as I did. My baby reminded me more of my father than Jock when I looked at him. He probably carried some of the features of his father, but even at this young age, he seemed to have inherited the appearances of my family. That was a relief.

I had written letters to the people who mattered to me, telling them what was happening to me. Soon I began to receive replies.

The aunt I had stayed with during my pregnancy gave me words of encouragement: "Thank you for your most interesting letter … It was wise to write and tell your friends. I think you will be more your own mistress if you live with your friend, don't you? I would love to see John but don't know when."

The words from my friends in West Yorkshire were less encouraging: "Many thanks for your letter. We were wondering what had happened to you. I think you will be foolish not to follow your family's wishes. It will be better in the long run for both you and the child. If you have the child adopted by some nice people, it will take their name and need never know it was illegitimate. Also, it perhaps will have a better chance than you can give it."

The letter I had most difficulty in reading came from my favorite dancing partner, still assigned to his tank troop:

"Thank you for your letter, which I received today. To tell you the truth, I haven't got over the shock of the news yet. I have read your letter seven or eight times since tea. You say in your letter if you don't hear from me you will understand. Well, as you see, I have written you as soon as I could. I must say your letter has altered my plans for when I return home. Needless to say, I am a very disappointed soldier tonight."

I received this correspondence at the same time I heard that the bombers were now flying bombing missions from the local airfield. They were contributing to the preparations that would enable Britain and its Allies to very shortly invade Europe. Early targets had been marshaling yards and gun batteries in France. To date, only one plane had failed to return.

Less than three weeks after my son was born, the Allied invasion took place, on June 6, 1944. For a time my family's attention shifted from me to the progress of the war. At about the same time, my mother announced that her closest girlfriend had died of cancer. Would I drive her to the funeral, which would be close to where we used to live prior to the war? My older sister would come with us to help look after my baby. I agreed.

CHAPTER 12

MICHAEL FROMM TOOK the slow route back to California. After the bombers began to fly in May 1944, he knew that his work with Number Four Air Group was over. It was time to move on. Following D-Day on June 6, 1944, he stayed around for a few more weeks to be certain that Germany would eventually have to surrender. He had no idea of what was happening close by to Mary Louise and the birth of her son John during May 1944. While Jock was open to sharing all other aspects of his life with Michael, he never once mentioned his sexual encounter with Mary Louise, and its consequences.

Michael had thoroughly enjoyed his time with the Land Girls in East Yorkshire. In fact, he had hoped to take one of them back with him to America. Unfortunately, those who were willing to go failed his good looks test, and those he fell in love with declined to leave their parents.

Michael was proud of his accomplishments at the airfield. He would watch the heavy bombers take off and return without problems. The runways were long enough and strong enough to take care of all situations. Even the planes that had to crash-land seemed to be supported by his work.

By July 1944, he had ceased regular contact with Jock McGregor but knew that he was close by, completing his Bomber Command assignment. At his last meeting with Jock, Jock had told him that he now spent more time with his family in the West Midlands and hoped to return to his family as soon as the war was over. They had also talked about staying in touch with each other after the war and maybe visiting each other once Michael was married. Michael was curious to visit this place called the West Midlands and to meet Jock's wife and two children.

Michael had also had a conversation with the youngest daughter of Jock's former landlady, who had worked at the airfield before the bombers began to fly. She had told him that she was now the only daughter living at home. Her older sister was happily married, and the middle one had moved away to live somewhere in West Yorkshire.

By September 1944, there was no reason for Michael to stay at the airfield any longer. He thought about returning home. The problem was that he might be conscripted and sent off to war in the Pacific Theatre. That front was still very active, and, from what he had heard, serving in Asia did not appeal to him. He had come to enjoy the Yorkshire countryside and felt at home with the local people.

He considered moving south to London, but less than a week after D-Day, the first V-1 or "doodlebug" had arrived in London. Bomber Command had failed to destroy this new weapon. Apparently these doodlebugs were launched from mobile launchers that could be moved around very quickly and hidden from the view of visiting bombers. Almost two hundred were being launched at London every day. The trauma among Londoners was serious, but the local population had quickly adjusted their way of life to this new threat, just as they had adjusted to the bombing during the blitz. As the Allies advanced across Europe, it was hoped that the launchers would eventually be pushed out of range.

He thought long and hard about what to do next. The increasing number of German prisoners of war coming to England gave him the answer. He decided to accept work with the War Agricultural Executive Committee. This organization had a significant presence in Yorkshire and controlled all agricultural production. Increasingly, prisoners of war were being put to work on the farms of England. Some 20 percent of national food production was expected to come from the sweat of these prisoners. Using his knowledge of the local farming community and his ability to speak some German, he was quickly hired and assigned to a camp responsible for holding German prisoners of war.

Previously the camp had housed Italian prisoners of war. However, following the Italian surrender to the Allies in September 1943, those prisoners had been moved to low-security camps. Some had even willingly volunteered to work until the war was over and had joined the Italian Labor Battalion in Britain. Those who declined the invitation were retained in camps but under less secure conditions.

Most of the current German "military guests" had traveled by ship to England after capture and then, after being processed, were taken to their assigned camp by rail. A few were airmen, captured before D-Day after failed bombing visits to Britain during which their planes were shot down. Groups of prisoners were escorted by the British military police from the rail station to their camp. Which camp they were assigned to depended in part on their "color code" after interrogation. Non-Nazis were graded white; those with uncertain loyalties were coded gray, and those with strong party affiliations were classified as black. The darker the grading the further away from London the prisoner was to be sent and the more remote the camp. Each prisoner wore a patch on his clothing to indicate the color he had been assigned.

As the weeks passed during the second half of 1944 and early 1945, and the Allies secured more and more territory in Europe, large numbers of prisoners were arriving. But there was a growing expectation among the guards that they would be less motivated to escape, since everyone expected that Germany would lose the war. However, this was not always the case. In March 1945, seventy prisoners at a camp on the British west coast tried unsuccessfully to tunnel to freedom. This was the biggest escape attempt made by German prisoners in Britain during the war.

Michael had to move to be closer to his new place of work. His previous landlord helped him find a new accommodation. Located very close to his assigned camp, it was another old manor house bordering the edge of a meadow that sloped down to a gentle, slow-moving river. It was a short distance away from the center of a nearby market town. He would often ride his motorbike to the town square to buy some fish and chips. He became an expert at ordering "one of each with scraps" at the little shop, which could be smelt long before it was seen, because of the odor of frying fish and chips. He was even able to interpret for a couple of prison guards who had come down from Scotland. When they ordered "two fish suppers," the owner of the fish shop had no idea what they were asking for. Michael thought it more than a coincidence that neither fish nor potatoes, the two staples of this very traditional British dish, was rationed in England at that time.

For a little over twelve months, Michael remained committed to this new occupation. He continued his work as Germany surrendered on May 8, 1945, followed by Japan on August 15, 1945. He helped with the administration of the camp on behalf of the War Agricultural Office. There were several rows of huts protected and kept secure by a barbed wire fence around the perimeter. It was Michael's task to assign prisoners to particular farms based on the farmer's needs, and to ensure that the prisoners were transported there by truck each day and returned safely to the camp each evening. Until Germany surrendered, it was usual to have guards accompany the prisoners. Some of the better-behaved "military guests" were given permission to billet on the farms when this was helpful to the farmer.

Because of his knowledge of German, Michael would often hear the latest gossip circulating around the POW camp. It seemed that most prisoners were content to wait until the war was over and then be officially reassigned to return to Germany.

There were many activities for prisoners to participate in at the camp. They could learn English, attend or participate in music events, and play soccer. Letters could be written and sent home but needed to be handed in unsealed so that they could be read and censored by the officials.

The single most serious deprivation for the prisoners was the ban on fraternizing with the locals. However, exceptions did occur, as evidenced by the many farmers' daughters who moved to Germany after the end of the war.

It was while Michael was working at the camp during the spring of 1945 that he received press cuttings from his parents detailing the death of President Roosevelt on April 12. His death had been announced by the British Broadcasting Corporation during the evening of April 12, and further information was published the following morning in the *Guardian,* Britain's national newspaper. Michael's parents were just two of many millions of Americans who admired FDR. Roosevelt had achieved so much, ranging from establishing a leadership role for America on the world stage to repealing Prohibition in 1933. He had also supported America's entry into the war in support of Britain, just in time.

It was now October 1945, and prisoners were starting to be selected for repatriation back to Germany. They were given the choice of returning home or staying in their host country. This became a signal to Michael that it was time for him to return to America.

He stayed on at the camp until the end of November 1945 but then resigned and decided to head for London. Petrol rationing stopped him from using his trusted BSA motorbike, so he had no choice but to travel by train. The railways had been the main means of transport during the war and had continued to serve a vital role as prisoners were repatriated, military personnel returned to their camps, and civilians returned home.

Michael advertised the sale of his motorbike in the front window of the fish and chip shop. It sold quickly, and he bade the bike farewell, pocketed the money he had been paid in the sale, and headed for the nearest railway station. Some hours later he was in Kings Cross, London. He stood most of the way during the trip, as the trains first traveled west and then south, and were packed with army, navy, and air force personnel, and only a handful of civilians.

Michael stayed briefly in London. His experiences of that city were very different to those that he was used to elsewhere. Bomb damage was rampant. He visited Westminster, St Paul's, Pimlico, the West End, and Hyde Park. Whole blocks of streets were missing, and elsewhere, buildings were badly damaged. Even Buckingham Palace had not escaped the German bombs.

Work had just begun on cleanup. Trucks full of rubble were moving among the cars and red double-decker buses in the streets of London as they slowly hauled away the bad memories of a war that was now over. People were mostly on foot or, in some cases, riding bicycles. The occasional taxi passed by. Bobbies patrolled the streets, handing out advice, giving encouragement, and helping keep the peace. The Underground trains were running, so it wasn't too difficult to get around.

Dirty, noisy steam engines belched smoke and soot as they carried their passengers to and from the rail stations that ringed the devastation Michael witnessed. Their piercing whistles would signal the start of each train's journey.

Michael managed to do some dancing, met a few nice English girls, and wandered into the occasional pub. Many of his fellow countrymen were in London, and he enjoyed meeting up with these Americans and exchanging stories. As the days passed, the uniforms of war seemed to be giving way to the return of civilian clothes.

Michael took in a soccer game, another sign that Britain was returning to normal. A Russian team was touring the country. He watched the team draw with Chelsea, standing in the stands with crowds of people, more than he had ever been with before.

He visited the beginnings of the countryside on the eastern borders of London. A Land Girl he had met in Yorkshire had invited him to stay with her family. She was now back home, and she and her family were trying to return to normal living. Michael took the Metropolitan Tube Line to visit her. It ran eastward, paralleling the north side of the river Thames. Terraced housing spread alongside this route, but every so often the houses would be punctuated by gaps where buildings had previously stood before being visited by bombs or doodlebugs.

Signs of recovery were scattered among this landscape. It could not easily be seen, but between the train and the river Thames was an automobile factory that had resumed the manufacture of passenger cars the previous month. During the war it had produced vans, trucks, tractors, gun carriers, and special-purpose engines. Remarkably, the blast furnaces that hugged the riverbank had survived. For whatever reason, the German bombers that had used the river as a compass for their targets to the west had overlooked this site for target practice.

Michael moved into his friend's small semidetached house, which was only a stroll away from yet another airfield. This one had been established in 1915 at the start of the Great War, when Michael's father was fighting alongside the British. This airfield's original purpose was to launch attacks against German airships, but during the most recent war, it had been converted into a fighter airfield. The camouflaged buildings were home to several squadrons, whose Spitfires had played an important role in winning the air Battle of Britain during 1940.

Now the airfield was losing its identity. Unlike the airfields that Michael was used to, this one was grassed over; there were no concrete runways. The very qualities that had made it a successful fighter station were beginning to make it redundant as planes became larger and heavier and required longer runways. By the time of Michael's visit, the airfield had become a Technical Training Command station.

Michael and his friend would occasionally go dancing in the nearby market town. His friend's older sister would accompany them. Michael was soon introduced to yet another English dialect, Cockney. In this case it was more a matter of different words being used than the way the speaker spoke them.

When needed, his two girl companions would translate for him. Both sisters were tall, very pretty, and wonderful dancers. Both claimed to be "going out" with steadies who should soon be home from the war. Michael's special evenings were those when he received a peck on the cheek from his friend as he and she went to their respective bedrooms.

Michael stayed with the family through Christmas. This was the first time in seven years that the family had been able to sit safely at the table and celebrate their companionship. There were few gifts because the stores were still largely empty. Room decorations were chains of colored paper that had been glued together and kept in storage since before the war.

The holiday fare was limited. Most of the food on the table came from the family allotment used for growing vegetables, and the duck came from the butcher, who had bought it from two duck hunters who were frequent visitors to the Thames marshes. But the happiness, revelry, and anticipation for the future more than made up for the shortages, rationing, and uncertainties that still remained as reminders of the war.

Now Michael needed to get home. As soon as 1946 arrived, he started to prepare himself for the long journey to California. He had thought of hitching a ride on a Liberty Boat to the East Coast of the United States, but most of these departures required him to travel to the south coast of England to join the ship.

Heathrow Airport, on the western edge of London, was much closer and would be opening as a civilian airport at the beginning of 1946. Airlines that had previously been flying out of locations on the south coast were now moving to London. The airport was only a sixty-minute tube ride and a short bus journey from where Michael was living. He could afford the ticket; he would be in New York far faster than if he traveled by sea, and flying by a land plane rather than a seaplane, in which he had flown before, would be a new experience for him.

Fifteen hours after saying farewell to England, he was home in the United States. He had arrived moments earlier, thanks to American Overseas Airlines and a DC-4 that had stopped over in Shannon, Northern Ireland, and in Newfoundland on its way to New York. Next, Michael traveled to the local Greyhound Bus Station to start his cross-country journey to Sacramento, California. He was excited; he felt as though he belonged here—everything seemed more familiar—and he could readily understand the people when they spoke to him.

Three days later, in late January 1946, he arrived home in Sacramento. His parents were delighted to welcome back their only child. Inside the house, everything looked familiar, but outside, he quickly began to notice the changing landscape. Repatriation might not be as easy as he had expected. But regardless of the effect of change, he would still need to rebuild his social life and resume his career as a transportation engineer.

His father had remained employed as an aircraft mechanic at the local air force base, where he had sacrificed long hours maintaining bomber and fighter aircraft. His mother, at the time Michael had left home, had never worked outside the house. But in the summer of 1943, she had responded to Rosie the Riveter advertisements and found employment. Initially she had applied for a job as a switchboard operator at a local cannery but was disqualified because of her German accent. The concern was that her voice might upset the customers. Fortunately, the cannery was so desperate for new staff that they found her a clerical job in the remittances department.

As Michael adjusted to his new surroundings, he was repeatedly amazed at how quickly the landscape was changing. The City of Trees was becoming a city of people. Gone were the open spaces and close neighborhoods where everyone knew everyone. As waves of people had arrived in Sacramento, the area had changed. The racial mix as well as the number of people had been impacted by this transformation. Tracts of little boxlike houses were being constructed on the city outskirts, and the orchards and fields of Michael's youth were rapidly disappearing under concrete and wood shingles. Businesses were moving to Sacramento to make use of the increased labor supply.

Early in the war, Sacramento had been a staging post for military personnel to equip and prepare for deployment to the Pacific war. Shortly afterward, skilled civilians had arrived, either as engineers or in other professions, to support the military and to replace the loss of local professionals who had been called up to the war front. Less skilled workers began to arrive to fill vacancies in local agriculture and to meet the needs of the new factories. The internment of several thousand Japanese during 1942 increased the demand for new labor. Finally, the Bracero Program had facilitated the transfer of large numbers of laborers from Mexico to work in agriculture and on the railways. As the war ended, many of these migrants chose to stay in the sunshine of California. Added to these numbers were the American Japanese citizens released from internment who decided to return home, and the decision of many retiring war veterans to stay in the warm climate of California rather than return to less favorable weather elsewhere.

Michael's first priority was to resume his social life. To do this, his father kindly lent him his car, a 1942 Nash 600. It had some effect with the ladies, but mastering the steps of swing dancing was far more impactful. Michael watched and read, and became familiar with all the different styles of swing. The Lindy hop was his favorite, and very soon he was welcomed on the dance floor and became a member of the Sacramento jitterbug community.

Fashion was important to him. He chose to dance with women who wore short skirts, exhibited tight waists, preferred colorful tops, and selected the short style of bobby sox. He developed relationships with some of the girls but none that became serious. Occasionally a partner would accompany him to other social events, to the movies, or flipping gramophone records to listen to the likes of Frank Sinatra, Perry Como, and big band music. Enjoying warm afternoons sipping frosty root beer floats at the soda shop was another favorite pastime. And Michael liked to attend the occasional jazz concert.

A joy ride into the mountains or down to the delta, with the appropriate picnic fare, was attractive to some women he met. Television was not yet a fixture in most homes, so people were not yet glued to their couches, watching TV for hours.

All in all, it was a very attractive but very different lifestyle in Sacramento from the one that Michael had known in Yorkshire. There was so much to do here in America; you always felt safe, everything seemed easily accessible, and most items for everyday living did not require ration books.

But the need to find employment would soon change Michael's life.

CHAPTER 13

By SPRING 1944 Jock McGregor was enjoying his expanded responsibilities with Number Four Air Group. He had moved out of the house of Mary Louise's parents and was living in accommodation at an airfield a few miles away from his prior residence. The new assignment initially encompassed a cluster of five airfields that included the one that Jock was building near Mary Louise's home, three other satellite stations, plus the parent base airfield a few miles away from the one under construction that provided all five locations with administrative support. His responsibilities were quickly broadened to include all airfields under the control of Number Four Air Group, giving Jock additional travel opportunities across the Vale of York, and a more satisfying workload.

He was very proud of the airfield that he had constructed from open green fields into a successful bomber station that was now participating in the war. It was the biggest project that he had ever worked on, and, he believed, it was an outstanding success. He acknowledged that Michael Fromm had played a key role in making this possible during the weeks after Jock had accepted his expanded role. Michael had assumed site responsibility and had regularly updated Jock on progress.

Bombers from this airfield had started flying raids on German-occupied Europe in May 1944 and were expected to continue these visits regularly until the war came to an end. Once the war was over, the airfield was likely to be turned over to Transport Command, and the bombers would cease to fly.

The months had passed by after the invasion of Europe; the war against Germany was won, and it was now July 1945.

Jock had not heard from or seen Mary Louise since he left her parents' house at the end of 1943, and he had made no effort to contact her. He was told that she had given birth to a baby boy and was no longer living at her parents' home, but he had no idea where she had moved to. Jock had never publicly admitted to fathering the child and knew that he wasn't named as the father on the child's birth certificate. He tried to dismiss the existence of Mary Louise and her child from his thoughts, but they would creep into his mind whenever he was thinking of his own family. The two of them were an infection that would not go away.

He was very angry with Mary Louise when she had taken legal action successfully against him in September 1944. She had obtained an order from the local courts that required him to pay her almost a pound a week in child support for the next fifteen years, reimburse birth expenses, and pay all court fees. He had refused to attend the court hearing.

The court order was served on him at his workplace by a police constable. Fortunately, this event occurred in the evening, so no one else was aware of the constable's visit. It was Jock's intention to challenge the court order and either have it canceled or have the amount of support substantially reduced. Until his appeal was heard, he decided to ignore the requirements of the court order and not make any child support payments. But he was continuously anxious that these proceedings might become public, and his friends and relatives would become aware of the sexual assault. After his argument with Mary Louise on the way to her aunt's when pregnant, he had decided to tell no-one about the events, including his wife and children.

His wartime assignment was now complete, and he had no idea when and in what capacity he would find new work.

He was on his way home to the West Midlands. His future was under his control. He rode the train home, since driving had not been an option. Although the basic petrol ration for private motoring had been restored a month earlier, during June 1945, the amount was still highly restrictive, limiting driving to only two hundred miles a month.

At least this was an improvement over what had existed before. All private motoring had been banned since July 1942. Petrol rationing was first introduced in September 1939, when the amount rationed was the same amount as was now reintroduced. Living in rural Yorkshire, on occasion, he had been able to bypass these requirements. There was a prevailing black market for gasoline. Petrol allocated for commercial and military use could not be separately traced and accounted for; consequently, people made money by selling some of their allocation. It wasn't legal, but there was no way of detecting the transfer. Jock assumed his access to the black market would disappear with his return to the West Midlands. He certainly had no intention of using more than half of a month's ration to drive home.

The greeting Jock received in July 1945 when he arrived at his West Midland home could not have been nicer. The front door stood open, with his wife and two children framed in the doorway. They all ran eagerly down the short driveway to meet him. His two-year-old daughter was in his wife's arms as his wife hugged and kissed him. His four-year-old son was tugging at his right pant leg and embracing it.

The McGregor home was a semidetached, three-bedroom house that had been built in the 1920s. It shared a wall with its neighbor but otherwise was self-contained and private. A small garden was at the back of the house, where his wife grew potatoes and vegetables. At the front of the house was a short driveway with no garage.

This style of housing was very popular with the middle class. The upper class typically occupied detached homes, and the working class mostly lived in two-story terraced housing.

Gwen, Jock's wife, had prepared a welcome home tea consisting of very salty potted meat sandwiches, a salad of lettuce, radishes, and spring onions, butterfly sponge cakes, and English jelly and trifle. All of this was accompanied by many cups of tea. Looking at his two young children and at his smiling wife, Jock reflected on how good it was to be back home, surrounded by his adoring family.

But to make this situation permanent would require Jock to find work quickly. Also, he did not want to jeopardize his current relationship by having to tell his wife anything about Mary Louise. Jock believed that his wife had no need to know and would not hear from anyone else. In the unlikely event that Mary Louise contacted his wife directly, he would deny the relationship. If Jock did tell her, it would only upset her, and it wouldn't change anything. So he decided to leave things as they were. But this didn't remove the personal anxiety that he felt over what would happen if his wife discovered that he had had an affair while in Yorkshire and was the father of another child.

During tea, he and his wife talked about current events. Jock asked about the many Americans that Gwen had talked about in her letters, and the status of the neighborhood air raid shelter.

"The Americans have all disappeared," said Gwen. "Once D-Day arrived in 1944, they all began to pull out and have never returned. As for the air raid shelter, it is now closed. We were lucky that so very few bombs were dropped in this neighborhood. There is not much to be rebuilt here, unlike in other cities nearby. It's much quieter now. Gone are the nightly gatherings of Lancaster bombers, that would circle overhead until they were in formation and then leave ready to bomb Germany."

She then asked Jock for his plans, and he replied, "I will try and find work very quickly. There should be lots of opportunities with so much rebuilding to be done. My plan is to concentrate on residential and infrastructure development, since that should keep me working locally. Times may be difficult for a while, but I am optimistic that everything will work out for the best. You should continue to stay at home and look after the children."

Gwen agreed with him.

They went out to the kitchen to share in the washing up and afterward, together, they put the kids to bed. During the visit upstairs, Gwen showed Jock where she had stored the gas masks during the war. She pulled out the baby's gas mask to let him see how it had entirely protected their baby daughter when the sirens had summoned her and the children to the air raid shelter.

To Jock, this was indeed home sweet home.

But finding employment was not as easy as he had expected. He initially accepted a position in the architectural department of a city planning office. He found himself drafting the layouts of prefabricated bungalows and developing specifications for more permanent housing. Occasionally he was assigned a more complex project, such as preparing blueprints for road construction, city gas mains, and installing new public water systems.

During this time his salary was less than it had been with Bomber Command. He was forced to draw on his meager savings, so he filed an appeal with the courts in Yorkshire to have his child support reduced or canceled. He assumed that the courts would inform Mary Louise. Until this matter was settled to his satisfaction, he decided to continue to ignore the payment requirements of the court order. However, he remained haunted by the knowledge that these proceedings were ongoing and continuously feared the consequences of public disclosure of what had happened.

By the late 1940s, the employment situation in civil engineering was improving. The Town and Country Planning Act of 1947 had given public authorities more freedom in sponsoring local residential and infrastructure projects, and the Special Roads Act of 1949 allowed new roads to be built that excluded access to certain categories of users. Previously everyone, including pedestrians and cyclists, had to have access to all roadways.

Jock was now employed by a rapidly growing company that concentrated on residential development, small- to medium-size road construction, and infrastructure projects. He worked long hours, often twelve to fifteen hours a day, six days a week. But he enjoyed the work. He received many compliments regarding the quality of his work, and the pay was good. He continued to smoke regularly to relieve stress and would occasionally drink a glass of whisky to provide added comfort. Hard work also took his mind off Mary Louise and her baby. At this stage his physical life had not been affected by his encounter with Mary Louise, but he felt its effect on his mental state.

He saw less of his own family during this busy work period but felt that this was a reasonable sacrifice in return for the high standard of living that he was able to give them. He bought himself a new car, a large touring vehicle, manufactured by Wolseley. He couldn't use it much at first because of petrol rationing, but it stood in the driveway as a symbol of his success.

In the early 1950s, once petrol rationing was relaxed, Jock and the family began to take longer trips and upgraded his Wolseley 18 to a Jaguar. By this time he had also developed a hobby in cinephotography and had started to make home movies starring his family. The early ones were made locally, but soon, with trips to Scotland, Wales, and the south coast of England, he became more creative with his productions and entered his best films in amateur competitions. Sometimes his films won prizes. He used the 9.5 mm film format that was popular before the war and operated a Pathescope camera and projector. Using this format, he was also able to show Mickey Mouse cartoons and Laurel and Hardy comedies at his home, along with his own family productions.

Jock particularly liked his summer visits to Weymouth and Lulworth Cove on the south coast of England. He and his family would stay at a Weymouth Guest House run by a woman who had lost her husband during the war. She was bringing up two young children on her own. This caused him to wonder about Mary Louise on occasion, but he kept his thoughts to himself.

There was much to do during these visits. The family would wade and swim in the sea, rent paddleboats, watch Punch and Judy shows, and eat ice cream. Jock preferred to stay on the beach and sit in his deck chair. His exceptions were the paddle steamer trips to Lulworth Cove, the SS Helier ferry to the island of Jersey off the coast of France, and looking in on the local bathing beauty contests.

His number one favorite was the all-day ferry visits to Jersey. The island was now back in British hands, having been occupied by the Germans from 1940 to the day that Germany surrendered, May 8, 1945. In the midst of its postwar recovery, the island had set itself the task of becoming the top honeymoon destination for British couples. During the German occupation, many of the islanders were deported, Jews were sent to concentration camps, and the fields were strewn with many thousands of land mines.

As the mid-1950s arrived, Jock continued his work successes. He hoped to become a partner in the firm and knew he was good enough for such a promotion. However, he never felt he received the same support at home as he did at work. His family frequently annoyed him with their pettiness over small domestic matters, and they never seemed satisfied with all that he did for them. This made him even more certain that he was correct in not telling his wife about the existence of Mary Louise. But thoughts concerning Mary Louise and her baby would never leave his mind.

Gwen would complain when Jock chain-smoked and drank more than a few glasses of whisky. Jock found that cigarettes and whisky had a calming effect on him and alleviated his anxieties about work, and sometimes about the existence of Mary Louise. He began to fall out with his wife. She often irritated him; sometimes she would only do what he asked her if he screamed and shouted at her. On occasion his temper would spill over onto the children. One time he asked his son to move his bicycle out of the rain into the garden shed, but his son refused. Jock became so angry he went out, started his car, and drove over his son's bicycle.

He continued to receive the occasional letter from Mary Louise, which he locked away in his private desk. These would alarm him because he was always worried that his wife would find one of them and open it. Mary Louise's letters usually asked for financial help, and, on some occasions, she would include a picture of her son. He found this all very annoying and wished it would stop, but he never wrote back to her. He had heard of no final decision from the courts concerning the child support order, but he believed he was justified in not sending payments until the order was legally enforced. He believed that his anger and impatience with his family was being influenced by his worries regarding Mary Louise. While initially his life showed no serious change as a result of his encounter in Yorkshire, he believed that its consequences were beginning to affect his behavior and personality.

Life generally in Britain seemed to be improving. The damage from the war was largely repaired, new homes had been built for displaced people, rationing had ended, memories of loved ones lost during the war were fading, and a new monarch had ascended to the British throne. Twenty-five-year-old Queen Elizabeth was now the queen of the United Kingdom, Canada, Australia, South Africa, Ceylon, and Pakistan. During her coronation on June 2, 1953, everyone across Britain had celebrated the event. Street parties were held, and red, white, and blue bunting was everywhere.

Jock and his family celebrated the coronation at the local school. A sports competition was held, followed by a party with cake and trifle that were served on long wooden collapsible tables; inevitably you met neighbors you had never met before. Jock and Gwen watched their son and daughter compete in the sack race, the egg and spoon race, and the three-legged race. There was much tumbling and lots of laughter. But again, Jock found his mind wandering back to Yorkshire and speculating on the whereabouts of Mary Louise and her child on this very important day.

Jock's work continued to remain busy. New funds to finance postponed projects became available. Housing developments, road improvements, and bridge-strengthening requests poured in. He had his choice of these projects. The more work he took on, the more he wanted; he was eager to do work that he had never done before. Also, he regarded work that was given to his competitors as inferior to that which he received.

He had his company bid on the installation of new seawalls in eastern England. This type of work had arisen because of the North Sea flood during February 1953. Some twenty-four thousand properties had been damaged by the floods, and hundreds of miles of seawalls had been breached. The North Sea surge had raced north to south along the east coast of England, where it invaded large stretches of lowlands and poured into the docks and over the islands near London.

While he was not successful in attracting any projects involving seawall construction, Jock remained at the top of his profession and saw his income continue to rise. However, he allowed his family situation to deteriorate while he poured all of his energy into his work.

Although there had been no recent correspondence from either Mary Louise or from the courts in Yorkshire, his mind continued to be haunted by this very private secret.

CHAPTER 14

A YEAR BEFORE JOCK McGregor returned home to his family in the West Midlands, and with my baby less than a month old, I, Mary Louise, in June 1944, drove my mother to her friend's funeral. Her friend had suffered from cancer for several years and had finally succumbed to the disease. She was to be buried in the village churchyard close to where my parents had lived just before the start of the war.

The drive took a little over an hour and consisted of driving along narrow country lanes that seemed to lead to nowhere. Fortunately, my mother knew the route and was able to guide me despite the absence of signposts. On the way she gave me an ultimatum.

"If you are not willing to have your child adopted, you really will have to leave home. Your father and I cannot live in the village if we allow you and your illegitimate child to stay with us. People in the village are already talking about us because some of them have heard a baby crying in the house. At church last Sunday, someone asked me if you had a baby and who was the father. I was made to lie in church."

I ignored my mother's remarks.

My sister Ava, who was sitting alongside the baby's crib in the backseat of the car, tried to soften my mother's threat.

"Mother, my husband and I live on a remote farm with no other houses nearby. The baby can come and live with us. Mary Louise can stay with you and visit her baby at our house. If people hear that I have a baby, they will assume it's mine."

My mother's reply to her was immediate.

"You will not do that. You and your husband want to have your own children. Having someone else's baby in your home will only cause trouble. Give the arrangement only a month, and either the child will be back with me, or you and the child will be back with me. Then I'll have three daughters and one baby living at home. If Mary Louise is going to keep the baby, she needs a much better solution than the one you propose. She can move back and live with Nan Dawson if she wants, but I don't see that as a long-term solution if she keeps the baby."

We continued our drive to the funeral. My mother had been a close friend of Bob Hutchinson's wife for many years, and they had gone to school together. Bob owned a very large farm close to the one we owned before the war. It had been usual for both families to attend church together.

After Bob's wife contracted cancer, she and her husband moved five years previously to a remote farm in West Yorkshire. Even after the Hutchinsons moved, the two women regularly met on market day when they were selling produce in town.

Now she had died. Since she and her husband had no children, Bob was being looked after by his sister, who lived a few miles away from his home, and had started to visit him regularly to clean the house, do his laundry, and keep an eye on him. She had provided similar help during the last few weeks of his wife's life.

Bob had recently been diagnosed with diabetes and was prescribed insulin to stabilize the illness. Daily injections of premixed insulin using a now standardized syringe had become his way of life. He injected himself daily in his upper thigh. For a farmer this procedure was cumbersome and time-consuming, and whenever he took too much insulin the effects severely interfered with his farming routine. Each day he had to sterilize the needle and the glass syringe and try and inject the right amount of insulin. The amount was hard to estimate. He had to assume his blood sugar at a level calculated by his doctor, consider the amount and type of food that he would eat during that day, and have some idea of the nature of the work that he would carry out. The physical component of farming during the mid-1940s could vary dramatically. More often than not he took too much insulin, which lowered his blood sugar, causing hypoglycemia. At a minimum, he would become tired, confused, and a little cranky; at worst he would pass out in a field somewhere or in a farm building and, worse still, suffer a serious seizure. There was no way of monitoring his sugar level. The doctor could conduct urine tests during his visits, but there was no simple "dip and read" urine test before the early 1950s. He had been told to stop eating fatty meats and concentrate on eating carbohydrates such as bread and potatoes.

He still had to work the farm. On occasion his sister had found him collapsed or in the midst of a seizure among the farm buildings or outside in the fields with his sheep and cattle. It was hard physical work for her to help him back to the house. She then had to give him food and cups of tea with sugar, but she was never sure how much sugar to provide. The most difficult situations were when the diabetic seizure made Bob verbally and physically abusive toward her. These were always unpleasant experiences. Afterward, Bob would have no memory of what had happened. She had told Bob that she was not willing to continue to be his housekeeper and nurse for much longer, now that his wife had passed. He needed to find a new solution for his personal situation that would provide him with the care and attention that he needed.

We finally reached the site of the funeral, a small stone church that dated back to the fourteenth century and sat in the middle of a field grazed by sheep. We left the car on the roadside and walked about a quarter of a mile across the field to the churchyard. The fenced graveyard surrounding the church had been carefully manicured, and the several chestnut trees provided shade during the summer months. Sheep's sorrel, marsh orchids, buttercups, and daisies gave additional color to this portrait of rich green fields, with a pale blue sky, dotted with fluffy white clouds that typified this part of the Yorkshire countryside.

Beyond the church passed a wide, fast-flowing river that ran through meadows inhabited by sheep, cows, and the occasional coarse fisherman fishing for freshwater nongame fish. Coarse fishing, for fish other than trout and salmon, was a daily event along these river banks, especially since the war had begun.

During the service my sister stayed in the car with my baby. On the way back to the car, my mother took a slight detour to introduce me to Bob Hutchinson and his sister. They smiled at me and shook my hand. My mother said, "Mary Louise, Bob and I have been talking, and he has a proposal for you. His sister likes the idea and hopes that you will accept the proposal."

Bob, who was about six feet tall, with graying hair, of slim build, and muscular from his years of farming, turned toward me and said, "Mary Louise, would you like to come and live with me? I need someone to look after me full time, and my sister cannot do that. You can move into the house, and, if you like, you can bring your baby with you. I need you to look after the house, prepare my meals, and help me with my illness. I will pay you a weekly allowance."

He looked at my mother, and they both waited for my reply.

After a few moments of thought, it seemed to me to be sensible to accept Bob's proposal. I replied by saying, "Yes, that is very kind of you, Mr. Hutchinson, so long as you are sure that I can keep my baby."

My mother replied, "Mary Louise, I still think you should have the baby adopted. But if you say yes to Bob, he will take good care of you and give your baby a good home, at least for the time being. I think it is a solution that will benefit all three of you."

Two days later, Bob Hutchinson drove to my mother's home to collect me, my baby, and my personal belongings. It was nearly a two-hour ride to his farm; there I was in July 1944, about to start a new life.

The work was very hard. Bob treated me well, but the farm was isolated and offered few homey comforts. On another farm, a short distance away, lived an old man and his daughter and son, both older than I was. Both farms were situated on a bleak, windswept landscape built of clay that clung to your feet whenever it rained, which was often.

There was no bus service and any escape from this constricted world depended on Bob Hutchinson having the time to drive me somewhere. I was not allowed to drive his vehicle. Because of the obligations of farming, Bob rarely had time to leave his livestock.

The only other company I had, at least until the end of the war, was the Italian prisoner of war who helped Bob, and several German prisoners of war who worked at the farm across the road. Their wolf whistles and shouts of "Hallo, fraulein" would usually annoy Bob when he heard them, so I would either have to come inside the house or move away from the window.

The brick farmhouse had three bedrooms upstairs and a kitchen, dining room, and sitting room downstairs. The house was attached to the farm's outbuildings. The first outhouse contained the laundry copper. This was a small square unit built of bricks; inside stood a coal furnace. The fire heated a large metal bucket that sat over it. The dirty laundry was placed into this bucket and boiled. The washing was then moved to a peggy tub, where it was churned manually with a posser. The clothes were then hung outside to dry and, finally, put through a mangle to press them. The last step was ironing. Two flat irons were heated over a fire; one would be used until it was cold and then replaced with the heated one.

The next outhouse was the toilet, with no running water, and beyond that were the milking rooms and the cow and pig sheds. Finally, there was an old barn that had been converted into a garage attached to the cow shed.

The house had no running water, electricity, or gas. A water pump a few yards away from the backdoor supplied cold water that needed to be boiled before it was drunk. Heating came from coal and wood fires in the kitchen and dining room. The only lighting was downstairs, provided by a combination of hand-carried paraffin lanterns and fixed gas lights running off bottled calor-gas. Candles were necessary to provide light upstairs.

Urine and worse was collected in small pots kept under each bed. Thursday night was bath night. A large metal tub was placed in the center of the kitchen, and everyone took turns bathing in it, using the same water.

The only entertainment came from an old radio that ran off an acid battery called an accumulator. Often the accumulator would run out of power halfway through a program. To listen again, we had to wait until the following Thursday, when the accumulator would be taken to town to be charged. There was no telephone.

I drifted into a routine, with different tasks designated for different days of the week. My baby stayed healthy. Bob Hutchinson appeared to appreciate the help I provided. During late summer, my older sister visited me. She asked to take my son back with her to her farm for a few days, and I agreed. It gave me a little less to do for a while.

We lived off the land. We slaughtered our own meat, usually a pig; we grew our own vegetables and fruit; we produced our own milk and butter; we could catch fish in the nearby pond, and my hens in their hen coops were generous with their eggs and flesh. We harvested a small field of wheat that gave us flour for baking bread. The occasional rabbit or duck that Bob would shoot added to the variety of our menu.

We also received more than our ration of sugar. A gentleman living some distance away who worked in a sugar beet factory would bicycle out to the farm every two weeks to collect two dozen eggs. In return, he would leave us two bags of sugar.

During September 1944 my father came to visit. He seemed a little more serious than usual and spent most of his time outside talking to Bob. When they came in for tea, and we were all seated around the table, my father started to talk. "Mary Louise, Bob and I have been having a serious conversation, and we have something important to say to you. We are both concerned about your personal situation and that both you and the baby face an uncertain future.

"As a result, I have asked Bob to marry you, and he has agreed. Your mother agrees that you should marry Bob. It is a very fine solution to your present predicament. Bob is willing to marry you because he thinks highly of you and because he needs your help in managing his diabetes. If you agree, he says you can keep the baby here in his home. His only condition is that he will stop paying you a weekly wage, but he will support you instead. We think that works well since the courts have ordered your son's father to pay you weekly child support."

I wasn't sure what to say. Here I was being asked to marry someone who, in his mid-fifties, was more than twice my age, was very sick, and lived in the middle of nowhere, miles from any community. On the other hand, if I said no to the invitation, I would likely lose my baby or be thrown out of my parents' home. Additionally, I had lost all of my boyfriends and no longer had any money. I thought quickly.

"If I do marry Mr. Hutchinson, I would like him to give me access to his car or for him to buy me my own car. I need a social life, and there are no buses to catch. I would also like to be able to visit you and my sisters from time to time. In addition, I need some training in nursing, since there are times when I do not know what to do when he is very sick."

Bob agreed to all my requests, except that I would have to use his car rather than have one of my own.

A few weeks later we were married, and I moved in with Bob on a permanent basis. He allowed me to become a member of the local Women's Institute; that gave me contact with other women living in nearby villages. I did not realize at the time that the institute also provided many educational opportunities and taught you skills that you need as a farmer's wife. I learnt how to sew and knit, improved my cooking skills, and was taught animal husbandry. On one occasion I even learnt pottery making.

The Women's Institute in England had been created back in 1915 to help women in rural areas work with their husbands and help increase food production during wartime. Because of the social benefits provided by the organization, the institute continued to thrive after the end of World War 1.

At the same time, I also signed up with the Nursing Reserves to become a qualified nurse. Bob's health condition was not improving. Many times I would find him collapsed, usually outside the house, often in a coma, needing assistance. Sometimes these incidents were easy to deal with, but on some occasions he would become violent and verbally abusive. I knew he couldn't help it, but his behavior often scared me. Both of us found it impossible to decide how much insulin he needed to take. As a consolation, I always had my baby to return to, and that made everything worthwhile.

As time went by, I started to reflect on the past and how it had brought me to my present state. I would think about my former boyfriends, who were around no more, and about the dances that I could no longer attend. I would think about my career and how it had come to a sudden end. I would think about my family many miles away and the loneliness of living with Bob.

And occasionally I would think of Jock McGregor, the person who had so changed my life. I had not heard from him since before the baby was born. I had expected to receive weekly payments from him, but not one had arrived. I had informed my lawyer of the missing payments. In turn, he had taken up the matter with the courts. While my immediate needs were being met, I continued to worry about my uncertain future.

CHAPTER 15

B late 1946 in America, Michael Fromm had found that finding
employment was much more difficult than finding girls. There were
few opportunities in Sacramento for people with Michael's skills, only
small-scope projects with limited durations. As he talked with people,
listened to the radio, and read newspapers, it sounded as if the state of
California was at the dawn of a new approach to road transportation.
But for Michael to participate in this new vision, it seemed as if he
would need to relocate.

A joint commission had developed a statewide plan for the
construction and design of California's highways. The intent of the
plan was to remove transportation bottlenecks that had occurred during
the war, to solve the impact of an increasing number of automobiles on
the roads, and to ensure that funding for highway construction was
distributed fairly across California.

The Los Angeles Metropolitan Area seemed the most advanced in
terms of planning and defining its needs. Existing surface streets in Los
Angeles were failing to meet the needs of increased traffic flow. While
there was a Los Angeles city bias toward an upgraded rail transit system,
regional opinion was strongly in favor of a freeway solution. Given what
was going on, it made sense for Michael to relocate to Los Angeles and
accept a position advising on highway and bridge design, and consulting
on the concrete compositions to be used in each construction. He
purchased his father's car, and by the end of 1946 was living close to the
beach in Los Angeles and working in his area of specialization.

The only continuing question mark as 1947 arrived was his social
life. Michael still hadn't found a steady girlfriend. He was looking for

the ideal woman with whom he could fall in love and live with for the rest of his life.

During March 1947, Michael received a letter from his friend Jock McGregor in England. Forwarded to him by his mother, it was a rather brief communication letting Michael know that Jock was back home, had been working for a city architectural planning department, and was happy to be reunited with his family. He asked Michael if he was married and what he was doing, and he offered Michael an open invitation to visit the West Midlands at any time. Michael replied with the details of his job and confirmed that he was still single. Subsequently, other than the occasional best wishes year-end holiday card sent, there was no further news from Jock.

The rest of 1947 saw Michael focused on his work. It was a busy time for construction design, and decisions had to be made on the strength and stress tolerances for paved surfaces, bridge supports, overpasses, and other parts of the planned freeways. His social life, which took a backseat, consisted primarily of walking the beaches, encountering the occasional beauty pageant by the ocean, and surfing as his primary source of exercise.

Surfing seemed to be growing in popularity and was supposed to be a doorway to meeting attractive women. Fortunately, the heavy redwood planks used for surfboards in the past were being replaced by much lighter balsam and fiberglass boards. So it was much easier for Michael to confidently display his slim, muscular, Adonis-like good looks while carrying his surfboard. He would solicit ideas on the best surfing locations from hitchhiker surfers he met. He occasionally envied their lifestyle, which allowed them to stay on the beach all day, but he continued to fail to find the woman of his dreams on the beaches of southern California.

It was during November 1947, however, that his social life took an unexpected turn for the better. He was on his way to spend the Thanksgiving holiday with his parents. A gift seemed in order, so after he left home, he pulled over into the parking lot of a nearby candy store and went inside to buy a box of chocolates. The people behind the counter were all dressed in white, and the smell of chocolate was heavy in the air.

As he waited his turn at the counter, there was one assistant who seemed not to be serving. She was stacking boxes and rearranging the candy display. He asked her to serve him so that he could quickly resume his long journey north. She shook her head and said in a strong accent, "I cannot understand; my English is poor."

Michael was intrigued. "Where are you from?" he asked.

"Ich bin aus Deutschland," she replied, with a look that suggested she found it embarrassing talking to Michael.

Michael replied in German, telling her that his mother came from Germany and that he was on his way to see her. After the initial shock of hearing German being spoken, she smiled.

"Sie sprechen Deutsch?," she said, seemingly pleased to have found someone who could understand her.

Michael told her how he had learnt German, his name, and that he lived close by. He said he would come in and see her again if that was acceptable to her. She said yes, and then added with a smile, "My name is Karen."

Michael returned her smile, said thanks to her, and then ordered the candy from an English-speaking assistant at the counter. Karen was a pretty girl, with light brown hair, had a pleasing figure, and seemed a little lonely. He had plenty of time to think about this experience as he drove north.

The following week, Michael went back to the shop. Karen was there, but she seemed very busy. He asked if she would come out for a drink with him one evening. She said yes. They fixed a date, and Michael agreed to meet her at the store at a set time.

That date was the first of many. She sparked a feeling in Michael that he had known her all of his life. He found it easy talking to her, and her personality was infectious. They laughed and smiled a lot. He felt pleased to be in her company. They sat, and she drank coca-cola, and he drank Schlitz beer, and then they walked along the beach and across the pier, where they rode on the carousel and played some of the arcade games. The weather was warm, and the lights of the pier sparkled that evening.

Michael told her about his early life, his years in England, and how he liked to dance and surf. He tried to explain his work to Karen, but she had a hard time understanding him. Michael knew only the English words for his technical responsibilities; the rest of his explanation seemed to confuse her. He asked Karen about her life as they sat looking across at the ocean.

She said, "I live with my parents, and I am an only child. We moved here a few months ago from China. My father is opening a printing business, and my mother has found work in a factory. I have been working at the candy store for three months. We like Los Angeles, especially the weather, and the freedom to do as we please."

Michael asked her about China.

"I lived there for six years," she said, in a tone that became a little more serious.

"We moved to China from Vienna, Austria, when I was only twelve. We lived in Shanghai. It was to do with Hitler. Earlier we had lived in Berlin. My father was a journalist from Vienna. My mother is German.

It was not a good time for us while we were in China, but at least we were safe from what was happening in Germany."

Michael continued, "Why did your parents take you to Shanghai? There were other places you could have gone."

She continued, "By the time we decided to leave Vienna, it was too late to go anywhere else. My father did not want to leave Vienna; he thought it would be safe. He was also responsible for the care of his grandmother, and she could not travel. My mother did seek permission to move to England, but my father was in prison by the time the permission was granted. My mother's sister had left earlier for London.

"Palestine was not an option, because my father was Jewish but did not consider himself a Zionist. Brazil had been suggested to my mother before we left Berlin. My mother told me that she refused to go there because one of the requirements was that we would have to change our religion to Catholic."

It was clear that Karen was finding it difficult to talk about her past, so they finished their drinks, and Michael drove her home. Soon they were going out regularly, sometimes to a movie, occasionally dancing, often just strolling on the beach and talking.

Michael met her parents on several occasions. Quiet people, they appeared to enjoy their privacy and were always kind toward Michael. They seemed to support the relationship that their daughter and her boyfriend were developing.

One evening after they had been dancing, Michael parked the car so he and Karen could look across the ocean from the beach. It was a star-filled evening; the shoreline lights added to the beauty. The waves were pounding in the distance, and there was the occasional cry from a beachcomber or, sometimes, from a seagull.

They kissed, cuddled, and talked about the events of the day. Michael asked, "Do you want to tell me anything more about your life before you came to America? If it's difficult to talk about, I will understand."

She replied that she and her parents had chosen never to talk about the past. Memories were too hard on their emotions. Karen was willing to say more about her life, but Michael should be prepared that this would upset her and might cause her to weep. She told him he needed to hug her while she spoke, and he did, gladly.

Karen began to speak. After Hitler marched into Austria in March 1938 to unite the two countries, her family situation rapidly deteriorated. She saw men being forced to scrub the streets, citizens placed in trucks and driven away, threats and abuse by German soldiers toward people standing outside their homes, children being forced to go to orphanages, and all Jews being ordered to wear the yellow Star of David on an armband.

Anti-Semitism had existed before Hitler's arrival, but it was now very visible and much more aggressive. Her father continued to believe that the family would be safe in Vienna and refused to wear the yellow Star of David. He was soon prevented by the authorities from practicing journalism.

The situation continued to worsen because of the next event.

Worried about the future, Karen's grandmother on her father's side had arranged for a courier to take money out of Austria so that it would be accessible to her sister, who was living in New York. Unfortunately, the courier had been caught and arrested. Shortly thereafter, her grandmother's home was visited by the authorities, and her grandmother was arrested.

Karen's father took charge, volunteering that he had made the arrangements. Karen's grandmother was quickly released, but then he was arrested instead. There was a trial, and he was imprisoned for an unspecified period of time. It was during this period that Karen said she would sometimes accompany her mother on her daily visits to see her father in prison. Home life deteriorated, food became scarce, and her mother spent many hours crying. The only good thing was that while her father was in prison, there was no man in the house. Elsewhere, the authorities would forcibly enter homes and arbitrarily arrest adult males and then have them deported.

About a year later, the authorities decided to release her father from prison, transferring him to a concentration camp. Karen remembered traveling with her mother on the tram to some office. There was an almighty argument. Karen's mother screamed at the officials that because her husband was married to a German citizen, Austria had no authority to deport him. The authorities conceded, and Karen's father was released to the safety of his home.

As soon as her father was back home, she remembers being called into the kitchen by her parents and told that the three of them would likely have to leave on a long journey. She had learnt later, while in Shanghai, that her parents had asked the Central Office for Jewish Emigration to approve a visa for them to move to New York. But this visa had been denied because of her father's past profession as a journalist.

At this stage, Michael could see that Karen was becoming exhausted and suggested that she should stop. She could tell him more later. She agreed.

Michael and Karen's romance continued. Michael gave Karen occasional English lessons, and she supplemented these by attending night school. He took Karen north to Sacramento with him during Easter 1948 to meet his parents. She had never visited northern California before. His parents liked her, especially his mother, who enjoyed the opportunity to refresh her knowledge of German. Later, he took her to his favorite dance hall and introduced her to jitterbugging.

On the way home to Los Angeles, Karen said, "Would you like to hear more about my time in China? Your father told me about his harsh times during World War I. Maybe you should know of the similar hardships that my family and I experienced during World War II,"

Michael told her to continue the story but only if it didn't hurt her too much. He was curious to know what had been happening to Karen at about the same time that he was riding his motorbike among the green fields of Yorkshire.

She began, "After my father was released from jail, my parents decided that we should all go back to Berlin. By now it was late 1940. We had some money that had been sent to us from New York, and my mother had relatives living in Germany whom she thought might be willing to help us. I overheard my parents talking about escaping from Austria by crossing the Yugoslav border, but my father believed that this was too dangerous.

"When we arrived in Germany, some of my mother's German relatives decided to travel with us, and everyone decided we should go on to Shanghai. I learnt in Shanghai that most countries by then had imposed restrictions on the entry of Jewish refugees; the British were even restricting the number of Jewish immigrants they would allow into Palestine. My family no longer had access to their bank accounts. Whatever silver and valuables we had in the house in Berlin were sold to a thrift shop, and we started our journey to Shanghai via Poland."

Karen's recollection is that the journey took place at the end of 1940 and that the family was in Shanghai by March 1941. By this point in her story, they were about halfway to Los Angeles. It was time to rest and eat. At lunch, the conversation turned toward work plans for the following week and Karen's expectations of Michael when he visited her parents for dinner the following Saturday.

They finished lunch, and soon Michael had refueled the car. They were back on the road to Los Angeles. Karen resumed her story: "We traveled to Poland because my mother had a family member still living there. At that time, Germany and the Soviets shared Poland through a nonaggression pact. The Soviets occupied the eastern part of the country, and Germany the western part. We traveled into east Poland and then on into Lithuania.

"Before we arrived in Lithuania, the Russians had entered the country in June 1940 and had annexed it as part of Russia. We had planned to obtain visas for Japan from the Japanese authorities, who had an office in Kovno, Lithuania. However, the office had been closed shortly after the Russian invasion. We had no alternative but to continue our journey without visas."

At this point, Karen stopped her story. She looked at Michael. "Are you bored?" she asked. "It is rather a long story, and I hope you learnt a little geography while you were in England?"

Michael replied that he knew of the countries she was talking about and was more saddened by her story than bored. He asked her to continue.

Continuing, Karen said, "Without visas, my parents decided to continue the journey but head straight for Shanghai. We traveled across a lot of Soviet territory and eventually arrived in Manchuria, which was occupied by the Japanese at that time. It is here that our world changed. We were met by physically abusive guards who were reluctant to allow us to continue our journey. They screamed at me as well as at my parents, but no one knew what they were saying. We couldn't turn back, so we had to suffer this behavior. Both the guards and we knew that Shanghai was still accepting refugees without visas, even though the Japanese had occupied the city since 1937. Finally the guards let us go. We then passed through Harbin and on to Dalian; from there we were on the last long leg of our journey to Shanghai.

"Initially, life in Shanghai was comfortable. We settled in the French Concession and became accustomed to the screaming, pointing, and bullying that we received from our Japanese hosts. We had money and lived in a boarding house. Food was adequate; we received breakfast and lunch every day. But after a few months, our circumstances changed dramatically. We heard that war had broken out between Germany and Russia on June 22, 1941, but the more significant event was on December 8, 1941, when the United States declared war on Japan. The American and British communities were immediately moved to internment camps.

"The Japanese moved us to a central area in the city, which became known as the Jewish Ghetto. There were many thousands of Jews living in Shanghai by then. At first the Japanese placed four to five people in each room, but eventually we were settled into our own small single room. Living conditions worsened. We had run out of money. It became a time for survival. People lost their dignity. The winters were icy cold, and the hot, humid summers exposed us to insects that would try to eat us. We had just enough food. The relief organizations would feed us daily. We were young; all of us stayed healthy. My father sold eggs supplied to him by a local Chinese farmer who cooperated only until the Japanese told him to stop. The Chinese were usually friendly toward us, unlike our Japanese hosts.

We had established committees to organize our community and to protect whatever human dignity was possible. My father was befriended by a Russian Jew who taught him how to bake Viennese kaiser bread. He would bake it, and my mother would sell it. My parents had brought a recipe book with them. They would often look at the pictures and dream of eating the food they were looking at. There were daily curfews that were ruthlessly enforced. There was a Japanese official who was very tiny. He seemed to think of himself as another emperor. I would see him sometimes grab a bench or something else that he could stand on, and then slap the person he had apprehended.

"I also remember the war coming to an end. Children would run out into the street or go up on the rooftops to shout for joy as they watched American planes dropping bombs on the city. It didn't occur to us that a misplaced bomb might fall on us, and there were no bomb shelters. Once the war was over, some of our relatives in America sent us money. We also have President Truman to thank for his kindness in opening the doors to allow us displaced people to enter the United States. And that's why I am here today."

With that, Karen took a deep sigh and smiled at Michael in a way that he had never seen before. If he had doubted that he was in love with her, there was no doubt in his mind after this moment.

The following Saturday, Michael arrived a little early at Karen's home and was instantly invited in to the front room by her father. With Karen seated beside Michael, the young couple and Karen's parents made a lot of small talk. This line of conversation continued until Karen poked her fingers into Michael's ribs. He knew what she wanted him to say.

Looking at her parents and feeling a little nervous, Michael asked, "Would you mind if Karen and I got married? I have great admiration for your daughter, as I do for you two. What may be far more important is that I am in love with your daughter. And I hope that she loves me." Karen looked at Michael; she smiled and nodded.

Karen's father spoke softly, with a heavy accent, "We would be delighted to welcome you into our family, Michael. There are not many of us here to celebrate, but what we don't have in numbers, we will make up in happiness. We can celebrate the creation of the state of Israel at the same time!"

A few weeks later, Karen and Michael were married in a civil ceremony, agreeing not to have a honeymoon to preserve their finances. Michael's parents sent him some money to help them purchase a new home. Three months later, Karen and Michael moved into a small house in Los Angeles south of where he had previously lived. They had a sweeping view north along the coastline and an inland view to the eastern edges of Los Angeles.

Michael silently thanked the Los Angeles Refugee Committee. The committee had given the family an ultimatum on arrival in the United States that it must go wherever the committee said or stop receiving aid. The family's preferred destination of New York was not an option. As a result, Karen and her parents had immediately found work and told the committee its services were no longer needed.

As Michael sat on the back porch that evening during August 1948, he gave thanks for a life that had treated him so very generously. His career was in its ascendancy, and he had found a partner who he hoped would be with him for the rest of his life.

CHAPTER 16

LIFE WITH BOB Hutchinson in Yorkshire, England, was tolerable, although he and I did not have much in common. I had been married eight months and we were celebrating the end of the war during the summer of 1945. The unpleasant episodes were when Bob experienced severe problems with his diabetes medication. Frequently he used too much insulin and ended up collapsed outside the house, either in a coma or suffering from a seizure. It was up to me to coax him inside and stabilize his illness by persuading him to drink cups of hot sugared tea.

I often felt isolated on the farm, and I missed my family and friends. Although I was unaware at the time, Jock McGregor had by summer 1945 returned home to his family in the West Midlands and Michael Fromm had transferred to work in a prisoner-of-war camp in East Yorkshire.

My membership in the local Women's Institute helped me adapt a little to my new lifestyle. I regularly attended the institute's monthly meetings and developed several new friends. I also became friendly with the people who lived in the farm across the road. Farming had become busier for all of us because the prisoners of war had by now been returned home.

Once a week I would get away from these surroundings with my son. Each Thursday, Bob attended the livestock market in the adjacent town. He would take me with him and leave me in the central marketplace to sell my eggs, homemade jam, and fresh vegetables.

I would also see Nan Dawson on occasion. She had given up work but was always in high spirits and gave me lots of encouragement with my new life. She regularly provided me with used boy's clothing supplied to her by her neighbor across the street. I would feel much better on the way home, including when we stopped at our regular store to collect groceries for the week and the accumulator for the radio, if it had needed charging.

My older sister Ava visited me several times at the farm during that summer. She knew two Land Girls who had known Jock McGregor. They told her that he had disappeared and was presumed to have returned home to his family. My assumption was that I would never see him again. Unfortunately, while this was a good assumption, he still found ways of interfering with my life and that of my son.

In October 1945, I received a summons from the local court to appear on October 24, to revisit the court order that had awarded me child support. Apparently Jock McGregor had returned home and was challenging the amount he was required to pay. He was asking for it to either be eliminated or at least reduced. I attended the court hearing and expected Jock to be present. He wasn't.

I explained to the court how I was now married but still had sole custody of my son. My husband Bob attended and told the court that he was not prepared to financially support my son. He would provide a home for my son but objected to any suggestion that he needed to provide financial support. The court considered what it had heard but apparently failed to persuade Jock McGregor to resume payments, since I received no new child support compensation.

Bob was exceptionally angry with me and with the court for this development. He told me that he had never intended to support my son, and he wasn't going to start now. I could keep my child in his home, on the clear understanding that when I did receive payments from Jock McGregor, they should be handed over to him.

Unfortunately, the courts in Yorkshire work slowly and, despite regular inquiries, no monies were forthcoming. My mother had an old address for Jock that she gave me. I sent him a letter and a picture of my son, hoping to make him feel guilty enough to comply with the court order. The idea did not work.

The months passed. Winter 1947 was probably the most difficult time for me on the farm. We experienced two months of harsh weather. Bitter east winds blew and brought large snowdrifts that blocked access to the farm. Coal and food supplies could not get through. With limited fuel, the house was ice-cold, and out in the fields, it was far worse. Sheep and lambs died, root food became frozen in the ground, and, to make matters worse, when the snow melted, we experienced extensive flooding. None of my family was able to visit me, and the weekly trips to the livestock market were no longer possible.

The most unpleasant aspect of my existence continued to be having to help Bob when he became ill because of his diabetes. He would not allow me to assist him with his injections, and there was still no method available to test his blood sugar level. He seemed to prefer to take too much insulin rather than too little. He understood that if he took too little he risked other physical complications due to diabetes, such as heart disease, kidney damage, deterioration of eyesight, and nerve damage. He preferred to risk comas and seizures, and have me help him, rather than risk the side effects of too much blood sugar. His coma episodes became more frequent and sometimes resulted in severe and violent seizures; he seemed to become more aggressive and uncooperative with me after the court hearing.

The next family challenge I faced was the surname of my son. He had inherited my maiden name. My mother told me that he would be bullied at school and picked on if he had a name different from my married name. People would know he was illegitimate and would likely tease him and call him nasty names. I didn't want that.

At the same time, I worried that if I changed his name, it would legally allow Jock McGregor to avoid making maintenance payments. My lawyer told me that a name change would have no effect on the court order. So I proceeded. During August 1947, my son's name was changed by Deed Poll to Hutchinson, and he has been known as John Hutchinson ever since.

Bob Hutchinson reluctantly continued to provide my son with food and a roof over his head, but there was a need also to clothe my baby, and I had no money to buy new clothes. This was another occasion when Nan Dawson stepped in to help me. She arranged to pass on her neighbor's son's clothes to me once he had outgrown them. That boy's name also happened to be John, so after I cut out the last name on the label, it seemed as if the clothes belonged to my John.

My son by now was walking and talking. My older sister and I spent many hours playing with him. For no particular reason, we began to dress him up as a girl and entered him in village fancy dress competitions. He often won, and it made us feel proud. When he was just nine and won the local summer fancy dress parade, he confided in me that he didn't like being dressed as a girl. Some of his friends at school called him a sissy. So that was the last time he wore a dress.

Bob and I had begun to visit my parents each Christmas. We would drive over on Christmas Eve to listen to the carol singers who visited each home in the village. Then we would return on Christmas Day for dinner with my sisters and their husbands.

On one occasion the driveway gate at my parents' home had been left open; my son wandered off into the village. He returned an hour or so later, his face and shoulders covered in cow dirt. I asked him for an explanation. He told me that he had met a young girl standing on the rungs of a farm gate. She had shouted at him to go away, said she wasn't allowed to talk to him, and then she picked up some soft cow dirt and threw it at him. I cleaned him up and chose to forget about the incident.

In September 1949, John started school. He was collected each morning at 8:00 a.m. by the school bus and driven five miles to his classroom. In the evening, the bus dropped him off about a quarter-mile away from the house, and he would walk home. The barking of our black spaniel would alert me to his imminent arrival.

School seemed to go well for John, although he made no friends because our farm was so remote. However, Bob taught him to ride a two- wheeler bicycle, which at least allowed John to cycle to the nearby villages, where he could meet other people. Bob was very patient teaching my son, although one time he let go of the bicycle prematurely. John wobbled forward a few feet and rolled off the bike into a bed of stinging nettles. He came home with red blotches across his face and on his arms and legs.

John also spent a lot of his time bird-nesting and helping our neighbor with his harvest, whether it was hay, wheat, or sugar beet. He also fished for pike and eels in the nearby pond. His bird-nesting came to a premature end with the passing of the Wild Birds Protection Act in 1953 that banned the hobby of collecting eggs. By then John had developed a very fine collection of eggs, and it was still possible to take them to school and trade them.

He would often bring home lapwing and moorhen eggs, even after the new law had been passed. He could tell when the eggs were addled, not usable to eat, either because they floated in water or the points of the eggs all faced inward to the center of the nest. We ate these eggs instead of hen eggs. This gave me more hen eggs to take to the market to sell, my main source of income.

Bird-watching remained legal, so that became John's new hobby. He also read a lot. One Christmas I bought him a pencil flashlight. I would often find him reading in bed under the bedcovers, using the flashlight. Bob did not like him reading in bed, especially using a candle, because of the fire risk.

I also started to teach my son about the value of money. He was given an allotment in the garden to grow lettuce, and then he could take what he grew and sell it at the local market when I went to sell eggs. He would charge two pence for a head of lettuce. I also had him pick rose hips in the hedgerows during the autumn. He would take these to school and receive three pence for every pound he picked. The rose hips were used to manufacture rose hip syrup, a vital source of vitamin C, due to the shortage of citrus fruits after the war.

We heard from his school that John would not eat meat. His portion of meat would be found under the lunch table. Rationing was still in force, and the school believed that this was a dreadful waste, even though, at that time, meat consisted mainly of gristle and fat. John's explanation was that it looked like the brawn that I fed him at home, and that he despised. I made brawn by pickling and then salting the contents of either pigs' or calves' heads.

John's love of nature kept him busy exploring the moorland on which our farm was situated. There was one occasion when he came home to tell me that he had discovered a new colony of wild animals. He thought the animals were larger than foxes and badgers, and asked if I would help him identify what they were. He took me across the field and showed me the site. It consisted of a series of holes organized in a square, and tracks leading away into the wheat field. I smiled and said, "John, those are not animal burrows. This is the site of an electric pylon; if you go across the field you will see another site just like this. Electricity is about to arrive on our farm!"

As a result of the cold winter in 1947, the government had nationalized the electric power companies, and a national grid or transmission system was under construction. A few months later, we had electricity on the farm.

As we entered the 1950s, most things in my life either remained stable or improved slightly. My son was apparently doing well at school; Bob had started to take me on vacations; my parents seemed to have finally forgiven me, and food rationing was ending. Talk of adoption for my son had long since ceased.

Unfortunately, my husband's illness seemed to be worsening, and the adverse effects of taking too much insulin were increasing in frequency. It would not be until the early 1950s when the daily testing of urine for blood sugar would become available for home use, and I would be able to monitor his blood sugar. Bob encountered a series of secondary complications during this period and had to be hospitalized for six months. Fortunately, a friend of Bob's who owned his own farm in a nearby village took care of our farm, including milking the cows by hand and feeding the pigs and ferrets.

I hated ferrets, even though they were important to my livelihood. They were used to catch the rats that invaded the hen huts and competed with me for the hen eggs. Bob would use a large gauntlet glove to grab the ferrets and place them in a tightly woven sack. They would be released near the rat hole and would disappear down the hole; then the rat, or rats, would appear quickly. It was my role to chase the rats while they were blinded by the daylight and, with a stick, send them off to rat heaven. The ferrets would reappear, return to the sack of their own accord, and be returned by Bob to their cage.

We also experienced an addition to our diet at this time. On our first trip together, in 1951, Bob and I had met a farm family visiting from Canada. They were in England to see relatives. We formed a friendship that led them to mail us food boxes after their return. They sent us cans of salmon. Meat would have counted against the food rations still in force at that time, but fish was not included in the rationing. It was a delightful change to eat tinned salmon for Sunday tea instead of the usual Portuguese canned sardines.

There was no change in my nonrelationship with Jock McGregor. He did not communicate with me, and there was no sign of any child support. But, still, I had my son.

Shortly after Bob returned home from the hospital, the agricultural authorities issued instructions to farmers in Britain that they needed to do a better job of feeding the nation. As a result, farmers were instructed to plough out their grassland and grow cereal crops instead. Bob's health would not enable him to do this. He was already experiencing an increased number of seizures. So the farm was sold, and we moved to a new home, located in a small village a few miles away. My first task in my new home was to paint and wallpaper the entire interior of the house.

It was a very comfortable home and had running water, electricity, even a phone. A bathroom was installed upstairs, near four comfortably sized bedrooms. After a little while, we bought our first TV. There was a small area of land attached to the house that allowed a few sheep to graze and hens to be raised, and I converted an old summer house at the end of the garden into an aviary to breed budgerigars. This became another source of income for me. Bob had much less work to do now and spent most of his time around the house. I became very active in the local church and continued my Women's Institute activities. I also continued my interest in nursing.

Whether it was wise or not, as Bob gave up farming, he raised the idea of having a family. By then he was in his mid-sixties. I doubted that this was a good idea, and the doctor expressed similar concerns given his age and health. But we went ahead anyway. By July 1955, I had a newborn baby daughter and a twenty-two-month-old son. This added to my workload, and I began to see less and less of John.

He passed the school examination that allowed him to start grammar school at about the same time my daughter was born. John would be bused into town a few miles away every morning and return home to me about five o'clock each evening. Most of my time was dedicated to my two young children and to Bob, who continued to experience comas and seizures. Sometimes Bob's abuse during these events would be focused on my son because of the continuing absence of maintenance payments from his real father. Also, unlike me, Bob had a low regard for education and preferred to see my son working for a living.

I assumed that my son was making good progress at school, but I soon discovered I was mistaken. At the end of his first year at grammar school in 1956, at age twelve, I received a bundle of school reports. Depending on the subject, my son was evaluated as "mediocre," "rather a low standard," "far below the standard of the class," and "he has very little aptitude for this subject." What dismayed me most of all was the summary evaluation from the headmaster: "Most disappointing. There must be a great improvement next term, or we shall have to ask ourselves if he is fit for the sort of work we do here."

This was totally unacceptable to me. I had not sacrificed the past twelve years of my life to produce a "mediocre" son. I wasn't sure what to do. I certainly couldn't help with his schooling; I had left school at age fourteen. And Bob had no interest in helping him. I did talk to a former headmistress who lived in the village; she agreed to provide private tuition for John in French and mathematics, and encouraged me to direct my son toward either teaching or banking. I spoke with my parents, but they did not have any suggestions. I decided to cancel John's piano and violin lessons because my thoughts of him becoming a great musician were fading. He needed to focus on his schoolwork.

I called the school secretary, who suggested that I might want to join the Parent-Teacher Association. I didn't know what that meant, but it sounded like a good idea. Within weeks of becoming a member, I had met the headmaster and could call him a friend. By the end of my son's second year at school, the headmaster had persuaded me to become the chair of the PTA. It was understood that my son would not be expelled if I took on these duties.

So here I was, at the end of John's second year in grammar school in mid-1957, with a new family, a sick but faithful husband, a son who was now able to stay in grammar school because of my efforts, my good health, my own car, and the qualifications and experience that would allow me to become employed, if ever I needed to work. Life for me, Mary Louise, was definitely beginning to improve.

CHAPTER 17

THE MCGREGOR HOUSEHOLD in the West Midlands during the early 1950s was comfortably well off. It prided itself on the luxury Jaguar car parked outside in the driveway, was home to two children who were very successful at school, reported no ill health or physical ailments, and was headed by Gwen, who tried to keep the wheels of domestic life turning smoothly despite Jock's occasional tantrums.

The year 1955 started with atrocious weather. Great Britain's big freeze that year had come onshore in early January. Deep snow and freezing temperatures struck throughout the country, leaving many communities cut off from essential supplies. Floods had returned to the East Coast of England, and road conditions everywhere were reported as treacherous. It had lasted eight weeks, without any signs of improvement. For Jock, this placed a hold on some of his projects, so for once, he was able to work shorter hours and only a five-day week.

His children both developed nasty colds that naturally transferred to their mother. Then Jock caught the same cold and found it hard to shake off. It interfered with his work; he found himself coughing persistently. He felt a little rundown and became increasingly annoyed with Gwen, who would suggest that he take time away from the office or at least not work as hard. Over time he began to notice chest pains even during regular breathing. He became listless and easily fell asleep at home. He was losing weight.

Gwen grew concerned. His cold seemed to be worsening rather than showing signs of improvement, and then he developed a mild fever. Eventually, one morning, Jock coughed up mouthfuls of blood. That was enough for Gwen; she called the doctor.

The doctor came and conducted tests and a thorough examination of Jock's chest. He asked Jock to arrange for an X-ray. When the test results came back a few days later, the worst was confirmed; Jock had been diagnosed with tuberculosis. He was still likely to be in the infectious stage and, therefore, was moved downstairs to a back room for isolation purposes. No one knew the cause of his illness. Maybe he had contracted the disease by inhaling respiration drops that had been exhaled into the air by another infected person. So many people had colds that winter this could easily have happened. The hope was that the tuberculosis would disappear after Jock took lots of rest.

Jock's illness created pandemonium in the household, and he had to stop working. There were worries that the family might also have contracted the disease. Gwen and the two children were tested with tuberculin through an injection in the arm. No bumps appeared around the spot of the injection, indicating that the disease had not spread to other members of Jock's family.

The first priority of treatment was to have Jock rest completely for several weeks, resting his mind as well as his body. He spent the next several weeks lying in bed in a semireclining position, his back propped up on pillows. His doctor insisted that he give up smoking, which he did reluctantly, but he seemed to compensate for this by increasing his consumption of whisky.

The windows of his room were left open to allow in fresh air. Gwen cooked him healthy food three times a day, occasionally relenting to serve him his fried eggs and french fries, his favorite dish of all times. After a month, he was allowed to spend an hour each day seated in a chair. He was granted a daily visit to the toilet for bowel movements, and he could have the luxury of a bath after the first four weeks of rest. He requested whisky, but the doctor told him to stay off alcohol while he was ill.

Safeguards were taken to minimize the risk of the disease spreading to other family members. His eating dishes, cutlery, towels, bed linen, toiletries, and other personal items were clearly marked to indicate that they were for Jock's use only. Anyone going into his room needed to wear a mask; the door to his room was kept closed at all times. His children could visit him but were kept well away from his bedside.

The family was told that complete treatment would likely take twelve to eighteen months and that Jock would likely have to be transferred to a sanitarium in a few weeks' time unless the disease disappeared of its own accord. If the illness continued, it was important not to stop the treatment too early, even if Jock felt much better. Premature ending of the treatment would risk the creation of drug-resistant strains of tuberculosis in Jock's body that ultimately could kill him. After nearly three months, tests showed that the disease had not gone away and that there was some indication of a collapsed lung developing.

The only good thing to happen to Jock during this period was the arrival of a second channel on English TV. In September 1955, the Independent Television Authority started to broadcast in addition to the BBC. The TV became very important to Jock as a source of entertainment and pleasure during his illness at home.

These were very difficult times for Gwen and for Jock's parents, who would visit him from time to time. Jock's reaction to his disease was unpredictable. Early on he accepted it and did as he was told. But over time, his behavior became more erratic and disobedient. At times Gwen had no idea how he would behave when she entered his room. As the weeks passed, he became sullen and depressed. He would ask for cigarettes but when refused, would instead demand whisky. He was impatient for the cure but would ignore attention to his personal hygiene and just sleep or watch television.

He was disinterested in the children. There were occasions when, no matter what Gwen did for Jock, he would be dissatisfied. He would argue with her and ignore her requests when she needed him to do something. He believed that he had contracted the disease while in Yorkshire. He had been exposed to untreated milk and had probably been infected by the cattle that had produced the milk. He would refer to books that he had read and argue that anyone with the least amount of intelligence would agree with him.

His spells of disobedience were the worst. He would refuse to eat his food, want to get out of bed and go outside, demand cigarettes and alcohol, and sometimes threaten to drive in to work. Gwen had hidden his car keys but was fearful of what he might do to her if she refused to hand them over.

During this same period she researched which sanitarium would be best for Jock's treatment, and made arrangements for his admittance. It would be expensive, and with the loss of Jock's wages, the household was already beginning to feel the economic pinch.

It was with a mixed sense of relief and sadness that Gwen found herself packing Jock's belongings in the car and preparing to drive to the sanitarium she had selected. The hospital had provided her with a long list of clothing requirements, including rubber boots and rain gear. It was situated in a Norfolk coastal village on the east side of England.

On a crisp autumn morning she left, with Jock supported by pillows, resting in the backseat of the car. He would be away from home for at least a year and possibly as long as eighteen months. It would likely be early 1957 before he came home. She would visit him fortnightly. The distance to the sanitarium was not great, but the narrow country roads were slow and poorly signposted. The children went to stay with their grandparents, her parents, while Gwen shuttled Jock to the hospital, and afterward during her fortnightly visits.

The sanitarium stood at the end of a long, narrow lane with its central white timber-framed building facing the sea. It could accommodate several hundred patients. Opened in 1899 as a sanitarium for well-off patients, it had been one of the first private hospitals of its kind to open in England and was fashioned after similar hospitals at the time in Germany and Switzerland. These facilities pioneered the open-air treatment of tuberculosis.

A number of movable wooden huts, referred to as airing huts, were scattered around the tree-studded gardens. Near each hut were smaller wooden buildings that served as toilets for the occupants of the airing huts. Looking like summerhouses on wheels, these accommodations allowed patients to spend all day in the fresh air without having to face into the wind that typically blew in off the North Sea. The location of the huts could be changed whenever the direction of the wind changed.

Warmth was provided to the main building by a coal-fed boiler that was located in an adjacent building, and was marked by a tall brick chimney. There were storage buildings and a separate block that served as the nurses' home. A tiny chapel was located on the ground floor of the main building.

The purpose of the sanitarium was to allow patients with tuberculosis to receive continuous supervised care under healthy sanitary conditions. Prior to the early 1940s, when the first antibiotic to treat the disease was discovered, treatment of what was sometimes called the "white plague" consisted of rest, fresh air, and the hope that the body's own immune system would kick in and defeat the disease. Death was the usual outcome if this treatment did not work.

With the discovery of the antibiotic streptomycin, followed very quickly by the discovery of additional effective antibiotics, it was now possible to treat the disease with a drug cocktail and not have to rely solely on the body's immune system. Antibiotics had to be taken for at least six-to-twelve months to completely destroy the bacteria, and the treatment was personalized according to each patient's condition, age, overall health, and other considerations. While the disease was life-threatening for those who contracted it, by the time Jock arrived at the sanitarium, tuberculosis was no longer considered a threat to public health.

Jock did not particularly like his new home. While the nurses were kind and caring, there was too much discipline and supervision to make certain that he conformed to the timetable of treatment. He would try to argue, but the nurses would ignore his objections and insist that he do as the doctors had ordered. His requests for alcohol and cigarettes went ignored. Sitting outside, watching the waves pound the beach, did little to improve his disposition. It was not possible for him to run away, and no one knew how long it would take to complete his cure.

Jock's wife regularly appeared each fortnight and gave him updates from home. She would bring him books and old newspapers to read, and share photographs of the children. She talked about finding a job but was worried about who would look after the children. Jock agreed that she should stay at home for the time being.

It was toward the end of his treatment in very early 1957 that Gwen arrived one afternoon at the hospital without her normal good spirits. She and Jock talked about family matters, but throughout the conversation Gwen appeared distant, her mind seemingly preoccupied. Jock finally asked her, "Is everything okay? You seem to have other things on your mind this afternoon. Is something wrong?"

Gwen appeared a little nervous and replied, "Yes, there is something on my mind. I have a letter in my purse that I need to give to you, and you can tell me what it's all about."

Gwen extracted a long brown envelope that had clearly been opened and went on to say, "About a week ago there was a knock on the door. I opened the door to discover two police constables standing outside, wanting to talk to someone. At first I thought something dreadful had happened to one of the children, or maybe to you. I asked them if there was a problem. They replied by asking me if you were at home.

"When I said no, they passed me this envelope, with the request that I give it to you. I asked them what it was about. They told me it is a summons for you to appear in court in Yorkshire in a few days' time. Some woman in Yorkshire and her husband are suing you for back payment in child support. I was shocked. I asked them if they had come to the wrong address and said I had no knowledge of the incident referred to in the letter. I explained that you were ill and living away from home. They took note of my explanation but asked me to deliver this envelope to you. I am to tell you that you must contact the courts in Yorkshire as soon as possible."

The blood drained out of Jock's face. He stumbled for words and began to sweat a little. Then he narrated a story of his time in Yorkshire and the events that had begun almost fourteen years earlier, in July 1943. The expression on Gwen's face continued to change as she reacted to this story. At first it was an expression of denial that this could never have happened. Then it was a look of disappointment and shock that this event really had occurred. And last of all it was one of anger, of having been let down, of being humiliated, of being taken advantage of by her husband, of being deceived.

She told Jock that she needed time to think about what he had just told her. Jock asked her not to say anything to the children or to other family members, at least for the time being. She agreed.

She didn't want the knowledge of her discovery to interfere with his recovery. She would wait until his treatment was over and then would expect a full explanation of why he had not told her before. She didn't want to break up the family, but what was intolerable was that Jock had hidden this information for the past fourteen years. She left feeling disgusted with him and drove home.

After she had left, Jock opened the envelope and read through its contents several times. He needed to decide what to do.

Gwen continued to visit him each fortnight, but the letter had chilled their relationship. She kept her promise of not telling anyone, but she no longer felt pleasure and happiness when she talked to Jock.

A few days before his release from the hospital Jock made his last visit to his airing hut. He acted on his decision to reply to the summons. He wrote to the court and to Mary Louise's legal adviser, telling them about his sickness and his loss of employment. He claimed that there was no way he could make payments in his present state. However, he proposed to begin payments as soon as he was fully recovered and was back at work. He would consider paying some of the arrears but argued that those payments should not include time when he was out of work.

Other than an acknowledgment that the letters had been received, he heard nothing further from the courts. The last few weeks of his stay in the sanitarium were worse than a nightmare. He had no way from that distance to address his relationship with his wife, and fretted over what she might do when he returned home. What he had kept secret for fourteen years was now known to his wife. His past was now very much beginning to affect his present, and no doubt would become an even greater influence on his future.

He felt depressed and wrongly treated. Here he was, in mid-1957, without a job, having lost his good health to a miserable and potentially fatal disease, and he faced the likelihood that he was about to lose his family because of an event that never should have happened. It was an accident of war. But it was affecting the remainder of his life. And yet, while he indulged in self-pity, he doubted that anyone else would be interested in his troubles.

CHAPTER 18

In JUNE 1957, Gwen collected Jock McGregor from the sanitarium. Jock enjoyed the drive home. He didn't think he would, but as he and his wife were carrying his belongings to the car, she said to him, "I think we should stay together. I will never forgive you for hiding the truth from me, but we have two teenage children who need our attention and affection. I haven't said anything to them yet, and I don't plan to, unless you want us to break up."

Jock's simple reply was, "Let's leave things as they are."

He was looking much older after his ordeal with tuberculosis and had become gaunt and gray. The sanatorium had told him that he was fully cured but that he would need the occasional x-ray to confirm that no further treatment was needed.

It was a sunny summer's day. There wasn't much traffic. He enjoyed all the sights of the countryside; he could watch the skylarks flutter over the meadows and listen to the curlews in the distance as the car drove among fields of recently mown hay, corn soon to be harvested, and green pastures, home to cows, sheep, and the occasional horse. They finally arrived at their semidetached home in the West Midlands.

Both children were happy to see their father, and Jock was pleased to see them. They were doing well at school and rapidly developing into young adults. His son was already going out with friends who could drive and was visiting pubs, clubs, and dance halls. Jock found this a little alarming. He told his son that in future he should not travel outside the boundaries of the town and be home no later than eleven o'clock at night. His daughter was hoping to visit Paris for a week with her school, but Jock told her that she couldn't go. He didn't have a job, and there wasn't enough money to pay for her trip. She was very disappointed. Both children thought he was a little mean and unreasonable.

Jock was tired after the long journey and went to bed early. It was so good to be back home and sleeping in his own bed.

For the next few weeks, he renewed acquaintances and rode buses and trams to see what was taking place in the West Midlands. He and his wife had talked about moving somewhere else, but she had been born in the neighborhood, and both of their families lived nearby. Substantial changes were taking place in the community. What was happening before his illness seemed to have continued. Flats or low-rise apartments seemed to be sprouting up everywhere, and slum clearance was still in progress. Apparently there was also overspill development that involved relocating families to the suburbs or even further afield.

Roads were being improved, and bridges were strengthened. Signs of commercial redevelopment were also visible. He had asked the firm he had worked for before his illness if they wanted him back. They apologized but advised him that they had no suitable vacancy.

The other significant change involved the continuing effects of immigration to the West Midlands. This had begun shortly after the war, with the arrival of people from Jamaica. Immediately following the war, Britain suffered a severe shortage of labor. At the same time, people returning to the West Indies who had fought for or supported their mother country found very few work opportunities there. The solution was to return them to Britain. The British Nationality Act of 1948 gave all Commonwealth citizens the right to enter Britain using their United Kingdom passports.

The shortage of labor persisted into the 1950s, and Britain continued to encourage immigration. Many industries advertised for workers overseas. Textile and engineering firms even sent agents to India and Pakistan to find new employees. The success of these practices was now visible on the streets of the West Midlands. Usually the employee would arrive, make the necessary preparations for his family, and then have his wife and children join him in his new country. Migrants from the West Indies had been the early arrivals, but now the largest group of immigrants came from the Indian subcontinent—Hindus, Sikhs, and Muslims. It was not unusual to see men wearing turbans on the buses, on the railways, or in the factories.

Immigrants tended to concentrate in areas of housing that were substandard and cheap. New immigrants appeared to be arriving continuously. Pressure was placed on education and on general services as a result of this steady stream of often non-English-speaking people. New workers' organizations and social societies were being established to protect the immigrants' culture and their well-being. There were also early signs of racial prejudice and discrimination from the white community. Newcomers were beginning to experience hostility, with estate agents often unwilling to offer them housing opportunities outside the immigrant neighborhoods. There were also cultural and language conflicts in the workplace.

These were all factors influencing Jock's decision on how he should resume his career. The local authority was ready to hire him, but only in a drafting role, which would return him to the level of responsibility that he had attained before the war. Other development and construction firms were interested in him, but he had let his formal membership in his professional institute lapse, and had never completed its courses. This caused them either to question his qualifications or to offer him a wage well below what he expected.

After discussion with the family and a promise from his parents to fund the business, he decided to establish his own planning, design, and construction firm. Initially, he would operate out of his home, but he would move to separate premises once it was established. His wife agreed to act as company secretary; he hired a qualified architect, and he appointed a friend's daughter as his administration and payroll coordinator. He was off and running, open for business, and using his network of contacts to identify suitable engineering opportunities. His preferences were for residential housing development, commercial development, and bridge and roadway improvements. He also needed to buy the heavy equipment necessary for project fulfillment. He was energized, enthusiastic, and confident that his venture would be successful.

During this time, Jock tried not to think about Mary Louise. He ignored the occasional legal correspondence that would arrive and did not make any maintenance payments. Soon their son would reach fifteen, the age at which payments under the court order ended. Hopefully this would release him from the misery of anxiety and guilt that he had felt for so long and that he had tried to ignore.

During the very late 1950s and into 1960, Jock's business grew and was successful. His business focus was on public-built and public-owned housing, known as council houses and collectively as council estates. He managed his many contacts in the public authorities to obtain business and built a reputation for well-constructed homes at a fair price. Much of his design and construction involved the building of low-rise blocks of flats or apartments, ranging from half a dozen units up to twenty or thirty flats in a block. Typically, the size of each apartment was one or two bedrooms. There was a ready need for these new homes because of the ongoing demolition of substandard housing and the replacement of housing destroyed during the war.

Jock also picked up other projects to add variety to his work. These included road widening, bridge strengthening, bus station redevelopment, and commercial area reconstruction. Replacing traffic lights with roundabouts to speed up traffic flow was a frequent request.

Some projects were a little less interesting, such as stair design for pedestrian bridges at railway stations and the building of bus stops.

Work demands were so high that Jock had no time to pursue his photography hobby; he had resigned from the Shakespeare Amateur Dramatic Society before he went to the sanatorium.

By the start of the 1960s, the nature of redevelopment had begun to change, and business was harder to find. Projects became larger than he could manage, and there was an increase in competition for the size of projects he could handle. On the residential side, development had moved to favor high-rise "tower" blocks. Government subsidies made this approach to housing more attractive, and more people could be housed in the same area. It was preferred by the local authorities since it would avoid their moving displaced families outside the city boundaries. Finally, for low-rise construction, there had been a big increase in the use of prefabricated materials that required little planning and no design.

There was also a decline in trunk road development and repair. Priorities were transferred to the construction of a national motorway, or freeway system. These were huge projects, typically beyond Jock's capability, and the motorways had the added insult of reducing the use of some adjacent trunk roads. Smaller projects were still available, but their number was declining. Jock persisted with his business, but he grew increasingly alarmed and worried over what was happening. Less income was flowing into his company, and more of his projects needed to be bid close to the breakeven point.

There were times when he felt annoyed and angry because of the way public authorities would insist on price reductions at the end of what usually would be protracted negotiations. It was almost as if they were conspiring to destroy his company. There was further alarm when the news broke that a new town was to be built a few miles away so that people could be relocated away from the city to allow the remaining slums to be cleared.

Over fifty thousand people would be relocated to this new development. But none of it was available for bidding by Jock. He could see his business starting to unravel and took out additional lines of credit secured by equipment or housing that he owned to continue to compete. He began to have some time on his hands, so he decided to make the best of what was happening to him and started the design of a new home for the family situated in the countryside of the West Midlands. He also found himself drinking more than he was used to, to soften his stress, and in place of the cigarettes that his doctor had banned after his illness.

He brought home his anxieties and seemed more depressed and angry the further away he was from his desk. He would have arguments with his wife over what was happening and what should be done about it. To Jock, she seemed to be spending money on the family as if nothing was happening to his business. His meanness even extended to his children. He required his son to start to work in the business, and he would blame him for lost deals and poor work. His daughter seemed to stick up for her mother, which he did not like and often criticized.

The stress caused by the firm's financial condition worsened when he discovered he had purchased stolen equipment that was repossessed by the original owner. He also suffered theft at some of his construction sites. Even the firm that he had worked for prior to his illness was giving him trouble. He undertook subcontracting on their behalf, but now they were having financial problems of their own. There was a rumor that the firm would be liquidated. Invoices due to him were being paid more slowly, and ultimately they were not paid at all when the firm was liquidated. He started to drink more often to soften his anger and moderate his depression. He took long liquid lunches and regularly bought whisky to take back to the office. Thoughts of Mary Louise would arrive and magnify his stress.

His wife was increasingly alarmed. He would come home late. He would buy stuff for the business that he didn't need. He didn't seem to care about the family.

Sometimes he argued that his business should become more diverse and be expanded. Then there were times when he felt he should close the firm, just walk away from it, and leave it to the banks to sort out. There were also times when he talked about selling the firm, making a lot of money, and moving the family to Spain or somewhere similar. When his wife would try to reason with him, he became belligerent and abusive and would sometimes threaten her physically. At other times he would storm out of the house and disappear for hours. His behavior became more and more erratic and extreme. In his down periods he would talk about ending everything as the best way to support his family. His physical behavior toward the family became more dangerous, and his use of alcohol became more constant. It reached a point where Gwen needed to talk to the doctor.

Initially the doctor prescribed the newly discovered antidepressant drug known as desipramine. Unfortunately, it brought with it a number of side effects, including agitation and regular headaches. It became apparent to the doctor that Jock was not responding favorably to this treatment. Gwen witnessed further deterioration in his behavior and worried that he might do harm, either to himself or to her and the children.

The doctor decided that Jock needed to be treated by a specialist because he needed psychiatric coping help and counseling to manage his depression and fits of anger and disobedience. Electroconvulsive therapy was now prescribed. Jock absolutely refused to accept this treatment.

There was no way that he was going to a "loony bin," as he called it. His parents supported his decision.

Gwen initially backed away from her plan, only to watch as Jock became even more violent and irrational at work, at home, and when he was driving. There was no way she and her children could live under these conditions. If he wouldn't accept treatment voluntarily, she would have to have him sectioned, or detained, in an appropriate psychiatric hospital. This was accomplished by Gwen and the doctor in a manner that was unpleasant for all. But had Jock not cooperated with the family, the police would have been called to take him to the hospital by force.

The hospital itself was a very fine establishment, liked by many of its patients, with a strong social component built around garden fetes, bingo games, trips to the seaside, and other activities. There were approximately twelve hundred psychiatric beds; both short-stay and long-stay patients were accepted. The large four-story brick building, which dated back to 1818, stood on its own grounds. The architecture included high ceilings and ornate windows, stairwells, and entrances. The many corridors connected a series of wards dedicated to different types of treatment and illness. Downstairs were cellars and isolation rooms, above was the central hall and pharmacy; a small chapel was on the second floor. Nurses and administrators lived on-site in flats and in a nurses' home.

Under the Mental Health Act of 1959, the doctors possessed the authority to treat Jock without his approval. He spent eight weeks in the hospital under observation and regularly received electroconvulsive treatment. On either side of his head electrodes were placed, through which he received a series of electrical stimulations. Each lasted less than a second. Several treatments were given to him every other day. Treatment was given under careful supervision and was considered the best available at the time.

It was believed that this treatment would help Jock with his depression and discourage his drinking habit. The diagnosis was that because Jock drank to relieve his depression, the alcohol was not the actual cause of his depression. If his depression could be treated, his desire to drink would be lessened. After some signs of improvement he was "deinstitutionalized" and sent home for continuing care and treatment.

Returning home after his illness, Jock came back to financial uncertainty, the need to do something to sustain his business, and strained relationships with his family. He resisted further treatment and claimed he was fully recovered.

The home he had started to build for the family was now complete, and he managed the arrangements that allowed his family to move to their new home. It was a large and impressive detached house, located some distance away from where he had lived since becoming married. His daughter was leaving home to train as an occupational therapist; his son continued to work for the business. The relationship with his wife remained tense and was made more difficult because Jock's parents had not forgiven her for having had him detained in the psychiatric hospital. He was drinking less but still exhibited unpredictable mood swings.

Jock had moved into a separate bedroom from Gwen in the new house. One morning a few months later, when she went downstairs, Gwen found that he had already left the house, taking with him a suitcase full of clothes and toiletries. The car was missing.

She was not aware that Jock had planned to be out of town. Her son went down to the office and confirmed that his father was not there. Jock's parents confirmed that he was not with them. Nobody had received a phone call from Jock. No one knew where he was.

Two days later there was a knock on the door. Gwen answered. Two serious-looking police constables asked to come inside. She invited them into the kitchen and prepared each a cup of tea.

"We have some difficult news to give you, Mrs. McGregor," said the more senior-looking policeman.

"What's happened?" Gwen asked, hoping it was nothing to do with the children.

"It's your husband. We think he's killed himself. We found his car parked next to the Clifton Suspension Bridge near Bristol. It's a dark-green Jaguar Mark X, registered in his name. A suitcase was on the rear seat. We have searched the river but have not found a body. That's not unusual, because the bodies of people who jump from that bridge often are washed up either on the Welsh or Irish coasts. We need a statement from you that we have notified you, and you have to sign for the return of his belongings. The car will be held until we have finished our investigations. It's taken us all this time to contact you because no address was in the vehicle."

She asked, finding it hard to believe what she had just been told, "Was there a suicide note?"

"No," the second constable replied, "but there was a book on the backseat with a piece of paper inserted in a page that describes a suicide. So we think that is what happened."

Gwen asked if they had any more information.

They said that the local police had been called out at first light the previous morning. A passing motorist had seen a car parked in a spot that is often used by people wishing to jump off the bridge. When the police arrived, the vehicle was cold, suggesting it had been there overnight; the car keys were still in the ignition. The suitcase was on the backseat and there was evidence that Jock may have eaten a sausage roll or pork pie before jumping from the bridge.

"We always investigate each incident, even though suicides are regular events on this bridge. The river was searched for several miles downstream, but nothing was found," said the older constable.

"Can you imagine why your husband would want to do this?" asked the younger policeman.

Gwen told him about the state of her husband's business and the financial difficulties, Jock's irrational behavior, and his recent treatment in a psychiatric hospital. The policeman took notes and had Gwen sign the receipt for the suitcase. He mentioned that many of the successful suicides at the bridge involved people with psychotic illnesses. He expressed his condolences to Gwen for her loss and told her that the search for the body would continue for three days.

Gwen immediately called Jock's parents and told them what had happened. They were as shocked as she was. She told her son and daughter that evening. They asked lots of questions regarding the suicide that she could not answer, and were clearly upset by the death of their father. They worried about their future, and she was unable to reassure them. The following day, Gwen and her son went to the office to start winding down her husband's business.

That was one of the worst days of her life. Her husband seemed to have debts everywhere. He had mortgaged the house that the family was now living in and appeared to owe much more than he was owed. In effect, he had jumped off the bridge leaving Gwen and the children with nothing. When she went through his personal items at home, she had to break into his desk, and discovered several letters from Mary Louise and a picture of a boy she assumed must be her son.

Jock's parents were not very helpful because of the disagreement over the psychiatric hospital. Gwen had to rely on her own parents for help and compassion. The family home was quickly repossessed, and the office was closed. Gwen's daughter dropped out of school in the south of England and became a student at a local teacher training college. Once the business was closed, her son found employment with another construction firm. Gwen and the children moved in with her parents.

By now it was 1964, and Gwen's life seemed to have reached rock bottom. She wondered if Mary Louise had in the past experienced similar feelings of being let down by Jock McGregor. And she thought about her son and daughter, who continued to be unaware that they had a half brother living in Yorkshire.

CHAPTER 19

By CONTRAST WITH Jock's life, my life, that of Mary Louise, was continuing to improve in West Yorkshire. I did, however, continue to face difficulties and setbacks that required patience and perseverance on my part. But overall my ambitions and opinions were beginning to prevail. My son John had celebrated his fifteenth birthday a few days earlier, in May 1959.

He was what was considered just "average" at school, but at least he had not been expelled. But during the prior year he ran with a group of boys who had all ended up in borstal or juvenile jail. Because he had a school bus to catch promptly each evening, he had avoided participating in the worst of the gang's behavior, and so had not been arrested. He had, however, been caught at school selling girlie magazines that he regularly stole from a nearby newsagent. Personally, I found this incident very embarrassing.

This particular Sunday morning I was in a field near my home picking up Babycham bottles, Britvic juice tins, beer cans, and the occasional empty container of spirits. We had held a dance as a school fund-raiser the night before. The marquee stood a few feet away, its white canvas coated with early-morning dew that glistened against the rising sun.

The money we raised went to help the school purchase a small passenger van. Older pupils had no way to conduct field trips, and yet regional matriculation exams increasingly required field experience, especially for students attending the two-year, six-form stream that was preparatory to attending university. The dance was a successful event, with many parents and their friends attending.

I feared that my husband Bob might interfere with the event and even try to disrupt it. His illness still gave rise to seizures, and at times he became violent. His anger had worsened because of my decision to keep John in school for his fifth year.

The court order requiring Jock McGregor to pay maintenance support had expired the day my son had become fifteen. It was still possible to sue for back payments, but the court was less interested now. Besides, Jock told the court in April 1957 that he had been unemployed for nearly two years, that he was still unemployed and recovering from a serious illness, and that he had no funds with which to meet his financial obligations. Because fifteen is the standard age when most pupils leave school, Bob wanted me to take my son out of school and find him work. I refused.

That evening he had threatened to disrupt the dance. I told him that if he did that, I would walk out on him with my son, and leave him with his five-year-old son and three-year-old daughter, to look after on his own. He knew I meant it, so he stayed away.

John had already begun to spend more time away from home. Two years earlier, my father had bought him a racing bike with dropped handle bars. It was yellow and black, with a four-speed derailleur. John loved the new freedom the bike gave him. On weekends he would cycle thirty to fifty miles each way and visit distant towns that he had never seen before. He would return home in the evenings exhausted and covered in salt from sweating.

Cricket had also become a passion. He played for two local village teams as an off-spin slow bowler. Apparently, he was very good. There was even talk that he should turn professional. This idea was dashed about the same time as the fund-raiser when he found out about his physical shortcomings: his fingers were not long enough. His small fingers could not adequately handle the ball in adult cricket. Both he and I were terribly disappointed, but he continued to play as a member of the village cricket team.

With sports no longer offering him a successful future, it seemed that all his eggs were in one basket. Only education could pull him out of the uncertain lifestyle in which he had grown up. To help fund his continuing education, I arranged an evening paper route for him. I also had him attend church each Sunday to pump wind into the organ. For this effort, he was paid one shilling each week.

One morning several weeks earlier, I had been talking to the school secretary. I commented on my financial difficulty in keeping John at school. She suggested that if I was on state-assisted child support, which I was, John might be eligible for free school lunches. Further investigation confirmed that I was eligible; I no longer had to give John five shillings a week for school meals.

He did not wholeheartedly welcome this change. It seems he had been missing some of his school lunches, purchasing three penny-worth of chips at the local fish and chips shop and pocketing the remaining nine pence as savings. So he no longer had that opportunity. Also, others at his lunch table would sometimes ask why he was receiving free lunches and make him feel different and inferior. But he soon adjusted.

Another privilege that came with this additional financial support was a free summer holiday to the seaside each year. In the past fifteen years, we had enjoyed only one family holiday of a week in a caravan, and more recently I had spent a few days in a rented cottage with my sisters and their families. However, John was usually absent from the rented cottage because he was busy playing cricket. Now he was able to spend ten days in a youth hostel at an upmarket seaside resort in northeast Yorkshire.

It was this opportunity that presented me with the same type of embarrassment my son had encountered over free lunches. When we arrived at the bus that was to take twenty boys and girls on this welfare journey, I discovered that the local press and radio were present. Cameras were clicking, and microphones were pushed into peoples' faces. Under no circumstances did I want my friends to know that I had fallen to this level of welfare support in order to enable my child to have a holiday. We went round to the back of the bus and hid for about thirty minutes until the bus's engine started, and it was ready to depart. The pictures that evening in the local newspapers did not include my son.

My friend, Nan Dawson, also continued to help me. She knew I was struggling for money. One day during a visit to her home in the city she told me that she had arranged for John to have free haircuts. Apparently she knew a local barber who was very successful and often won male hairstyling competitions. He needed men and boys on whom to practice, so she volunteered John, and the barber accepted. For the next few years, John regularly visited this hairdresser to receive his free haircuts so long as he allowed the barber to choose the hairstyle. Typically he would leave with blow-dried hair swept up at the forehead and forced back into waves across the top of his skull. Sometimes I would collect him from Nan's after school; on other occasions, he would cycle to school and cycle home after his haircut.

There were consolation improvements to my life that compensated for the challenges I faced in bringing up my son. My mother and father had returned as my loving parents and as strong supporters of my personal goals. They would even stay at my home and volunteer to look after my children. When this was not convenient, they would solicit my sisters, who were both married, to take care of my children in their homes.

This gave me opportunities to develop my work skills by volunteering at several nearby hospitals and to deepen relationships with my friends at the local Women's Institute. In the late summer of 1959, it also allowed Bob and me to spend six weeks traveling across Canada and the United States. The friends from Canada we met in England a few years earlier had sent us ship and rail tickets to make the trip possible. At first Bob was reluctant to accept this level of generosity, but eventually I persuaded him to accept.

These simple acts of kindness from various people gave me the energy and confidence to do what I believed in, and never to concede defeat. The visit to Canada and the United States gave me an insatiable lust for travel that would continue with me for the rest of my life.

However, I still had not addressed the problem that my son was just "average" at school. This assessment did not sit well with me, given my ambition for him to enter into the sixth form and go on to university. I had exploited as much as I could my relationship with the headmaster and my influence on the Parent-Teacher Association. The headmaster told me that he had done all he possibly could to help, and it was now up to my son to want to succeed.

I came up with the idea of monitoring his study hours and rewarding him for the amount of effort he put into his homework. I asked him, and he agreed, to keep a record of the additional number of hours, by subject, that he studied, not including regular school. For every fifty hours he accumulated, I would pay him a pound. It was in his interest to be honest with his reporting. During the year he spent many hours in seclusion in the sitting room of our home preparing for his exams.

Bob remained irritable and mean at the thought that the result of all this extra study would keep my son at school. His belief was that since he was providing a home for my son, he should have a say in what my son did. Bob's annoyance displayed itself during the winter months when he would interrupt my son's studies to turn off the electric fire, the only source of heating in the sitting room.

But my son stayed with the program, even if it meant wearing an overcoat during his study time. By the narrowest of margins he passed a sufficient number of exams to move into the sixth form. I was so proud of his accomplishments!

As an additional reward, my father and I came up with sufficient funds to buy John his first car, a very old, preowned Wolseley Eight. It was a black four-door sedan with a windscreen that could be opened. The car didn't go very fast, and the handbrake was suspect, but its capabilities were a big advance over the bicycle. Ahead of his seventeenth birthday, when he would legally be allowed to drive, we would visit one of the many derelict World War II airfields, so John could practice driving up and down the disused runway. He soon became familiar with the steering, the clutch, the floor pedals, and the instruments of the vehicle; as a result, a few weeks after reaching age seventeen, he passed his driving test.

By now my son was participating in sixth-form studies. Reports from the headmaster were that he was doing well. He had chosen the natural sciences because they were aligned with his hobby of ornithology and his interest in biology. They also happened to be the subjects in which he did best. Geology was a new subject, but it seemed he had a natural ability for this science. He could look at a hillside and, without reference to a stratigraphy map, could describe the different layers of rock that made up its profile.

On weekends he would sometimes disappear in his car and visit his favorite nature reserve on the southeast coast of Yorkshire. He would tell me of mist-netting and ringing migrant birds and adding new species to his list of birds seen during his lifetime. With up to fifteen thousand migrant birds passing through the reserve every morning during spring and autumn, it was easy to add new species to the log.

He was so engrossed in this hobby that he managed to miss the Cuban missile crisis. It was only after he left the bird reserve at the end of October 1962 that he discovered that much of the world had spent thirteen anxious days wondering if a third world war was about to begin.

This passion for bird-watching continued during his university years, helped by the coincidence that he was accepted as an undergraduate at a university within an hour's drive of the reserve. He had sacrificed cricket by this time for girls and ornithology. It seems he even combined his two interests on occasion; for example, the girl who was eventually to become his wife had her first date with him out at the reserve. My son introduced her to bird species such as wheatiers, winchats, redstarts, and waxwings, and then, for dinner, prepared undercooked hot dogs on the roadside using a camping gas stove.

It was easy to be mesmerized by the history and solitude of the reserve, which consists of a narrow spit of land made of sand and shingle, about three miles long, located at the southernmost tip of southeast Yorkshire. In some places it was less than fifty yards wide, with the sea pounding on its eastern edge, and the mud flats of the river estuary marking its western extremity. The air was salty and clean. The vegetation was windswept and comprised largely of low-growing plants and shrubs, especially Marram grass.

During the late afternoon of January 31, 1953, the location signaled the start of serious damage caused by the North Sea floods. The sea breached the seawall defenses in several places but failed to breach the shingle spit. The following year, strengthened protection was built using local materials drawn from what became known as the canal bank.

The reserve was also a treasure trove of history. It was the location where Henry Bolinbroke landed in 1399 to dethrone Richard II, an event recorded for posterity by William Shakespeare. Gun batteries with barracks were established in 1805 during the Napoleonic Wars, and the reserve was the site of serious defense installations during both the First World War and the Second World War. During World War I, forts were built on either side of the estuary, along with coastal artillery batteries. The forts were reactivated during World War II and were regularly attacked by the Luftwaffe. Indeed, it was here in the winter of 1939 that the first British casualties of the war occurred on English soil. By the time of my son's visits, the military purpose for this land had ended, and the area had been converted into a nature reserve.

For myself, I continued to develop my work skills by attending various seminars organized by the Women's Institute and local hospitals so that I would be prepared for employment when the time came. During this period, my father died. My mother then looked to me as her primary caregiver. In exchange, she spent time looking after my children when I had other matters to attend to.

I had long since forgiven her for the difficult times she helped create when John was born. She had little need to look after John now because he had discovered parties and dances and was out most evenings. During the day, he was at school. I would encourage him to go to parties and dances in the village to avoid unnecessary driving and indirectly to see what he was up to. He seemed to be following my youthful practice of going to dance halls and would go to all-night events that ended with breakfast.

At the end of his two years in the sixth form, he passed all of his examinations and was offered a place at the university that he had ranked as his number one choice. Once again, there was a financial obstacle. He qualified for a public grant that would cover tuition and maintenance costs, but he needed money to support his daily living. The decision was made that he should take a year off school before starting university.

Using my hospital contacts, I found him a hospital porter position at a nearby medical facility. His responsibilities were varied but helped him develop a strong discipline for work. Sometimes he would be in charge of the morgue; sometimes he would prepare patients for surgery; sometimes he staffed the needs of the emergency room, and often he would be required to scrub and polish ward floors and remove soiled linen and food waste from these same wards.

After the year was up, it was time for him to transfer to university life. It was very hard for me to say good-bye to him. I drove with him to the lodgings where he was to stay during his first year and then returned home by train. Every few weeks he would return home for a weekend visit, and he seemed to be adapting to an environment of which I had no knowledge. President John F. Kennedy had been assassinated the Friday before one of the weekends in late November 1963 when John came home. We talked at length about what had happened, its implications, and the sadness felt by so many people.

My life was to take another significant shift less than six months after my son had departed for university. During late February 1964, Bob complained of feeling unwell. I called the doctor. After various examinations and tests, the doctor decided to have Bob admitted to hospital. I followed the ambulance and, once at the hospital, made certain that my husband was comfortable and had everything he needed. Then I drove home. The phone was ringing as I arrived home. It was the hospital. Apparently the doctor had gone in to examine Bob and discovered that he had died in his sleep. I was later told that postmortem examinations indicated that he could have died of one or several different causes, and not directly and solely because of his diabetes.

My sense of loss was overwhelming. My brain was numb, so I could not think, and little issues for the next few days appeared insurmountable. I called the village vicar on hearing of Bob's death and asked him to my home to give me comfort. His arrival was almost instant. He reassured me and supported me as I informed my children of Bob's departure. I heard myself weeping quietly as I spoke to them, as much because my children had lost a father than because I had lost a husband.

I then contacted my son's university and asked them to instruct John to return home immediately for family reasons. As soon as he arrived, I told him of the death of Bob.

I sought to avoid making decisions and allowed a degree of self-pity to take charge of me. After the funeral, my husband was buried next to his first wife. He had died at seventy-seven, and I, now at the age of forty-one, faced a new and uncertain future. Bob's will had left all his property and monies to his children and nothing to me. While I would contest the will, and ultimately gain access to the house and a minimum stipend to support my children, I would need to find employment to secure an adequate standard of living.

My mother was still alive to look after my two young children, and my years of study and volunteer work caused the local hospital authority to ask me to consider becoming superintendent and home warden for its three largest hospitals. This would put me in charge of the day-to-day operations of the three hospitals and all employment matters. It was twenty years since I had last worked full time in paid employment.

I sought John's advice. He was supportive, so I agreed to a three-month trial at the hospitals. I loved everything about the job from the very first day. My other love was travel. And this passion I could also now accommodate. Starting the year after Bob's death, it became a requirement that I spend at least one holiday overseas each year. The first year I was traveling to ten countries in Europe; the second year I took a cruise to Africa, and the third year I made a trip to Scandinavia and the Soviet Union. In the Soviet Union, I was asked to visit a teaching hospital a few miles outside Leningrad to provide advice on its operations. While it was technically inferior to the hospitals I was used to, the ultraclean surroundings, the passion to learn, and the kindness of staff dispelled any feeling of distrust that I had been told to expect during my visit.

My life was beginning to transform. I could never make up for all that I had lost, but here I was, living in my own home, with a loving family, receiving regular income, in good health, and with a son that I had fought to keep, who was now attending university, something that no one in my family had ever accomplished before. I was a fortunate person.

I would let life take its course.

CHAPTER 20

T$_{HE}$ $_{PHONE}$ $_{RANG}$ in the entry hall of Michael Fromm's Sunset District home in San Francisco. It was a rainy day in October 1964. The winter wet weather arrived early that year.

"Hello. Do you know who this is?" said the voice at the other end of the line.

"No," replied Michael, as he searched his memory to place a name with the peculiar accent to which he was listening. He knew it to be an English "black country" accent. Who did he know who lived there? The name of Jock McGregor came to mind.

"It's Jock McGregor from England. Do you remember us working together in Yorkshire during the war? Those were good times. I am sorry that I lost close contact with you. However, I hope your mother shared the Christmas cards that I have been sending you for the past few years. She gave me your current address, and it was easy for me to track down your phone number. I am coming to America later this month, and I wondered if I could come and see you."

"Yes, I remember you from the airfield." replied Michael. "I recall that you went home to your family in the West Midlands. I assume you still live there. Is your wife coming with you to the United States?"

An emphatic no was Jock's answer. "It's a long story, but she thinks I'm dead. I moved to the island of Jersey a few weeks ago, where I have begun to paint. But I find life here a little dull, and I hear there is a lot more going on in San Francisco. Would it be okay to meet you and possibly stay with you until I find a place to rent?"

The thought of hosting someone from Europe and reviving relationships with Jock McGregor were attractive to Michael. He recalled the regular chats in the English pubs with Jock during the war. Jock had always supported him back then. Additionally, he and his wife Karen had become Anglophiles. Karen had reconnected with her aunt in London after the war. Her aunt had married in England and had a son about the same age as Karen's daughter. Also, Karen had tracked down two school chums who came from Vienna to England as part of the Kindertransport begun immediately prior to World War II.

In 1938, the British Parliament had passed a bill that waived certain immigration requirements for unaccompanied displaced children in Europe, who ranged in age from infant to seventeen. A refugee organization volunteered to take responsibility to choose, organize, and transport predominantly Jewish children and to find them homes in the United Kingdom. The first trains left Vienna on December 10, 1938, and a few days earlier from Berlin. Nearly ten thousand children were transported and placed either in foster homes, with relations, in hostels, and at farms. The last known transport was of forty children by boat from the Netherlands on May 14, 1940, the same day that the Dutch army surrendered to the Germans.

At the end of the war, after Karen's friends discovered that their parents had not survived, they decided to remain in England. They were relocated and lived within a few miles of each other in north London. Karen communicated with them by mail on a regular basis, and they met, either in London or San Francisco, every two to three years.

Michael had stayed in touch with the Land Girl who still lived east of London. She had married her prewar boyfriend when he returned home from Germany. They had moved into a new home built a few miles away east of London, in a new town that had been constructed after the war to accommodate people displaced by the war damage and slum clearances in London.

Michael and Karen, and their daughter, Sarah, would usually stay with these friends in the years that they were able to visit England. The Land Girl was now a teacher at a nearby comprehensive school, and her husband worked in production control at a nearby tractor factory. The English couple did not have children. They owned a large afghan hound that frequently managed to escape but was fortunate enough to be found and returned each time. The woods, the red brick houses, the small green fields, and the quaint Essex towns contrasted sharply with the cream buildings, golden grass, orange groves, and ever-growing bustling conurbations of the Bay Area.

After checking with Karen, Michael informed Jock, "Yes, it's fine for you to visit us for a few days at the end of the month. Do you know your arrival date?"

"Yes," announced Jock. "I am booked on the British Overseas Airline flight that gets in around teatime on October 26. I will meet you at the Airline Bus Terminal on O'Farrell Street around 7:30 p.m., if that is convenient. I can't wait to see you and catch up on the news. It has been a long time."

Michael replied, "I'll be there at 7:30 p.m. You will recognize me by my 49ers baseball cap and London T-shirt. We can walk over to Market Street and use Muni to get home."

With that, Jock ended the call, and Karen and Michael sat down to discuss what they might do with Jock when he arrived. They would show him the sights of San Francisco, take him up to Marin and the redwood groves, and maybe also make a trip south, to the Santa Cruz Beach boardwalk. The regular winter rains would begin very soon, and it didn't make sense to travel farther afield until the warm, dry weather of April/May returned.

The flight was on time. Jock arrived at Michael and Karen's home about 9:00 p.m., and Karen showed him to his room. He looked a little

173

tired and, not surprisingly, had aged since Michael had last seen him. But for a fifty-year-old, his body was trim, and he was in good shape. He was clean-shaven and retained most of his hair, except for a bald spot on the back of his skull. The hair showed some gray, but his blue eyes remained bright and alert.

Michael had also remained slim and was about the same height as Jock. He sported a small moustache. Both men shared a sarcastic, self-deprecating sense of humor. Karen had not put on weight and remained well-proportioned. She wore a permanent smile, and her pleasing face was framed by a short pageboy hairstyle.

They introduced Jock to their daughter, Sarah, who was fifteen and had just started her first year at senior high school. It was her sophomore year, since it was only a three-year high school. She already had the form of a young lady and had inherited her mother's engaging smile. Her hair was dark and shoulder-length. She carried herself gracefully on a pair of exquisite legs, revealed by her preference for wearing short skirts. She welcomed Jock to America and wished him a pleasant stay in San Francisco.

Over breakfast the following morning, Jock and the Fromm family exchanged updates on their family histories. Jock explained how he had contracted tuberculosis ten years earlier and how this had interfered with his career. He also told Michael of the time during the war that he had had "an affair" with the canteen manager at the airfield, and how she had given birth to a son nine months thereafter. He wasn't sure whether to believe her that the baby was his. Her name was Mary Louise, and she was the daughter of his landlady. He hadn't told his wife about what happened, but she had discovered anyway while he was away in hospital being treated for his tuberculosis.

Michael and Karen were shocked by this story and queried Jock further to better understand his reasons for hiding the affair from his wife. Michael confessed that he had been unaware of the affair during the time he was in Yorkshire; he mentioned to Karen and Jock that Jock had always appeared deeply attached to his family. Michael could vaguely remember Mary Louise as a very attractive woman, but she was someone who always was off-limits to his dating.

"Were you in love with Mary Louise, or was it just one of those wartime affairs?" asked Michael. "She always seemed a very nice person to me but not someone who would be unfaithful to her boyfriends."

"It was more of an unplanned affair," replied Jock. "The incident occurred one night after I had been drinking following a meeting with the air commodore. He had forbidden me from returning home to my family until the airfield was completed. I didn't think much of the incident until a few weeks later when her parents confronted me with the allegation that their daughter was pregnant and that I was the father.

"The courts unfortunately agreed with Mary Louise; she took legal action against me, but I always had my doubts. She went to so many dances when she was at home with her parents that it was hard for me to believe that I was her only lover. I was ordered to pay child support but regarded this as unfair. My wages after the war were very low, and I had my own family to support. I lost all contact with Mary Louise after I moved out of her parents' home except for the occasional letter from the court and her legal adviser. When I became sick and was out of work, it was impossible for me to pay anything."

"But if you had doubts about the pregnancy, why didn't you share the situation with your wife when you returned home, and tell her about the baby and the court decision? Wasn't it dishonest to hide the affair from your wife, only to have her find out about the child by accident?"

"Maybe," said Jock. "But if I had told her, I could have disputed being the child's father, but I couldn't claim that the affair had never taken place. None of us had any idea what would happen to us after the war. Mary Louise's illegitimate child was one of many thousands born during the war. It seemed to me that any confession to my wife about the affair would risk our marriage, and I didn't want that to happen. Telling my wife wouldn't have benefited Mary Louise in any way. I loved my children, and I didn't want to lose them. My thoughts were that what my wife didn't know couldn't cause her any harm. Maybe I was mistaken, but history is already written. I cannot go back and change the order of events."

Michael nodded as he reluctantly accepted Jock's explanation. His doubts remained regarding Jock's integrity. It seemed to him that Jock had been exceptionally selfish in hiding the facts from his wife and not taking responsibility for supporting his illegitimate son. At the same time, Michael remembered that Jock had been a good boss during his days in Yorkshire, had always been patient with him, and had encouraged his activities with Land Girls. There was something very engaging about Jock that made it difficult for Michael to dispute Jock's judgment and risk losing a good friend.

Jock continued his story. He told Michael and Karen that after his battle with tuberculosis he had formed his own company with the help of his parents but that the firm had failed because of theft, fraud, and the poor quality of its staff. His wife had been unsupportive and very critical of him during this time. When he became worried and depressed over what was happening, his wife had accused him of being mentally sick and had had him forcibly placed in a mental asylum. He had been deeply angered by this treatment, and his parents had agreed with his point of view.

After being discharged from the hospital, he had helped his family move into a very nice new home that he personally had built for them. But his wife continued to argue with him and criticize his business abilities as his firm continued to suffer. She didn't seem to appreciate all that he was doing to try and support her and their two children. Life at home became intolerable.

Jock decided to leave home and disappear by pretending to commit suicide. This way he could leave behind his failing business and escape from his unpleasant home life. He pretended to jump from a nearby bridge that crossed a steep gorge and a river. It was a well-known location for suicides.

Jock said that he believed he had left sufficient funds for his wife and children to live a good life. He had also taken funds from his business to provide himself with the financial support that he needed. At the same time he had decided to give up civil engineering and focus on the creative activities that he enjoyed.

He had moved to the island of Jersey, a place that he often visited with his family during the 1950s. In Jersey, he had discovered a passion for painting. He now wanted to pursue this hobby in San Francisco, which he thought would allow him greater creativity. He might even make a good living by selling his pictures. He also believed that the Bay Area offered him a more tolerant environment. He had thought of becoming a writer but had decided that painting was a more satisfying activity than writing novels.

He confessed that he had not made contact with his family since the sham suicide and had no intention of informing them of his whereabouts. Michael and Karen speculated on the motives behind this deception and suggested to Jock that at some time in the future he might want to change this decision and call them. He listened to them but seemed to shrug off their advice.

Michael then told Jock how he and Karen had met, married, and very quickly had been blessed with their only child. Karen had continued to work at the candy store until they moved from Los Angeles to San

Francisco; Michael explained how he had been responsible for assisting in the development of the Southern California freeway network.

He had moved to San Francisco in 1959 after more than ten years as a transportation engineer, working on the construction of the Southern California freeways. Major structural engineering advancements had been made during his tenure, and he was proud of his contribution. However, the pace of development began to slow as a result of growing public opposition to road construction.

Freeway routes had initially been developed without consideration for local interests and potential impact on neighborhoods. They were viewed as part of a regional and statewide infrastructure that overrode local concerns. But by the late 1950s this situation was changing, as freeway revolts led to the modification or cancellation of new freeway routes. Several Southern California freeways that Michael had been assigned to were negatively impacted by community opposition.

At about this time, Michael had been approached by a university in San Francisco that was developing an engineering school and wanted to recruit instructors for undergraduate courses that focused on specialist aspects of civil engineering. Michael accepted one of these positions; he was very happy to be a member of academia. Work was only a few minutes away from his home, unlike in Los Angeles.

He had found out that opposition to freeway construction was even more intense in San Francisco than in Los Angeles. There was a plan to build a double-decker freeway westward across the city through the Golden Gate Park and through an area to the east known as the Panhandle. It would connect to a north-to-south freeway that had not yet been built. Earlier in the year, a neighborhood group was formed to campaign against the freeway and had arranged a rally in Golden Gate Park. Other neighborhood groups had come out in opposition to the freeway; petitions and thousands of letters had been sent to the Board of

Supervisors. As a result, it looked very unlikely that the freeway would be built, although there remained powerful groups in the city that were still pushing for the development. It was hoped that the Bay Area Rapid Transit system, known as BART, just being constructed, would remove the need for these freeways. However, BART would not be operational until the early 1970s. Michael confessed that he liked to stay in touch with the practical aspects of his science as well as its teaching.

Karen took over the conversation and told Jock that she had transferred into banking when she moved to San Francisco. She was a business services teller in the neighborhood branch of a major San Francisco bank. With both parents working, she and Michael shared a common concern for the welfare of their daughter, who was at a difficult age when she was easily influenced by her friends and was finding it difficult to balance her social interests with her academic responsibilities. It was apparently normal after school for Sarah and a group of her friends to spend too much time in a local diner talking about whatever girls of fifteen and sixteen talk about.

During the rest of his first week in San Francisco, Jock was left to wander around the city on his own. It was convenient for him to use the municipal transit system that ran close to the Fromms' home. He spent much of his time at Fisherman's Wharf; it seemed so peaceful and so different from anything that he was used to. He would look out across the bay and watch the commercial ships sail silently by, either to dock in San Francisco or in the opposite direction to visit distant ports in Asia. He would wander around the crab stands and watch as the day's catch was boiled, cracked, and cleaned. Cioppino with a slice of sourdough bread was a whole new culinary experience for Jock.

He spent an hour at the Wax Museum that had opened two years earlier, and then drifted through the gift shops. He visited Ghirardelli Square, adjacent to Fisherman's Wharf, which was in the process of opening as a tourist attraction. The buildings dated back to the prior century when they had been the headquarters of the Ghirardelli Chocolate Company. The company had moved across the bay, and the square and its historic brick buildings were now being remodeled to form an integrated restaurant and retail complex. Earlier plans to replace the buildings with apartments had been scuttled.

The prison island of Alcatraz stood some distance away from the shoreline in an abandoned condition. After twenty-nine years of operating as a maximum security penitentiary, Alcatraz was closed and abandoned by the Federal Bureau of Prisons on March 21, 1963. The high cost of operating the prison had eventually brought about its closure. The prison was not to open to the public for another nine years, in large part because of objections from Native Americans and their supporters.

By the time of Jock's arrival there were already claims from Sioux Indians that the island should be returned to them. Reference was made to the 1868 Treaty of Fort Laramie between the United States and Sioux that promised that all retired, abandoned, or out-of-use federal land would be returned to the Native people from whom it was acquired. Because of its closure six months earlier as a penitentiary, it was believed that Alcatraz qualified for reclamation. This claim contributed to the delay in reopening the prison to the public. In March 1964 the island was occupied by a small group of Sioux for four hours. The group offered the federal government the same amount of money that the government had initially offered them—a payment of $9.40 for the entire island. From November 1969 to June 1971 another group of protesters took charge of the island. Approximately fourteen protesters broke through a Coast Guard blockade and landed on the island. They were subsequently joined by a significant number of others. By late May 1970 the government had cut off all electrical power and telephone

service to the island, and in June 1970 a fire of disputed origin des.
many of the buildings on the island. The number of occupants bega
decline, and a year later a group of government workers forcibly remov.
the remaining fifteen people.

For Jock, the weather remained dry during the first few days of his
visit. People were motivated to leave their homes and stroll the wharf,
enjoying the fresh bay air. An array of colorful hats was worn by many of
the women walkers. In the distance, the Golden Gate Bridge shimmered
its international orange in the afternoon sun.

Jock used this time to investigate where he should live. He found a
newly opened hotel a few blocks away from Fisherman's Wharf where
he could stay if the Fromms tired of his company. He would also
need a car, so he visited the local dealerships and decided to purchase
a preowned Volkswagen Beetle. He hoped he could afford the 1960
model, with its push-button door handles and its air-cooled rear engine.

He asked Michael's opinion of the car the following Saturday
morning.

"I think it's a good choice," said Michael. "VWs are reliable, good-
looking, and have plenty of room. But if you're buying a car, what are
your plans for living in San Francisco?"

"Would you mind if I stayed with you a little longer?" asked Jock.
"I have started to look for an apartment, but so far I haven't found
anything that I like. If you want me to move out sooner, there is a hotel
that I found that I will move into temporarily."

"Not necessary," said Michael. "You are welcome to stay with us
until you are ready to move into your own place. I apologize that we are
not good hosts during the week because of our work, but we are happy
to show you around the Bay Area on weekends. Sarah can also show
you places if you have a car."

This arrangement was very agreeable to Jock. He thanked Michael, and they talked of the places that Jock would like to visit. His first ambition was to drive across the Golden Gate Bridge, visit Marin and maybe Muir Woods, which he had heard so much about. That became their plan for the following weekend.

Michael, Karen, and Jock managed to get as far north as the Point Reyes National Seashore. The scenery was amazing; Jock had never seen anything quite like it. Standing near the Point Reyes Lighthouse, he looked north across the peninsula at the wild coastal beaches, with cliffs carved into promontories and bays. He searched the sea for sight of a passing gray whale migrating north to Alaska, but on this day, none were to be seen. The three stopped on the way home in Inverness, a place in which Jock thought he could settle. As they traveled through Marin, they visited the redwood grove at the base of Mount Tamalpais and also stopped at the Mountain Theater. It was too late in the year for the annual theater production, but Jock made a note to return the following year.

He also experienced his first Thanksgiving dinner at the end of November. Karen did the cooking. It was the usual turkey with sweet potatoes, stuffing, vegetables, and cranberry sauce, followed by pumpkin pie. Michael's parents drove over from Sacramento to participate in the celebration. Karen's parents had decided to stay in Los Angeles and visit friends who they had first met in Shanghai.

The following weeks, with his newly acquired VW Bug, Jock traveled out of town on days when the weather was kind. In late January 1965, on an unusually warm Sunday, he and Sarah visited the Santa Cruz boardwalk. Her parents agreed to the visit, although Michael worried silently over Jock's honesty and trustworthiness. But he had no desire to fall out with his daughter or with Jock, and both seemed to enjoy each other's company.

Jock had never ridden before on anything like the Giant D, Sarah persuaded him to take the ride because of the spectacular vie the Monterey Bay that he would enjoy from the top of the attractio. One ride was sufficient. They wandered along the beach and splashec their feet in the ocean. Jock very much enjoyed being with Sarah. She seemed so much nicer than what he could remember about his own children.

Just before they left the boardwalk, they overheard on the radio that Winston Churchill had died that same day. Jock talked to Sarah about how important Churchill had been in Europe in winning the war when he and her father worked at the airfield. He commented that if the Nazis had won, it was hard to imagine what would have happened to Sarah's mother and her parents in Shanghai.

On the way back, they stopped at a hamburger café that was well known to San Franciscans. Jock had never experienced such tasty food on a bun.

"Where else should I visit?" he asked Sarah as they were nearing her home.

"You still have a lot to see in San Francisco. Until the warmer weather returns, I think you should stay local. Then you can travel east to Sacramento and to the Gold Country, and maybe to Lake Tahoe or Yosemite. At this time of year, it is ski season in the mountains. Do you ski?"

"I have never had time to learn," replied Jock, "and at my age, it's probably too late to start now."

Sarah continued, "If you like, sometime I can show you around my school."

"I would like that," was Jock's answer.

The following week Jock met Sarah after school; she showed him her classroom and other buildings. The coeducational school was built just before the United States entered World War II. The three-story building had approximately fifty classrooms, a library, and a cafeteria, and a football field was nearby. Also, a series of bungalows had been erected to accommodate the growing number of students.

Sarah introduced Jock to a few of her girlfriends and a couple of boys she knew who were on the school's golf team. Despite the school's success at golf, the team members were usually looked down upon as sissies by most of their peers. Sarah confided in Jock that one of the evening hobbies she and her girlfriends enjoyed was to go into town and hitchhike. They would pretend to be out-of-towners, and if they were lucky, they would be shown around the city and bought soda drinks and ice cream by good-looking young men.

Jock continued his sightseeing in San Francisco, visiting such places as Lombard Street, North Beach, Golden Gate Park, the Sutro Baths, Coit Tower, and the cable cars. He also found his way to the Cow Palace, which had been constructed in a style that reflected the livestock pavilion built in San Francisco for the 1915 International Exposition. Hence it became known as the "palace for cows" and eventually was named the Cow Palace.

He had missed the Beatles, who had appeared at the Cow Palace in August 1964 at the beginning of their first American tour. The enormous indoor arena was also the site of the 1964 Republican National Convention. At the time of Jock's visit, it was also the home of the local basketball team, the San Francisco Warriors.

Jock was beginning to connect with the underground culture in the city. The beatnik generation was morphing into the hippie culture that was rejecting many of the past norms. There was an emerging advocacy for change and a growing unwillingness to be pushed around by authority and politicians. Opposition to the Vietnam War was the catalyst for people coming together, but the collective demand for change went far beyond the war. There was the civil rights movement, the need for environmental change, support for women's rights, freedom of sexual expression, challenges to traditional authority, a desire for a new generation of music, art, and literature, and a curiosity to experiment with psychoactive drugs. Jock began to enjoy his time in San Francisco and believed he had made a wise choice in deciding to move from the island of Jersey to the Bay Area.

CHAPTER 21

IN MARCH 1965, Jock moved into his own apartment, which was about three blocks away from the Haight-Ashbury district of San Francisco. He planned to resume his passion for art and benefit from the freedom of San Francisco's emerging new liberal culture. His accommodation was a bottom-level flat in a three-story apartment house near Fulton and Arguello. It was a stucco building with a small entrance lobby. The living quarters were rather scruffy but spacious. There was one bedroom, a combined living and dining area, a well-equipped kitchen, and an updated bathroom. He shared a back patio area with his neighbor.

He was located close to Golden Gate Park, and parking was nearby, as well as access to public transit. A grocery store was within walking distance. The nearby neighborhood contained a number of old Victorian houses whose exteriors were beginning to transform from their postwar battleship gray to a multitude of bright, vibrant colors. The trend had begun a couple of years earlier when a local artist had used vivid greens and blues to paint the exterior of his house. Other residents had quickly adopted this new style, and these colorful Victorians were becoming known as the "painted ladies."

His next-door neighbor was named Greg. He lived alone and appeared to be in his late twenties. He had long, dark curly hair and sported a full beard. His dress code was jeans, a tie-dyed T-shirt, a black belt, and brown flip-flop sandals. Sometimes he wore beads around his neck; sometimes he didn't. He had stayed in San Francisco after graduating from a local university, and after a couple of years working for an insurance company, he had decided to drop out of conventional life. He was carrying a draft card when Jock first met him but talked of burning it ceremoniously when the right occasion arose. He seemed amused by Jock's accent and liked listening to Jock as he spoke. He agreed to show Jock around Golden Gate Park and suggested that Jock visit the San Francisco Art Institute to collect advice on how to start his American career as an artist. Greg's passion was listening to music, and he volunteered to introduce Jock to some of the local emerging bands. He suggested that Jock grow a ponytail and told him where to buy comfortable modern clothing.

It was late in May when the two met for a tour of the park. By then Jock had obtained art materials and sufficient advice from the Art Institute, and Greg had destroyed his draft card the previous day during a rally at the University of California in Berkeley.

Greg was curious to know why Jock had decided to move to America.

Jock answered, "I don't know how long I will stay here, but I needed to leave my past life behind. It had always been stressful; there was too much pressure to support my family, and I just got sick of it all. I wanted to be my own person, create something, and be respected for who I am. I find I become irritable with people who don't agree with me or criticize me. I sometimes become impatient and lose my temper with individuals who want things their own way or who are stubborn and petty-minded. Then I feel upset and depressed. Here, I hope to be my own person and be able to channel my efforts in whatever direction I choose. I already feel a level of freedom and tolerance that never existed in England. At home, I would drink and smoke a lot; here, at least drinking doesn't seem to be necessary."

Greg asked him, "So what's your opinion on things over here? What's your view on the Vietnam War? What about civil rights? What do you think about our lifestyle? How much of a rebel are you, or do you just want to be left alone to do your own thing?"

"I want to fit in, but I am not here to fight for causes or to demonstrate for change. I do oppose the war, and I can't comprehend why America discriminates against and segregates some of its people. I like watching the rebellion, but I prefer to be an artist and not an activist. Hopefully I can do this here," said Jock, with slight hesitation.

With that, Jock and Greg wandered across the road into Golden Gate Park, which was crowded with people. Just after they arrived in the park, Greg left the regular pathway and led Jock up a small incline that featured an unimpressive view of some of the park buildings and the radio tower some distance away. The area was occupied by a large group of mainly young people who were sprawled on the grass enjoying the sunshine, chatting, and listening to music. Many of the men were dressed like Greg; the women wore brightly colored tops, long skirts, and scarves around their heads. A few peace signs littered the hill, and someone had hung an antiwar poster on a tree. What was most apparent was that they looked content and in no hurry to move. Greg pointed out several who seemed to be smoking pot, and others who he said were "tuning in" on recreational drugs.

For the next few hours, Greg and Jock walked through the park. They visited the tourist places, such as the Japanese Tea Garden, the De Young Museum, the Botanical Gardens, and the Academy of Science, but also strolled the wide-open spaces such as the Polo Fields, the Speedway Meadow, and the Panhandle. Returning to the apartment, Greg promised to introduce Jock to the emerging music scene later in the week.

A few days later, they visited a variety of concert halls, clubs, and ballrooms where mainstream music, folk music, and the emerging San Francisco sound could be heard. New clubs were opening up to showcase the new wave of San Francisco rock bands that were coming onto the scene. These same bands would hold open-air free concerts for anyone who wished to attend. It was still early days for this music, which was considered more complex, more powerful, and more open to improvisation than either the newly arrived "Liverpool beat" or the traditional folk music that was now aligned with the antiwar movement. In concert halls such as the Fillmore, music was much more of a psychedelic experience, with strobe lights, light projections, and uninhibited dancing.

Returning to the apartment on a warm summer's evening, Jock and Greg sat outside on the patio, exchanging stories from their past. They nibbled on nuts and drank water. Greg asked Jock if he had ever used marijuana.

"Yes, once," replied Jock, "but I started to cough and stopped inhaling."

"Would you like to try some now?" invited Greg.

Not sure whether this was a good or a bad idea, Jock hesitated.

"Let me bring out the pipes, and you can decide as we go along."

Without waiting for an answer, Greg went into his apartment and quickly returned with two glass pipes, a bag of weed, and a box of matches. He filled one of the bowls, handed the pipe to Jock, and then lit it as Jock puffed gently on the stem. He did the same for himself. Jock found himself coughing as he inhaled, but he persevered, increasing the duration of each inhalation. After about five minutes, he began to feel the effects. At the same time, Greg refilled his bowl to give him a second hit. Jock felt light-headed and a little dizzy. He experienced a sense of calm. His mind began to race, and he started to visualize the art he would paint. He needed to take a drink of water because his mouth was dry. It all seemed like a mellow high.

But as the effects began to wear off an hour or so later, he began to feel anxious, upset, and a sense of panic over what he was doing and who he was with. He felt guilty. He became incoherent for a time. At one stage, he no longer recognized Greg. He accused Greg of stealing his

T-shirt and tried to remove it from Greg's back. Greg resisted and left the patio. Jock felt increasingly tired and eventually fell asleep outside on the patio.

Greg saw Jock the following morning.

"You seemed to get a little agitated last night. I hope you're okay," said Greg.

"I'm fine; it was a good trip, and thank you for the experience and marijuana. Sorry if I scared you with my delusions."

And that was the last time Jock saw Greg. He heard from others that Greg had moved over to the East Bay to join the antiwar protesters. Jock continued to smoke the occasional reefer that he bought up on the hill, but he would do so on his own. He settled in to his art and paid occasional visits to Mendocino and Sonoma counties, where he would try to capture the colors of the forests and seascape. He occasionally called to see the Fromms. They would always appear pleased to see him, and Sarah would quiz him on the music he had heard and the hippie fashion he had seen. He occasionally would buy her a necklace or a headband from the people in the park.

He also heard about the communes that were beginning to appear between San Francisco and the town of Mendocino. He visited several of them but always felt out of place. They made him feel old. Some of the free love he witnessed made him feel envious.

On one occasion a couple of girls, probably in their early twenties, had propositioned him to go with them up to the top of a ridge lined with old oak trees that overlooked their commune. It was a beautiful, sunny day. The ridge looked westward across a narrow valley toward the ocean. The girls and some friends were holding a freedom festival. He felt a little apprehensive as he stumbled up the incline to this cluster of young people. Drums and a guitar were playing, and several women were dancing. Other people lay in a circle. A couple was engaged in lovemaking; some were deep in conversation, and yet others were trying to control their young children. The oak trees stood sentry over the event, and the golden grass rolled down the hillside in a thwarted attempt to find water. A lone turkey vulture sailed overhead, seemingly watching all that was happening below.

Jock lay on the forgiving grass, soaking up the sun, squinting at its source, and watching all that was taking place with simultaneous emotions of astonishment and envy. The two girls shared their names with him and introduced him to a third girl who was traveling with them. They called over a group of boys who had driven up in the same van from San Francisco a few days earlier. They were here to celebrate the freedom of nature and to thank the land for its food provided during the past year.

One of the boys took a clear plastic bag out of his pocket and began passing it among the group. The bag contained a number of tiny tablets in a variety of colors. When Jock asked what was in the bag, one of the girls replied, "Acid. Most of us want a hit today. You should try it. But if this is your first time, don't use more than two or three of the dots. The color doesn't matter. Put them under your tongue and then swallow what's left after about fifteen minutes and then wait."

"What will they cost me?" replied Jock. "Who do I need to buy them from?"

The girl replied, "These are communal dots. We each pay something each month, and then we get to use the dots until they are all gone. Today's trip is on us; enjoy it. It's our way of thanking nature. But be careful if you haven't done this before. The effect is likely to last six to twelve hours, so you need to spend the night here. If you want, the boy with the bag will sell you more dots tomorrow before you leave. He makes them himself."

With that, the bag arrived. Jock extracted three pink dots, or tabs, and placed them under his tongue. He then lay back on the grass to await the consequences. Someone passed around some food. He took an apple and tore off a piece of bread but declined the cheese. He ate, drank water, and waited.

Nothing much happened for the first thirty minutes; conversations continued among the group, and a couple started to dance. Jock found it easy to relax in the warm sunshine. The people who had adopted him were sensible and kind. He felt safe, comfortable, and content.

When it arrived, the hit was strong. It seemed to Jock as if he was being transported into another world. How long he would remain there he did not know. He became much more aware of his surroundings. The guitar playing became softer and more melodious. He found thinking difficult. He started to feel disoriented and confused. He babbled at his friends and they seemed to babble back.

The hills were beginning to move and distort, as if struck by an earthquake. Where the hills joined the sky, a kaleidoscope of color was beginning to emerge. At first it was a simple range of reds, but this quickly transformed into a rainbow of bright, ever-changing colors. Jock soon gave up trying to think and sacrificed his mind and body to the euphoria that had taken charge. Geometric patterns began to appear and migrate across his vision. He let his consciousness sink deeper into this new mystical world of beauty, form, and color.

The euphoria seemed to last forever. He laughed out loud at what he saw and spoke incoherently to anyone who would listen. The visualizations grew more intense. The experience began to change.

The flashes of color and patterns of light took control of his mind and began to cause fear. He started to doubt that the experience would ever end. He had no way of controlling the images. The hallucinations began. He lost all sense of reality. The imagery took on a negative presence. Out of the fairy-tale lights emerged a scene of multicolored falling bridges and torrents of purple-green water running in all directions.

Mixed in with these images were the pink faces of falling, screaming people. The faces would look at him as they passed by and then disappear into the raging water. He began to recognize faces he knew; he saw his wife, the faces of his children, and the anguish on the face of his parents. His own face appeared, without expression. These images kept returning and recycling across his mind, time after time, without an end. He began to scream that he was dead. Dysphoria took control of his emotions. He encountered an overwhelming sense of depression. There was no way he could alter this experience.

Jock became hysterical; he screamed and shouted. He tried to find sanctuary from the images by climbing trees and threatening to jump. The falling faces followed him wherever he went. He became violent, lashing out at the air and anything within his reach. He scratched at the soil with his fingers, trying to dig a hole in which to hide.

He felt attacked and agitated, and shrank away from his new friends. They surrounded him, talked to him calmly, and had him lie down. They told him everything would be okay. They restrained him within the circle whenever he tried to escape. He slowly became less aggressive, and eventually the two girls whom he had first met were able to lead him to the commune buildings below. One of the girls gave him her mattress for the night. His symptoms continued to distress him but became less severe.

Jock slept little that night, suffering from the occasional flashback that would repeat the earlier images in ten- to thirty-second episodes. During each episode, Jock would lose all control and start shouting and screaming at the top of his voice, trying to run away from the images. Members of the group took turns acting as "trip sitters" throughout the night to keep him safe indoors. In the morning, Jock felt exhausted, tired, hungry, and in need of a bathroom.

By early afternoon, Jock had recovered sufficiently to be ready to start his journey home to San Francisco. He was still not thinking rationally and continued to find difficulty speaking in clear, coherent sentences. He was not sure he remembered how to drive his car. The two girls took charge of his departure. They helped him find the driver's seat, gave him directions to San Francisco, pushed a small plastic bag containing two dots into his back pocket, and kissed the side of his face in appreciation of his visit. Despite his inability to continually focus on the road, he somehow managed to drive himself without incident back toward San Francisco.

Sometime later, he found himself exhausted and lying on his bed in his Haight-Ashbury apartment. He became hungry and ate what he could find in the refrigerator. His visual flashbacks continued without warning. He tried to control his behavior, but these experiences would leave him shaking, confused, and with an overwhelming sense of sadness.

He determined to stay away from drugs and, in the future, focus only on his art. He would visit Golden Gate Park from time to time but became an observer, not a participant, in the hippie culture that flourished all around him. Occasionally the music he heard in the park would trigger another flashback, but these became less precise visually and easier to tolerate.

He commuted between his apartment and Mendocino, where he spent most of his creative time. This small community, seated on a hilltop overlooking the ocean, would trigger new ideas for artistic experimentation. His art reflected his love of nature, but his use of nontraditional colors helped him construct abstract interpretations of his visual experiences. Efforts to sell his pictures through galleries and directly to the public met with mediocre success. However, he was doing what he wanted to do. He was confident that very soon his reputation as an artist would lift him to the same level as that enjoyed by the most successful postimpressionist painters.

He would show his best paintings to the Fromms, and found it therapeutic to explain the meaning behind each painting and how he visualized his interpretation of nature. His preference was for oils, although he did on occasion experiment with watercolors. Oil paint gave him the harsh, strong colors that were impossible to obtain with watercolors.

It was during one of these art discussions that a very excited Sarah asked him if he wished to go and see the Beatles. The band would be playing at Candlestick Park on August 29, 1966. The father of a friend at school had bought a block of tickets. Her parents wouldn't be going, but there would be a mix of parents and schoolgirls attending the concert. Michael indicated his support for the invitation, but only so long as Jock agreed to return his daughter directly to her home immediately after the concert was over. Jock accepted the invitation and its conditions.

The conversation then turned to a discussion of local San Francisco politics and who might have started the fire that had destroyed the Sutro Baths a few days earlier. The baths, which stood adjacent to the Pacific Ocean on the western edge of the city, had been an important recreational destination for San Franciscans since they had been opened to the public in 1896. They had been built by a former mayor of San Francisco, Adolf Sutro. The large structure consisted of a massive glass enclosure of iron, wood, and concrete, forming seven swimming pools maintained at different temperatures. The baths were situated in a small beach inlet below the surrounding cliffs; the swimming pools were fed by water from the ocean. They could accommodate ten thousand people at any one time. Eventually the baths had succumbed to financial failure, and two years earlier they had been closed, with plans to replace them with high-rise apartments. The cause of the fire was still under investigation.

After finishing his second glass of whisky, Jock thanked his hosts for their hospitality, repacked his paintings and put them in the rear seat of his car, then drove back to his apartment, a short distance away.

CHAPTER 22

THE BEATLES EXPERIENCE was something new for Jock. He had never attended a major concert before. All the screaming and hysterics of the young girls was a little off-putting, but he enjoyed what little he could hear of the performance. He sat beside Sarah, and when they could, they chatted about various matters.

He confided in her his experiences with various drugs; she sympathized with him. She told him how she and her girlfriends would pretend to be high on marijuana. They would nod their heads, repeatedly flick back their hair, roll their eyeballs skyward, and claim to be "stoned." Some of them ironed their hair to keep it straight as part of this charade.

With their attire of fashionable dark navy peacoats, double-breasted and hip length, and bottles of Red Mountain wine, they usually persuaded their escorts of the honesty of their claims. In reality, Sarah had never smoked marijuana. It was the wine that gave her the buzz. At less than two dollars a gallon, it was cheap and well worth suffering the sour, bitter taste. Marijuana had been offered to her, but she worried about her parents' reaction if they ever found out.

It was a fairly cold evening, as the fog blew in off the ocean during the wait for the Beatles to come onstage. Immediately after the performance was over, they headed for the exit. Jock offered to see Sarah to her house and then planned to walk over to his apartment once she was home. She accepted. On the bus to Sarah's house, their conversation returned to hippies, drugs, and music. Sarah talked about the many new bands emerging in San Francisco, playing at such venues as the Fillmore,

Avalon, and Matrix. Her favorite was a newly formed band that was popularizing psychedelic rock and was about to release its debut LP.

Jock talked about his painting and the difficulty he was having in making a living out of his art. He planned to keep his apartment until the end of the second-year lease but then would have to decide on his future plans. He also talked about the growing opposition to the use of recreational drugs. A bill was under discussion in the State Senate in Sacramento that would ban the use of LSD. There was a substantial amount of disagreement among the legislators, but it looked as though the bill would pass. In his neighborhood there was already talk of arranging a public event to celebrate the use of this drug in defiance of the new law. The level of confrontation between the local police and the hippie community seemed to be on the increase, and the event would be a way of signaling a desire for peace and harmony. Jock wanted to attend because of the destructive effect this ban could have on the hippie community. Users would either have to give up LSD or face criminal prosecution. The price of LSD was likely to increase substantially.

Sarah asked if she could come along with him. He said yes, so long as her parents agreed, and that it was understood that she would not use drugs. She could pretend but go no further.

A Pageant Rally would be held in the Panhandle in Golden Gate Park starting at 2:00 p.m. on October 6, 1966. It would not be antigovernment despite approval of the new law, but rather was to be a celebration of community awareness and international fellowship. The posters announcing the event encouraged participants to arrive with flowers, feathers, beads, flags, costumes, and incense. With some reluctance, Michael agreed that his daughter could attend, so long as she met Jock outside his apartment immediately after school and stayed with Jock at all times.

Jock would be responsible for her care and security, and must personally escort her home immediately after the event was over. These conditions were accepted by both Sarah and Jock. Jock would attend the start of the rally but would return to the apartment to meet Sarah outside his home.

Jock discovered that there was already a major celebration taking place when he arrived at the Panhandle shortly after two in the afternoon. It was a cool, clear day. He was dressed in patterned pants and a purple cotton shirt, wore sandals on his feet, and multicolored beads around his neck. He had pinned a band of flowers to his bandana to wear around his head. He found the two tabs of acid that he had been given a few weeks earlier, and shoved them into his pocket.

People dressed in hippie attire were already singing and dancing, some of them leaping around in circles in a drug-enhanced haze. Spontaneous points of music broke out among the crowd. Usually it was the sound of a guitar or drums, but occasionally a saxophone could be heard. The first issue of the new hippie magazine with its psychedelic artwork was available. The Magic Bus with its hand-painted psychedelia had joined the celebration. Bread shaped like coffee cans was available for the hungry.

The size of the turnout seemed to grow continuously. Jock wandered among the crowd, looking, and breathing air perfumed with the smoke of reefers that were circulating among the crowd. Some people appeared to be taking hits of LSD. He thought he should join them, so he took out the two tabs from the plastic bag he was carrying and placed them under his tongue. Soon it would be illegal to do what he was doing. He hoped not to experience the same type of hallucinations that occurred when he first took the drug, and he planned to have met Sarah and returned to the park ahead of any serious effects from the drug.

He returned to his apartment during late afternoon. Sarah arrived a few moments later. She had borrowed some hippie clothes from the elder sister of one of her friends. She wore a long russet patterned skirt with a matching vest. Underneath the vest was a long-sleeved orange blouse. Her loose, long dark hair was secured by a floral patterned headband, and her ankle and pendant bells signaled her movements. Her brown leather sandals completed the outfit.

She was almost too beautiful and too well-dressed to be taken into the park. This was confirmed by the looks she received on arrival. Jock and Sarah found a quiet corner to sit in and enjoy the music as a series of rock bands began to perform. Periodically Sarah would be dragged off the ground by people nearby and made to join in the dance festivities. During one of these dances, someone passed by and offered Jock more acid. He took two more tabs and ingested them. Soon Jock could feel the start of his trip.

As before, euphoria was his first experience. There were no visuals. He felt a close, comfortable connection with the people around him. He remained lucid and coherent. He felt no body weight; it was if he was floating on air. He dreamed sweet thoughts. He smiled; he grinned; he laughed, and he spoke a lot. Sarah passed him a drink, and he thought it was maple syrup. He joked with her. He felt energy pulsing through his body. He had lost all sense of time. Life had taken on a beauty that was new to him. He looked around as the trees slowly began to move, the sky danced in unison, and people began to float. Colors were intensifying, becoming deeper and brighter. He was euphoric.

Sarah was still dancing. The music had become louder; everything appeared in more detail. Then, as he smiled at his surroundings, everything began to fuse together and then break out into different shapes and patterns. The grass turned purple and then neon-green;

the trees became orange and brown, and the sky was a pinkish-blue. Everything he could see began to throb like a beating heart. The shapes and patterns began to mutate and move and turn in clockwise circles. The trees would melt, be consumed by the patterns, and re-form, and people would float by as if blown by the wind.

The dysphoria and fear began to return to Jock. The patterns began to repeat themselves and stretch downward as if to take hold of him. They stared at him through odd-shaped eyes; they talked to him, but he could not understand. He began to sweat and feel cold at the same time. The neon-green grass rippled beneath him and then arched upward, carrying Sarah into the ever-changing shapes above him. She became part of the patterns. She looked down at him. She cried out his name to him. The patterns sent out their branches to imprison her legs and hold her tight around the throat. She belonged to them now.

Jock began to panic. He yelled her name and in gibberish asked her to come down. She could not. He kept screaming her name. The real Sarah heard him and returned to his side; he tried to bite her as she tried to comfort him. Her dancing partner came to her aid and experienced similar treatment. Jock by now was shaking uncontrollably; his body color was changing; his eyes were rolling without control; he would not stand, and he had become incontinent. He was no longer able to recognize Sarah.

Sarah was not sure what to do. Others nearby suggested that Jock be taken to a hospital. He was carried to the edge of the park, kicking and screaming; a taxi is stopped, and Sarah, Jock, and Sarah's dancing partner get in the backseat. Jock sits in the middle. He tries to jump out of the taxi. He experiences difficulty in breathing, but eventually they arrive at the emergency room of the general hospital. Jock is admitted for tests and observation overnight. Sarah returns home by taxi and tells her parents what has happened. They call the hospital, which advises

Michael that Jock is undergoing a series of examinations, and it will be best to visit him the following morning.

Early Friday morning, Michael and his wife drive over to the hospital. They are uncertain whether Jock will be discharged, so they take the car in case they have an extra passenger when they leave. As they enter the intensive care unit, they are intercepted by a nurse.

"Are you here to see Jock McGregor?" she asks.

"Yes," replies Michael. "Is everything okay?"

"He is making good progress," the nurse assures them, "but the doctor wants to talk to you before you go in to visit your friend."

She ushers Michael and Karen into a nearby waiting room. A few minutes later the doctor arrives, looking a little harassed and carrying a manila-colored file.

He starts, "Are you Mr. McGregor's next of kin?"

"No, we are his close friends," is the reply from Michael. "He has no next of kin in America. His wife, children, and parents all live in England, and we don't know their whereabouts."

"In that case," says the doctor, "let me tell you what is happening to your friend, and then you can pass on this information to his family once you have traced them. Mr. McGregor suffered a serious seizure yesterday evening that was probably brought on by the drugs he was taking. He should fully recover, but there are other aspects to his condition that you need to be aware of. We think that he is likely to be suffering from manic-depressive illness or melancholia. That is what we think brought on yesterday's attack.

"He has a good chance of full recovery, but he will need close care and attention. He must stay off all recreational drugs, and he should stop drinking alcohol. He may still continue to experience psychotic symptoms such as hallucinations and delusions, but these should reduce over time. It's possible that he may also need psychotherapy to lessen the seriousness of his symptoms. We know only a little about this illness, and while there are some medications, they all seem to carry the risk of unsatisfactory side effects. On the other hand, if nothing is done for the patient, there is a risk of severe depression and the possibility of suicide."

The doctor looked at Michael and Karen to assess whether they understood what he was saying, and if they appreciated the seriousness of the situation.

"In summary," continued the doctor, "I believe the patient needs to go home to England as quickly as possible. His home doctors can assess his condition and develop an appropriate set of treatments for his disorder. Do either of you have questions? Please accept my apologies if this has been a shock to you."

"I think we understand," said Michael. "Is there anything we need to do now? Will he be safe if we keep him at our house for the next few days?"

"Yes," replied the doctor. "By all means take him home and make sure he gets lots of rest and sleep. He may encounter flashbacks, but be patient, remember his behaviors are symptoms of a mental illness and not a result of his personal selfishness or meanness. If you have any serious problems with him, bring him back here. You should also know that at the moment he has no memory of what happened yesterday and that this memory may never return. He also appears to have some type of long-term memory loss. He doesn't recall anything about himself and his family. The only information he has been able to give me is his parents' name and address. At least we think the address is his parents."

"Are there symptoms that we should watch out for that might be an indicator of imminent abnormal behavior?" asked Michael.

"Yes, there are," replied the doctor. "Unfortunately, there are many symptoms, and they are different for manic behavior than for depression. Over the past twenty-four hours we have seen depressive stage symptoms such as sadness, irritability, uncontrollable crying, difficulty concentrating, insomnia, thoughts of death, and loss of energy. Symptoms for mania, some of which your daughter observed last night, range from excessive happiness to restlessness, rapid speech, sudden shifts from joy to anger and hostility, and impulsiveness. Drug and alcohol use can aggravate these symptoms, and some people with mania are also known to sometimes display an increased sex drive. So please be careful."

Michael and Karen thanked the doctor for the information and went into the ward to see Jock. He lay half-asleep, listless, and initially he was unaware of their presence.

"Jock, we are here to take you home," said Michael, trying to sound positive and enthusiastic. "Sounds like you had a tough time yesterday. Let's get you out of here. Sarah will help us look after you."

"Who is Sarah?" were Jock's only words.

Once Jock was back in the Fromm residence, and comfortable in bed, Michael and Karen sat downstairs together to discuss their next steps. They asked Sarah to stay upstairs and listen, in case Jock had any aftereffects from his previous day's experience.

Their first decision was who to contact in England. The hospital had been able to obtain the address of Jock's parents, and Michael's mother was able to provide Jock's former address because of the Christmas cards she had received. However, when they tried to call the phone number of Jock's home, it had been disconnected, presumably because the family had moved. Michael decided to write to Jock's parents and ask that they call them in San Francisco.

It was early morning a few days after the note was sent that the phone rang. Michael answered.

"Is that Mr. Fromm?" came a woman's voice from the other end. Michael immediately recognized the accent.

"Yes, it is," replied Michael. "Is that Mrs. McGregor?"

"Yes," was the answer. She continued, "I received a card from you asking me to call you. What's it all about? I don't think I know you."

Michael explained who he was, including having worked with Jock during the war and being his longtime friend. He was contacting her on Jock's behalf and hoped she didn't mind.

"But my son is dead; he committed suicide well over two years ago. How can you be calling on his behalf?"

Michael understood the delicacy of the situation.

"Yes, I had heard about the suicide, but did they ever recover the body?"

"No," was the woman's answer in a confident tone. "The police never did find his body, but they were certain he had jumped because of what his wife told them. Are you saying something different?"

Michael was a little uncertain how best to continue the conversation. Clearly he was going to spring a huge surprise on Jock's mother. He began hesitatingly.

"Mrs. McGregor, this is not easy for me to say, but your son is alive. This is no hoax call. He came to visit me and my family about two years ago here in San Francisco, and he has stayed here ever since. He lives here in San Francisco. He told me what happened to him before he moved to America but had me promise that I would never tell anyone. Anyway, now that he is ill, albeit not seriously, I need to break my pledge to him."

"What's wrong with him? Where is he now?" asked Mrs. McGregor.

Michael replied, "He is staying with us at the moment. He was recently taken ill and was hospitalized. He is recovering, but the doctors here say that he should return home to England. I can't really explain the details of his illness, but it's something to do with his mental state. He has been very depressed recently and had what seems like a nervous breakdown. It was so bad that it affected his memory. He should recover, so the doctor says, but he needs medical help and family supervision. He could remember you and your home address but not much else. If I put him on a plane here in San Francisco, can you and your husband meet him in London?"

"My husband cannot meet him; he died about a year ago. And I am not sure that I am well enough to travel; I suffer from arthritis. I should be able to arrange for a cousin to come and meet him. When will he return home?"

"What about his wife and children? Could one of them meet him?" asked Michael.

"No, I don't think so," said Mrs. McGregor. "His wife is now living with her parents, and I don't believe she has forgiven him for what he did to her. And his two children are now married and will no doubt also be angry and upset when they find out he is alive. He messed up their lives in the years before the suicide and then left them penniless. Do you have any idea of the treatment that he needs?"

Michael thought carefully. "There is not much else I can say. The doctor talked about him having some form of psychiatric care when he returns and that he will need to have help to stay on the treatment."

"When will he come home?" asked Mrs. McGregor.

"I will arrange for that quickly and call you as soon as I have details. If you think of any other questions, call me back. Forgive me for surprising you in this way. Jock is a good friend of mine, and I am sorry that his health has made it necessary for me to send him home."

A few days later Michael called Jock's mother and gave her details of the Pan Am flight that Jock would be traveling on in late November. Michael and Karen cleared out Jock's apartment, canceled his lease, and moved his paintings into their garage. His personal belongings were packed, ready for Jock's journey home.

The whole family accompanied Jock to the airport. Michael told the airline of Jock's condition and that someone would meet him at Heathrow. He stressed that under no circumstances should Jock be given alcohol or allowed to smoke. The family waited with Jock at the gate until the flight was called, and Jock disappeared onto the plane.

On the way home, both Michael and Karen breathed a sigh of relief. Jock had caused them a great deal of consternation and had lost their confidence when he had failed to look after Sarah. She was safe, fortunately, but no thanks to him. Maybe they would visit Jock or his wife the next time they were in England if Jock had repaired relationships with his family. That visit, though, may be some time away. Sarah was already in her senior year at school and was applying to universities. Berkeley was her first choice. The money needed for tuition, either at Berkeley or elsewhere, and the need to monitor Sarah's lifestyle, might delay their trip for a little while.

They also wondered about Mary Louise and what had happened to her after Jock moved out of her parents' home. Where was she now? Maybe Michael should visit his former airfield in Yorkshire and try to track her down. Karen said that she would like to see his old haunts, the places where he lived while she was living in Shanghai with her parents.

CHAPTER 23

I<small>T WAS THE</small> summer of 1972, and I, Mary Louise, remained living in Bob's house in West Yorkshire. I had been able to resume my life since my husband's death but was unable to recapture my lost youth. I had no reason for complaint. All my decisions in life had been mine to make, although the circumstances under which they were made were often outside of my control.

My son was now married and working in the south of England. He had completed his university education, obtaining a joint honors degree in geology and geography. He had been approached to stay on at the university and conduct research into oil exploration micropaleontology. His decision to leave higher education was driven by his need for adequate income and not because of any disrespect for academia. My older sister attended his graduation with me. It was a reward for both of us that, after more than two decades of perseverance, we had enabled him to reach this level of distinction.

My sister remained happily married, living on the farm that she moved to immediately following her wedding. Over the years she had added some pounds to her frame and had experienced a slight walking disability, but she always displayed a sense of fun and happiness when she was with me. She would repeatedly coax me out of my doubts and depression whenever I thought that I could not accomplish something.

My younger son was studying horticulture at a local college, and my daughter was training to be a nurse. I had continued to be employed at the hospitals for seven years but had reluctantly resigned my position at the start of 1972. I maintained my passion for travel, taking leaves of absence from work whenever I ran out of vacation. I would arrange for substitute managers if my absences were lengthy, and occasionally my younger sister would deputize for me. She had married many years earlier and was also a farmer's wife. She liked the company of people and the urban feel of my workplace and gladly deputized for me when I asked. Whenever she or one of my substitutes would experience a serious problem at work, I would receive a phone call wherever I was.

My second husband, John, and I married during late July 1970. We spent all of our time together but lived part of the time with my children and other times at his home.

We had met two years earlier. I was sent to London to attend a hospital conference but missed my train home. A doctor colleague I knew offered me a bed for the night and invited me out for dinner. A small group of us were eating in the restaurant that evening. John joined our table, and I was introduced to him.

He was a real estate investor who had come down to London for a few days to visit the annual motor show. I could tell that he was well off, but it was more than his money that attracted me. He had a passion for travel, and he loved to dance. Our relationship blossomed during the following two years. We traveled constantly together whenever my work would allow me. My mother would move into my home and take care of my two youngest children while I was away.

My husband John was a few years older than me, about my height, had remained trim except for a slight paunch, and boasted a complete head of silver-gray hair. He had blue eyes, like my father. He was extraordinarily self-confident and could be very direct with people. With me, he modified this approach and was always caring and considerate. He had lost his wife to cancer, and his children were now grown up, married, and pursuing their own independent careers.

Living with John was very different from my life with my late husband Bob. John was in good health, was much younger than Bob, had a far more stable personality, loved to socialize, treated me as an equal, and liked to do the things that I liked to do. But nonetheless I had a great deal of respect for Bob. Despite all the difficulties, without his willingness to help me when we first met, who knows what would have happened to me and my son?

John and I traveled extensively. John possessed a fear of flying, known as aerophobia, which would always influence our plans. Just the thought of flying would cause him to sweat, become disoriented, and make him irritable. He also experienced anticipation anxiety so that even a preliminary discussion that involved flying could cause those symptoms. I gave him books to read, and he attended a course that lessened his phobia, but it never went away completely. We never knew what caused it.

Before we married we had taken several cruises together, including one to the Mediterranean and the Black Sea, and another to New York and back. We also toured Canada, the West Coast, Mexico, and back to the East Coast by Greyhound bus, and most recently we had cruised among the Channel Islands just off the coast of France. Our favorite Channel Island was Jersey.

My lengthy absences from work were tolerated by the hospitals, but John never accepted the idea that his travel plans should compete with my work obligations. Our marriage in 1970 was celebrated with a world cruise, courtesy of the Peninsular and Oriental Steam Company. The ship left Southampton, traveled across the Atlantic to the Panama Canal, sailed up the West Coast to California and Vancouver, then to Hawaii, and on to New Zealand, Australia, and Southern Asia. Its last stops were in Africa and Portugal. This four-month cruise was followed by a month's driving tour of Sweden and Norway, a Danube cruise, and a visit to the Isle of Wight, off the south coast of England. And today we were about to leave for ten days in Scotland.

"Mary Louise, your sister and her husband are here. They have put their suitcases in the car. We should leave for Scotland by no later than late this afternoon. Your mother has arrived as well. Which bedroom do you want her to sleep in?" John asked from downstairs.

I went down to greet my sister, her husband, and my mother.

"How are things on the farm?" I asked my sister's husband.

"Lambing is over, and we are waiting for harvest time. Our eldest son will look after the farm while we are away. He has the address of the hotel where we are staying; I told him to call us if he runs into any difficulties."

My mother stood in the shadows in the kitchen, her small suitcase on the floor beside her.

"Mother, thank you for helping out," I said. "Please use the spare bedroom on the left-hand side at the top of the stairs. You should have a peaceful, quiet time here. My daughter is away visiting London, and my son will be attending classes every day. The neighbor said he would keep an eye on you and come over each day to make sure you are well. He usually brings us some of his milk each morning. If you need food, the traveling store stops outside on Tuesdays and Fridays."

My mother thanked me for the instructions and then gave me an airmail envelope, saying "This arrived for you."

There was US postage on the envelope, which was addressed to me at my mother's home. I placed it in my purse.

We left the house at about two o'clock that afternoon. We hoped to drive to Berwick-on-Tweed, located on the England/Scotland border, and stay there for the night. We would finish our journey to Aviemore in the Highlands of Scotland the next day.

John had decided to drive during the journey. Cars were very important to him. He always bought a new car each year and had become a fan of the Rover P-6. The updated series of this model, known as the Mark II, was launched in 1970. He had purchased the version with the larger 3500 V6 engine that was made of aluminum, an innovation in its day for automobile engineering. Rover had recently been purchased by British Leyland, and there were worries that the Rover brand would lose its independence and be integrated into its mother company. The vehicle was fast, comfortable, and safe.

As we drove, John asked me, "What's in the letter your mother gave you? Is it from someone we met during our last visit to America?"

I took the letter out of my purse and examined the front and back. The return address said San Francisco. I opened the letter, which was from a Michael Fromm. I read it and then summarized the contents to share with everyone in the car.

"It is from a Michael Fromm and his wife, Karen, who live in San Francisco. They want to visit me. He says that during the war he worked on the construction of the airfield near my mother's house and hasn't been back since. He plans to bring his wife on a visit and show her where he used to work. Michael has booked them into the same hotel that he lodged in during the war. They will be here from August 15 to 21. He wants me to contact him at the hotel and is offering me dinner, plus dinner for anyone else I care to bring along."

My husband John quickly reacted. "That's a good idea. I'll take him up on a free meal, if you want to go."

"I'm not sure," I said. "I don't really know him, although, after all these years. I am curious to know what has happened to him. I remember him as one of the senior engineers at the airfield."

I decided I would get the hotel's phone number when we arrived in Aviemore and call there to set a date for our meeting. I could always cancel at the last minute. I did like to meet new people, and there was always the possibility that new friendships would lead to new places for us to visit.

We made it safely to Berwick-on-Tweed and stayed at a very nice guesthouse overlooking the North Sea. The following morning, we left early and crossed the border into Scotland, then traveled via Stirling and Perth toward Aviemore. We took the picturesque route along the base of the Ochil Hills for our journey to Perth. On the way we stopped for lunch at a place called Tillicoutry, known as "Tilly" to the locals. We ate at a very nice café, where we ordered the gray-colored steak pie with gravy, green beans, and mashed turnips, and drank several cups of tea. It was not our best meal in Scotland but probably the most traditional. We would have ordered haggis, made with a sheep's stomach stuffed with the sheep's internal organs, minced with onion, oatmeal, suet, and spices, but it was not on the menu.

A few hours later, we were in Aviemore. The town had been developed as a tourist resort during the 1960s after the Aviemore Hotel was destroyed by fire. The Aviemore Center was opened in 1966. The intent of our visit was to do some light hiking, some shopping, enjoy the local pubs, and possibly be taught some Highland dancing. Aviemore was also the first ski resort to open in Great Britain; the first chairlift opened in 1961, but there was no snow during our visit.

While in Aviemore, I called the hotel where the Fromms planned to stay and left a message that my husband and I would visit Michael and Karen on the evening of August 19.

At the end of our few days in Scotland, we drove directly home, with no overnight stay on the way. We had encountered thick mist and low clouds in the Highlands, but a dry, sunny day with puffy white clouds in a sky of blue accompanied us home. For me it had been a very relaxing tour. I no longer needed to return to work, and I had a husband who cared for me and bought me whatever I asked for.

CHAPTER 24

At seven o'clock in the evening John and I arrived at the Fromms' hotel. It was only a few miles away from where both my sisters and their husbands lived, but for John and me, it was more than a two-hour drive. Michael and Karen were waiting to meet us in the dining room.

After brief introductions, Michael asked, "What would you like to drink?"

I ordered a gin and orange, and John ordered a glass of wine. Our hosts both drank warm beer, something their friends back home said they should try. They had driven up from London a few days earlier in a rented Avis car. The hotel they had selected for their stay occupied a corner lot. It had been in use since the days of Elizabeth I, but had been modernized and was well-maintained. Their room was on the second floor. The dining room was small, quaint, and quiet, and offered traditional English fare—roast meats, fried fish, and pies and pasties. Once we had ordered our food, the important conversations began.

"We are delighted to be here," said Michael. "I hope my letter didn't startle you. This is my first time back to Yorkshire in almost thirty years. We visit England every three to four years, but we normally stay with friends near London. From what we have seen, there is a lot new around here but also much that I remember."

John asked, "So where have you visited since you arrived, and what did you do during the war?"

Michael explained his responsibilities for the construction of the runways at the nearby airfield during the war and his subsequent work at the prisoner of war camp.

"It seems that everything has been allowed to fall into ruin," said Michael. "Yesterday we strolled around the airfield; it appears totally abandoned. The buildings were derelict, grass was growing out of the runways, and rusting equipment lay around everywhere.

"We visited the prisoner of war camp the day before, and it's in a similar state of abandonment. Most of the sleeping huts look like I remember them, but the place is also derelict. The only places that the English seem to care about are their very old historic sites. We have visited towns such as Beverly, York, and Selby, which seem steeped in history. But it appears that if the history is less than a hundred years old, no one cares about preserving the site."

It was my turn to ask a question.

"I really don't remember you from the war years. What do you remember about me, if anything?"

Michael replied, "I didn't know you well enough to speak to. I worked with the planning director, a person called Jock McGregor, and we would sometimes see you in the canteen. I also called at your parents' home to take Jock to the local pubs. He was your lodger at the time. Jock visited me in San Francisco a few years ago, and we talked about you."

I felt a little alarmed over the content of these conversations and wondered how much Michael might know about my relationship with Jock.

Michael hesitated. "How much should I say to you? Jock talked about personal matters and how well he knew you, but I don't want to embarrass you."

I guessed what he might want to talk about. So I replied, "It's all right. My husband John knows about my past. He knows what happened with Jock before I married my first husband and the difficult times I had during my first marriage. He has met John, my son. He knows that Jock is his father. However, I have never talked to my son about his past because of how I feel whenever I think about what happened back then. I have always told my son that Bob Hutchinson is his father."

Michael then explained in detail what had happened during Jock McGregor's two-year stay in San Francisco. In particular, he talked about what Jock had told him about his relationship with me and about Jock's illness at the end of the visit. Michael said he had planned to visit Yorkshire much sooner but had been busy putting his daughter through university. She had graduated a year earlier from Stanford University. Her degree was in chemical engineering, and she was now working for a large oil company in Texas.

He went on to say, "When Jock was with us, he told us about his doubts as to whether he was the father of your son, how the uncertainty haunted him and affected his personality, and how he hid this secret from his wife for fourteen years. He very much loved his wife and children and, therefore, chose not to disclose your son's existence to his family.

"It seems that when his wife eventually found out, her relationship with Jock quickly deteriorated. And when his business failed in the early 1960s, so did their marriage. But I don't think they were ever divorced. During the marriage he suffered from tuberculosis. He also told us that his wife had forcibly sent him to a mental hospital because of his behavior and that, more than anything, ended his relationship with her. It also ended her relationship with his parents because they disagreed with her decision.

"Apparently the situation at home became so difficult for Jock that he pretended to commit suicide and disappeared to the island of Jersey before moving to San Francisco. He wanted to start a new life as an artist in America. Unfortunately, he was not successful."

Michael asked me if I knew any parts of this story. I told him that most of what I was hearing was new to me. I had had no contact with Jock McGregor since before my son was born, although the courts had told me that he had suffered from tuberculosis during the mid- to late 1950s. I asked Michael what else he knew about Jock.

Michael continued, "After Jock returned to England, I lost all contact with him. I sent a few letters addressed to him at his mother's address, but they were never answered. Most recently I did receive a letter but from the new owners of his parents' old house. They told me that Jock's mother had died and that Jock had moved out to live in a council-owned apartment, and gave me an address where they believed Jock was living. I have written to that address but have heard nothing. Also, I don't know what happened to Jock's wife and children."

"So I assume that we will never know the end of the story?" I commented to Michael. "Maybe that's a good thing. I have established a very satisfactory new life, and I have no desire to go backward."

"I am not sure that you are correct," said Michael.

"What do you mean?" I asked.

Taking a deep breath, Michael remarked, "I was intending on my way back to London to call at the address where Jock is believed to be living. But something happened while Karen and I were in London. We read this article in one of the newspapers there."

Michael took a newspaper clipping out of his inside jacket pocket and handed it to me. After I read it, I passed it to John. The article read as follows:

Man Found Dead in Car

A middle-aged tourist from England was discovered today dead in his car in eastern Yugoslavia. There was no sign of foul play, but investigations are continuing.

The vehicle in which the deceased was found is a Ford Anglia Estate wagon. It was parked at a camping site frequently used by foreign tourists visiting this part of the country. The body is believed to be that of a Mr. McGregor, whose home is in the West Midlands. His passport, wallet, and personal belongings were all recovered from the vehicle. His next of kin have been informed.

John and I were speechless.

Michael resumed. "There is no proof that this is our Jock McGregor, but it sounds awfully like him. I am still thinking that on my way back to London I should visit the address I was given to see what I can find out. I don't know where his wife currently lives, but we do have Jock's recent council apartment address. I also have an address that Jock gave me when he was living in San Francisco for the house he built for his family—the house they had to move out of when he disappeared."

Michael finally delivered his last surprise for the evening.

"If you two would like to come with us, you are welcome. I am not sure it's a good idea for you, Mary Louise, but it might help us all find out ultimately what happened to Jock."

I wasn't sure I wanted to do this, and John replied for both of us.

"Let's think about the idea overnight, and I will call you in the morning. This has all been a little overwhelming for Mary Louise and me. We need time to digest and decide what to do."

John's proposal was accepted.

The following morning, John and I discussed the idea. I still had doubts about the wisdom of the visit. At the same time, it might help bring closure to this period of my life. I finally accepted the invitation, told John yes, and he called the Fromms at their hotel.

The following morning, with the mist still rising off the fields, we began our journey in a convoy of two cars, headed first south and then westward to the West Midlands. Before we left, Michael called ahead to reserve rooms for two nights at a hotel that, according to the map, was about midway between the two addresses we had obtained.

CHAPTER 25

I HAD NEVER VISITED the West Midlands. I knew Coventry and the East Midlands, but this part of England had never been a destination of mine. I was struck by how the many towns and cities that dominate this part of the country merge into each other and suffocate the fields and forests that once reigned supreme here.

I was also impressed by the diversity of people I saw on the streets. This feature was about to become even more pronounced. Idi Amin, who had become president of Uganda the year before, announced earlier in the month that he would expel the fifty thousand Asian residents who possessed British passports from his country. Many of these displaced refugees would start arriving in England the following month. Amin had shifted his country's allegiance from the West and was now being backed by Libya, the Soviet Union, and East Germany.

The West Midlands' economy was clearly centered on engineering. Visually, that made the area unattractive to me because of the many factories and the dirt and smoke that they produced. Unemployment was taking its toll. Earlier in the year the number of unemployed people in Britain exceeded one million for the first time ever. This was the opposite to the shortage of labor experienced immediately after the end of the war. Labor unrest was spreading throughout the country; just in the previous month there had been a highly disruptive national dock strike.

We stopped at our first address, supposedly the current home of Jock McGregor. It was a dingy, dirty apartment complex with street-side parking of questionable safety. John worried about what might happen to his car. The apartment was located on the eighth floor; it was locked and appeared empty when we arrived.

An Asian-looking woman and two children were walking down the outside corridor. Michael caught up with them and asked, "Do you know who lives here?"

"I don't know his name," said the woman. "He has lived there for about two years but keeps to himself. He doesn't seem to have visitors. He drives a Ford Anglia Estate wagon, which is missing from its regular parking spot. He disappears for weeks on end with the car. I have no idea where he goes. Recently some people were here that I have not seen before. They seemed to be moving out a lot of his belongings. But where to, I don't know."

Michael thanked her. She nodded, took her children by the hand, and began to descend the stairwell. There was no-one else nearby.

We couldn't find the caretaker, so we decided to drive on to the second address. Hopefully its location would not be as dreary as this neighborhood, where cracked windows, graffiti, garbage on the stairs, and peeling paint were the standard features.

The home at the second location was altogether different. It was an individually designed detached house set on a substantial plot of land located in a very old picturesque village. The village was dominated by a church and its tower, which sat on a hilltop surrounded by houses, many dating back to the Middle Ages.

The house we were visiting had been built much more recently. It was approached by a lengthy driveway with a lawn on one side and shrubbery on the other. The front door was recessed and double-glazed. We parked both cars in the driveway, and Michael got out of his rental car. He told John and me to stay in our car, went to the front door and rang the bell.

After a few seconds, a woman appeared. She and Michael appeared to engage in serious conversation; after a while, she went back inside the house. Michael waited. She returned with a piece of paper and pointed in a direction back beyond the church. Michael thanked her and then came over to our car.

"What happened?" I asked. "Was she helpful?"

"Yes, she was very helpful," replied Michael. "We are lucky to find her at home. She is usually at work, but took today off to prepare for the family vacation that starts tomorrow. She has lived here for eight years and bought the house from a woman who was the original owner. Apparently her husband fell into financial problems, and they had to sell the house to settle some debts. The woman and her two children moved in with the woman's parents. This sounds very much like our McGregor family. The new owner kept the woman's new address in case she had to forward any mail. We may be reaching the end of our search, although it seems we have to return close to where we just visited."

Michael appeared to believe that the journey was about to be successfully completed.

The next town was nestled between two much larger cities. Only a small portion of its northern border was in the countryside; the rest of the town simply fused into the adjoining conurbations. Apparently originally it had been a small, independent agricultural community; during the reign of Elizabeth I in the 1600s the town had begun its journey into the Industrial Age. This was due to the proximity of both coal and iron ore. By 1665, it had become the home to about 150 families who were engaged in the making of gridirons, currycombs, bolts, latches, and coffin handles. Gridirons, sometimes called griddles, were manufactured for cooking purposes, and currycombs were used for horse grooming. Over the centuries the town had become famous for its locksmiths and lock manufacturing.

With Michael leading the convoy of two cars, we eventually found our third address. It was a home in the middle of a street of terraced Victorian houses. The front doors opened immediately onto the public sidewalk. None possessed garages, but each seemed to be very well-maintained.

Again Michael checked with John and agreed to initiate the investigation. He knocked on the door, which was quickly opened by an elderly man wearing little more than an undershirt and a pair of oil-stained trousers. A conversation followed. At one point Michael took out a piece of paper from the top pocket of his jacket and appeared to write down something. He thanked the man, who returned inside the house, and Michael then walked over to talk to John.

"What's the news?" asked John.

"Well, I think we are making headway, but it seems the search continues," replied Michael. "This is not where Jock's wife lives; this was her parents' home. She apparently used to live with them, but after they died a little while ago, she moved out, and the man I spoke with bought the house. He did, however, know her new address. It's in a small town that is not far away from the first address we visited."

John suggested that we resume our search in the morning and that we should check into our hotel now and make it an early night. Michael agreed. Again in convoy, but with John leading this time, we found our hotel, which was an old converted manor house. We checked in for our two-night stay.

CHAPTER 26

THE FOLLOWING MORNING, after a large English breakfast, we set out in John's car to resume our search. We left Michael's car at the hotel, since we would return that evening.

It took us about thirty minutes to find our fourth address. A relatively new semidetached house built of brick, it appeared to have the traditional three bedrooms upstairs and three rooms below. Entry was through a side door reached by using a short, narrow cobblestone driveway that also led to a small garage and carport. The front garden had been converted into a well-manicured expanse of green lawn. We all four got out of the car and walked up to the front door. John rang the bell, and we waited. Finally a woman appeared behind the glass door, peered out, and then gently opened the door.

She was well-dressed, probably in her mid-fifties, about my height, and appeared recently to have had her hair permed. She was stocky but not overweight, had a round face and wore no makeup. John later told me that she looked a lot like me but carried a little more weight and was a few years older than me.

John started the conversation.

"I hope you don't mind us all suddenly appearing like this, but by any chance are you are the ex-wife of a person called Jock McGregor? For reasons that we will explain to you, we have been trying to trace a Mrs. McGregor who we understand lives in the West Midlands and was the wife of Jock."

She looked at John quizzically. She wondered if this was a strange way to start a sales pitch to sell her maybe a set of encyclopedias or some kitchenware.

"Yes, that is my married name, but for the past few years I have been using my maiden name. I have not lived with my husband for nearly ten years, and I have had no contact with him for about the same amount of time. But what is the purpose of your visit, since I don't recognize any of you? Are you looking for him or for me?"

Michael then spoke. "First, my apologies, Mrs. McGregor, that we should all suddenly appear like this on your doorstep. We appreciate you talking to us. I am from America, and I used to work for your husband during the war in Yorkshire. We were building an airfield together. I am trying to trace his whereabouts. After the war, he and I lost personal contact with each other until the mid-1960s when he came to the United States and spent time living with us in San Francisco. The last time I saw him was in late 1966 when I put him on a plane headed to Heathrow, London. I am currently on vacation with my wife, Karen, and I had hoped to trace him during our visit to England. When he was with us in San Francisco, he became ill and had to be sent home. Hopefully he is still okay."

Michael continued, "I should also like to introduce you to a friend of mine, Mary Louise, who has traveled with us from Yorkshire. She and I worked at the same airfield as Jock during the war, and we met up a few days ago when I was visiting the north of England. She and her husband, John, have accompanied Karen and me to prevent us from getting lost in this part of the country. Mary Louise also knew Jock."

The mention of my name seemed to trigger a memory in Mrs. McGregor as evidenced by her facial expression. She looked a little startled and stared at me.

"You had better come inside, and call me Gwen, please," said Mrs. McGregor. "I think you have found the right person, but I am curious to know why you have such an interest in my ex-husband."

In single file, we entered the house. We were ushered into the front sitting room and each offered a chair. As soon as we were seated, we more formally introduced ourselves. Gwen volunteered to make us some tea and departed to the kitchen for a few minutes. We looked at each other, pleased with our success at tracing Gwen but afraid to speak in case we said something that she could overhear.

Gwen soon returned to the room holding a tray with five teacups, a pot of tea, milk, sugar, and a plateful of chocolate-covered biscuits. She poured tea for each of us, offered around the biscuits, which we all declined because of the big breakfast we had eaten earlier, and then opened up the next phase of our conversation with, "So where should we start? Do you want me to talk about myself or my ex-husband or both?"

In reply, Michael suggested, "Maybe we should talk about who we are, our family situations, and our knowledge of Jock; that way, Gwen, you will gain a better sense of why we are here. And then we would like you to talk about Jock."

Gwen agreed, and Karen started the storytelling. She told Gwen about her Austrian background, how she had met and married Michael, how she and Michael live in California, and, finally, what she and Michael do for a living. She also talked about their only child, Sarah, and her recent college graduation. She finished with the details of their current vacation, where they had been, and who they had seen.

Karen asked Gwen if she had any questions. Gwen said no but wished Karen and Michael an enjoyable conclusion to their vacation. Gwen mentioned that she rarely visited London and had only once been to Yorkshire. That was nearly thirty years ago, during the war.

Then it was my turn to talk. I felt uncomfortable and a little embarrassed. I explained what I did during the war, that Gwen's ex-husband Jock lodged with my parents, that I had been married at the end of the war, that my first husband had died, how I had met John and when we had married. I also talked about my love of travel, and some of the places that John and I had visited.

This was the easy part of my presentation; then I continued with the more difficult part. Gwen seemed to anticipate what I was about to say.

"I also have a son named John. He is now in his late twenties and was born in 1944, just before D-Day."

Feeling some tenseness in my chest, and not sure how Gwen would react, I continued, "Your ex-husband is his father. I think you know this, and that Jock told you about his child in Yorkshire. He never agreed that he was the father, but he is. Regrettably, he never financially supported my son and never participated in his upbringing; he never met his son. He disappeared from my life before John was born. Until Michael and Karen visited me, I had no idea what had happened to him. I never told my son about his real father. My son is now married and living near London. I have always told him that my first husband was his father."

I was glad to be finished with the story. John looked at me and smiled. Then, turning to look at Gwen, he asked, "Were you aware of this child in Yorkshire? Did Jock ever mention him to you? We think he did."

"Yes" replied Gwen, "I found out about your son quite by accident when Jock was away in hospital. The discovery was a huge shock to me. Jock had refused to talk about what happened in Yorkshire. It was only when the police told me that I was able to confront Jock and learn the truth."

John thanked her for the information and said it was very much in accordance with what Jock had told Michael in San Francisco. He then asked, "And what about your personal situation?"

Gwen replied carefully and thoughtfully, "I live on my own. Both my parents died quite recently. I never divorced Jock and never remarried. I have two children; both are married, but I see them on a regular basis because they each live nearby.

"Jock and I lived together for about twenty-five years, but during the last few years, living together became intolerable. He eventually walked out on me and arranged the false suicide, and that's about the last time I had any contact with him. Both my children have children of their own, so I am a four-time grandmother. They have been told by me not to have any contact with their father because of what he did to us."

Looking at me, Gwen then asked, "And what about you, Mary Louise, do you have any grandchildren?"

"No," I replied, "not at the moment, but my daughter-in-law is pregnant and is expecting a baby girl at the end of the year. She only told me a few days ago. She discovered she was pregnant during a vacation to Tenerife. My other two children are not yet married."

"So what happened to your son after he went to university?" asked Gwen. "It seems that you, Mary Louise, and I have both suffered similar experiences involving my ex-husband. In your case he walked out much earlier than with me, but we both seem to have ultimately suffered the same fate. Each of us was left with a child or children to raise and without the funds to help us be successful.

"I am proud of my achievements and those of my children. My son married eight years ago and is a very successful manager at a large construction firm. It was founded in 1960 at about the same time that my ex-husband's firm was beginning to encounter problems. The training my son received from his father did help him pursue a successful career in construction. The firm's headquarters are just down the road from here, and he and his family have recently moved into a larger home nearby. My daughter has also been successful and became a schoolteacher. She now stays at home to look after her four-year-old and eighteen-month-old daughters. But what about your son, Mary Louise?"

I started my story. "My son also has been successful, although I rarely now see him. He and his wife are living in Essex, just outside London."

Michael interrupted me. "We have just been staying with close friends in Basildon, Essex. Does your son live anywhere nearby?"

"Yes," I said, "about two miles up the road in a place called Billericay. They have just moved there and live in a house behind the main street."

"Wow, then next time Karen and I are over here, we can visit them? What do you think, Mary Louise?"

I replied in the affirmative, although I did not disclose my concern. John knew nothing of his past, and if Michael Fromm was to visit him, I would need to do a lot of explaining before the meeting. But I would deal with that challenge later.

Continuing my conversation with Gwen, I added, "John has been working for a large automobile manufacturer just outside London ever since he graduated from college in 1966. He was accepted into the firm's graduate trainee program. After about six months, he found himself in the Personnel Department responsible for assisting with labor relations negotiations.

"He has since moved over to the staff relations side and is about to be promoted to industrial relations manager, responsible for both staff and labor. He enjoys his work, appears to be very successful, and works long hours. My husband John and I have visited him and his wife on several occasions, and I plan to visit again when the baby arrives. My daughter-in-law is still working as a teacher at a nearby secondary school; she will give up that work when the baby is born."

Michael by this time was beginning to appear a little impatient and took charge of the conversation. Looking at Gwen, he asked, "Do you know what happened to Jock when he returned home from San Francisco in late 1966? I never heard from him after seeing him off

229

at the airport. Nor did I hear from his parents. Did you ever see him after he returned? It sounds as if you never tried to get back together with him."

Again Gwen thought carefully about the words to use as she answered Michael's questions.

"When he returned, I wanted nothing to do with him. He arrived home safely at the airport and was met by his cousin. His mother took him back in. I think she was pleased to see him and hoped he would look after her since Jock's father had died the year before. I don't know what Jock did about the mental illness that you mentioned. I think he was seen by doctors, but I believe he ignored their advice. His mother was a forgiving person, unlike me.

"My early years with Jock after we married were wonderful, and they continued like that until just before he became ill with tuberculosis. The relationship then began to unravel, and once I found out about Mary Louise, our relationship virtually ended. I put up with him for the next few years, mainly for the sake of the children. During this period his behavior became extremely erratic, unpredictable, and oftentimes very unpleasant. We would have some very difficult episodes together. He drank a lot, and I was never sure if his behavior was caused by the alcohol or was because of the stress at work, or both. There were occasions when I needed my daughter to return home from college to help curb his anger and because he always seemed a little calmer when there was someone else living in the house.

"His time in the mental hospital was an awful experience, and when he walked out and pretended to jump off the bridge, that was it. Good riddance, I thought! While we were left with nothing, I at least had my freedom. My parents did all they could to help us. His parents ignored me. There was no way I wanted him back when I discovered that the suicide was a hoax and that he was back living with his mother.

Whatever happened in Yorkshire in 1943 seems to have affected my husband just as much it did Mary Louise, albeit in very different ways."

"So did you see him at all after he returned?" asked Michael.

"No, I didn't. His mother and I had stopped speaking to each other after I had him sectioned to the mental hospital. She never called me after he returned, and I had no desire to call her.

"I think Jock and his mother would get into huge arguments once he moved in to live with her. I heard from other sources that there were times when he would set fire to books and destroy anything that reminded him of his past.

"He always expected his mother to support him financially, and, therefore, he didn't work once he returned from America. Apparently there was a period when he became a born-again Christian and supported his local church with its fund-raising. But that ended when he had a major argument with the vicar over what to do with the money. Jock never set foot inside the church again.

"I don't think there was any improvement in his behavior after he came home. Before his mother died, she bought him a Ford Anglia Estate wagon, which he used for touring Europe. It was a pale blue one and had the larger engine that he needed because of the long journeys he took. He had the collapsible backseat converted into an area big enough for him to use as a bed.

"Back in the early 1950s, he loved touring England with all of us; by the early 1970s, he was touring Europe, but on his own. I really don't know where he traveled to; I heard he would disappear for weeks at a time."

Gwen fell silent, seemingly a little exhausted after the lengthy discussions and her very thorough explanations.

We refilled our teacups and passed around the chocolate biscuits.

It was now my turn. With some hesitation, I said, "I hope this question doesn't upset you, Gwen, but while Michael was in London, he saw a newspaper article that reported that a Mr. McGregor had been found dead in a car in Yugoslavia. Is that our Mr. McGregor, or someone else? If it is our Jock, do we know what happened?"

Without hesitating, Gwen replied, "It is our Jock McGregor. But I don't know whether we will ever learn the full story of what happened. Apparently he was visiting Yugoslavia. According to his passport and some other papers we found in the car, he had entered the country south of Trieste in Italy, and had traveled down to Dubrovnik and from there eastward. He would have passed close to where Richard Burton was filming *The Battle of Sutjeska*. Burton's wife, Elizabeth Taylor, I think was also there. Jock was something of a movie buff, and he might have wanted to visit the movie site. The movie commemorates the Second World War battle between Yugoslavia and Germany in which the Nazis tried unsuccessfully to destroy Major Tito and his Yugoslavian Patriotic Army. Jock was always interested in the war after his time working with the Royal Air Force. Another reason for the visit might have been to see Queen Elizabeth II, who is visiting Yugoslavia during early October.

"Anyway, for whatever reason, he had managed to reach the border with Romania. He tried to cross the border there. I have no idea what would have attracted him to visit that country, other than his general curiosity. It seems he found himself in an intense argument with the Romanian border guards, lost his temper, and screamed and shouted at them, and they turned him back.

"He returned to the campsite where he was staying and told this story to the tourist who was camped next to him. The following morning, that same person went over to Jock's car and found him dead inside. The authorities were called; their diagnosis was death by natural causes. His body was flown back to England, and the insurance company is recovering the car. I am still in the process of cleaning out his apartment."

"Did they ever determine the cause of death?" asked Michael.

"It was diagnosed as a pulmonary embolism, a blood clot in the lungs. We don't know exactly what caused it. We assume it was a blood clot, but it could have been a lesion resulting from his fight with tuberculosis, like a fat embolism. This is only speculation. If it was a blood clot, it is more likely to have been triggered by the long car journey than the result of losing his temper with the border guards."

"Why did the authorities contact you and not another relative?" asked John.

"Because we never divorced, so legally I am the next of kin. I think the police tracked me down through his sister who is still alive. Anyway, I have had to deal with this unfortunate affair. But now it is nearly over."

"What burial arrangements did you make?" asked Michael.

"I had his body cremated and his ashes taken to the church close to the house that that he had built for us in the early 1960s. That village was always his favorite place."

"I think we have been there," said John. "Is it the village with the church on the hilltop?"

"Yes," said Gwen. "Maybe you would like to go up to the church for a visit? It will bring our story to an end, and it's a nice day to drive out in the countryside. Mary Louise, you can see the final resting place of the father of your son.

"I really am so very sorry for what happened to you. Both our lives have been greatly affected by Jock McGregor. It seems to me that Jock allowed his mania to destroy his career and his depression to wreck his home life. I would like to think that everything that occurred was beyond his control because of his mental illness. But I doubt that this is true. I also think that he could never leave behind the memories of what happened in Yorkshire with you, Mary Louise. Personally, I cannot forgive him for his dishonesty, his unwillingness to accept medical help, and the fact that he left you and me penniless and responsible for his children.

"So shall we go and visit the church?"

We all nodded in Gwen's direction, then cleaned up the teacups and returned the uneaten cookies to the kitchen. We left to drive to the church. Michael and Karen went with Gwen in her car, and John and I followed in ours.

We reached the church with its imposing tower. Seated on top of a hill, it was built of red sandstone with a historic interior that included a Norman font, a frieze of knights in battle, and two pipe organs. The church bells chimed the time of day every hour. The church reminded me of churches back in Yorkshire. It dated back to the seventh century and the times of the Anglo-Saxons, the same people who had occupied east Yorkshire before the arrival of the Vikings in 866 AD.

After touring the inside of the church, we went outside to the spacious graveyard, which extended down the hillside to the west.

"Where did you place Jock's ashes?" I asked.

Gwen looked at me with what I thought was a smirk, but then a grin appeared.

"I didn't leave his ashes in the urn. I asked the vicar to choose a breezy day to scatter Jock's remains throughout the graveyard, no place in particular. I didn't want to watch. So I didn't really give Jock a final resting place. Or, I did, in a way. He is buried nowhere but rests everywhere. It seems a fitting tribute for a man who seemed to possess so many personalities.

By now it was early afternoon. We invited Gwen to come across the road to a local pub. She accepted, and we all drank beer and wine and feasted on a ploughman's lunch, comprised of cheese, onions, pickle, salad, and bread. Afterward we said our farewells to Gwen. Michael invited her to come and visit Karen and him anytime in San Francisco. I offered her my Yorkshire hospitality.

We returned for another early night at the hotel, so both John and I and Michael and Karen could get on the road to our respective destinations early the following morning. We did not have breakfast and said good-bye to Michael and Karen as they started their journey to London and then onward to San Francisco. We left about fifteen minutes later; John did the driving.

It had been a very emotional three days for me. I was tired but content. I looked out across the green fields of England and marveled at the cattle and sheep grazing peacefully. The wheat fields were turning yellow. We passed villages that had remained largely unchanged since before the war; we passed through towns and cities that had changed because of the war, with new housing developments and factories replacing those that had been destroyed by the German bombs.

Our freeway system was still being built, which allowed us to experience both the speed of the highway and the leisurely country driving that went along with the twisting narrow roads. I reflected on life.

I thought of what might have happened if I had not visited my parents that day in July 1943, of what might have happened if I had said yes to Jock when he had asked me to marry him, of what might have occurred if I had listened to my parents and had my son adopted, of where I would be if Bob's wife had not died of cancer, and of what my future would have been if I had walked out on Bob during one of his tantrums. I drifted off to sleep as John drove us home.

EPILOGUE

As THE AUTHOR of this novel, I hope that you the reader have enjoyed your time travels with my mother and father. They were difficult and different times back then. I considered it respectful to end the novel in 1972, the year my father died. However, I probably owe my readers some clarity on what is true and what is fiction in the story, and there may be some interest in knowing what happened to Mary Louise and her son after 1972.

Much of what you have read about Mary Louise and Jock is true. Names, places, and some dates have been altered to afford privacy for family members, but most of the main events described in the book did in fact take place. Only Michael Fromm and the air commodore are fictional. Jock managed the construction of the last bomber airfield to open in Yorkshire, the sexual assault did take place, and Jock did return to his family in the West Midlands after the war; he never voluntarily told his wife of the illegitimate son he left behind in Yorkshire, his career did evolve as explained, he did contract tuberculosis and was sent to a sanatorium, he was sectioned to a mental hospital a few miles away from his home, and he did pretend to commit suicide by appearing to jump off a bridge over the River Avon near Bristol. Following the faked suicide, he disappeared to the island of Jersey, where he stayed for three or so years. We will likely never know what happened to him while in Jersey. He apparently painted, although none of his canvases appear to have survived. His transfer in the novel to San Francisco is fiction. At about the same time in the book that he returned to his parents' home from San Francisco he actually returned home from Jersey. He claimed to have lost his memory in Jersey, and the only information he was able to give the Jersey authorities was an address, which turned out to be that of his parents' house. He returned to live in his parents' home, and when his mother died, he moved to live on his own in a rented council apartment. Jock's death occurred as explained in the novel although no one knows exactly what happened or why he was in Yugoslavia. He was buried in the manner described by Gwen.

Mary Louise never talked to him or saw him again after late 1943 and before I was born. Her experiences until the early 1970s were very much as described in the book although it has been necessary to speculate on how some of these events took place. She never discovered the whereabouts of Jock McGregor and told me that she never received any child support payments from him. In December 1982 she inquired of British Social Security the status of Jock and was told that he had died on August 7 several years earlier. The office advised her that the possible place of death might have been the West Midlands, but it had no knowledge of a death certificate. Whether she made any other efforts to trace Jock, I do not know. The three items of correspondence mentioned in the novel that she received at the time of her son's birth were actually written, and the baby expenses listed in the book were indeed incurred. Nan Dawson, her benefactor at the time, did exist, as did Nan's neighbor who supplied the boy's clothes. Bob Hutchinson was a diabetic and lived twenty years with the disease, frequently suffering from the side effects of too much insulin.

Michael Fromm was created to link the separate lives of Jock and Mary Louise. However, the historic comments built into his life are largely based on fact. The story of his wife, Karen, fleeing from Vienna across country to Shanghai, China, is based on a true story experienced by a couple who were married at the time and who lived in Vienna when the war started. My own years of living in both northern and southern California helped me construct the events that occurred in Sacramento,

Los Angeles, and the Bay Area. The meeting of Gwen, Mary Louise, and Michael in Gwen's home in the West Midlands at the end of the novel is entirely fictitious. However, Gwen's report of Jock's life after he returned from San Francisco and his death and its consequences are based on her daughter's recollections.

After 1972 Mary Louise continued to live with her second husband. They traveled extensively. In July 1974 her second husband died. The day before, the two of them had spent many hours visiting Scarborough on the coast of Yorkshire. They were both weary because of the travel. The following morning her husband awoke complaining of a pain in his chest, and within ten minutes he was dead. My mother never again remarried. She spent the next few months visiting friends and relatives and, after the travel, decided to accept short-stay nursing assignments. As a result of this work, she was propositioned to accept a more permanent position looking after an elderly man of significant prominence in England who lived in London. She accepted. She also found time to look after the children of prominent landowners and industrialists. The final years of her career were just like her beginnings when she worked as a live-in home help after leaving school. Mary Louise moved to London and eventually moved into a Chelsea apartment, allegedly bought for her by one of her benefactors. She spent the remainder of her years living in London. She found time to dance, and she traveled frequently. Her hobbies expanded substantially once she stopped work.

While living in London, she was able to see more of her son, since he lived only about thirty miles away. She was present at the birth of his second child and occasionally traveled with her son and his wife on vacation for babysitting purposes. At no time did she tell her son anything about his origins and his real father. On occasion when he asked why his birth certificate did not list a father, she would reply "Bob Hutchinson is your daddy."

Her son lived a successful life, thanks to the education he had received and the strong sense of integrity, ambition, and hard work that had been instilled in him by Mary Louise. He also had had the good fortune to inherit the intelligence of his father without all of his father's character shortcomings. Following university he moved south to work for the automobile company that Michael Fromm had noticed at the end of the war when traveling to see the Land Girl and her parents on the east side of London. He was accepted into the company's management trainee program and quickly found himself a career in personnel management, or what is today called human resources. This career path took him into banking with an American bank early in 1978, and just over a year later he was asked to transfer from London to San Francisco. This he accepted. And his life forever changed. He, his wife, and their two children settled in the United States, first living close to San Francisco, then in Los Angeles, and then back in San Francisco. Other than a three-year return to London in the late 1980s, he and his family have spent the remainder of their life living in the United States. After leaving banking at the end of the last millennium, Mary Louise's son went on to work for Stanford University. He subsequently took up consulting, and for the last few years he has worked for the University of California.

It was not until December 2007 that Mary Louise decided to talk to her son about his origins. He was staying with her in London, and it was the night before he left to return to San Francisco. The conversation took several hours, and at times it was difficult for Mary Louise to remember all the details and not to become upset by having to recall her story. Most of what she said is already embodied in the novel. Among the facts that she got wrong was the name of Jock's son, and she believed Jock's wife was a famous opera singer. It turned out that his wife had sung Gilbert and Sullivan for the local opera society and had been invited to Paris to pursue a professional singing career. However, this plan was first derailed by her marriage to Jock and then by the outbreak of war.

Mary Louise talked to me about the "awful time" she experienced with her parents when they learnt of her pregnancy, and she said that the worst day of her life was the day she married Bob Hutchinson. She went on to summarize the unplanned encounter with Jock and its consequences as "a great shame; I had no choice; I had to get married. I had chances to marry nice people, but that was not to be."

At no time during the evening did I ask my mother why she had kept me at birth rather than have me adopted. I worried that this would upset her and would be insensitive to the many struggles that she had endured to raise me. However, it was clear throughout the conversation that abortion was not an option at the time. In contrast, it was also certain from her comments that if the same events had taken place under today's circumstances, I would not be here to write this book.

The following morning, she asked me how I felt. My emotions were under control despite the realization that I was fortunate to be alive. I was pleased that at least I knew about my father, and I was curious to investigate his background. I was shocked that I was born illegitimate and as a result of a rape; but on the other hand I felt very, very thankful that I had survived birth due to the courage of my mother. My mother painted a picture of the importance of my father that made me want to discover more about him as soon as I returned to San Francisco. We left her apartment, and she accompanied me on the Underground to Heathrow Airport. It was the last time I saw her alive. She died one year later.

Once I was back in San Francisco and had absorbed most of what I had been told, I thought I should inform my wife. However, before doing so, I thought I should check with my mother to be certain that she approved of my plan. Her e-mail reply said "No, John, I think you should not say anything at this point. One talks to another, and in no time it is in Yorkshire." To the very end my mother was ashamed of what happened to her and seems to have fought for and supported me as penance for her own perceived shortcomings.

My immediate private investigations on the Internet showed me that my father was not the important person that my mother thought him to be. Also, his son had not been a TV presenter as thought by Bob Hutchinson and my mother. In the 1950s Bob Hutchinson would instantly turn off the TV if he saw who he believed to be Jock's son presenting the news on a particular evening. The assumption was that the son was financially supporting his father and helping his father avoid making child support payments; none of this was true. I felt very disappointed by these findings and wanted to know more, since clearly my mother had not provided the full picture. But I obeyed my mother's wishes and took no further action at that time.

Following my mother's death, it was my opportunity to further investigate my roots and see what else I could discover. My father's real name was distinctive, so that gave me hope that I would discover additional information. I also told my wife about my conversation with my mother and what I was up to. She was surprised to hear so much so late in our marriage. However, her attention was on other matters. She had already begun her own fight with cancer, which ultimately took her life.

I tracked down the birth date of my father and then obtained a copy of his marriage certificate. With the help of Ancestry.com I also obtained a copy of my father's birth certificate. But it was far more difficult to track down the details of his children, and I could find no trace of a death certificate, either for him or for his wife. It was time to obtain help. So I advertised and received an offer from a genealogist living in England. I accepted the offer. I told her everything my mother had told me. She went to work.

A few weeks later she was beginning to have success. In October 2009 she reported back to me that she had discovered the marriage details of my grandparents, and from there she had been able to confirm the birth of my father and also the birth of his elder sister. She could trace his sister's marriage, the children who were born, and his sister's death, but it was difficult to track my father. All efforts to find a death certificate had been unsuccessful. She concluded that my father "either did not die in Britain or had died after 2005." From my father's marriage certificate, she was able to trace his two children; she could confirm their marriages and their children, but she could not discover any of their current whereabouts. It seemed that Jock's daughter had divorced and remarried, but she couldn't be certain. Ultimately, she traced a death certificate from 1993 that appeared to be my father's wife. We assumed that they had not divorced, and the address shown on the certificate was close to an address belonging to Jock's sister. It also showed that the person who had died was a widow, so we could assume that Jock was deceased.

We also checked with the UK Institute of Civil Engineers. They had no record of my father being a member in 1954 or thereafter and had no record of his qualifications. My mother had also mentioned that my father may have been a professor at Oxford University, but this information proved to be inaccurate. The breakthrough came when the genealogist received a copy of the death certificate for the person that she believed to be Jock's wife. It showed that the death had been reported by a man who possessed the same name as was shown on what we believed to be my father's daughter's second marriage certificate. Even more important, an address was given for the person who reported the death. It was now sixteen years later, but it was possible that the person still lived at that address. He did, and it was soon confirmed that his wife was indeed the daughter of Jock and Gwen. It was now for the genealogist to contact my half sister to see if she would communicate with me. Miraculously, she agreed. Much of what is in the novel concerning Jock McGregor comes from her memory.

Several lengthy e-mails were exchanged between me and my sister, and I was shocked and amazed as I learnt about the difficulties my father and his family experienced. The stories were unreal, the sort of stuff that people normally invent. It seemed as if my arrival in this world had dramatically affected the life of my father as well as that of my mother. The one overriding thought that kept returning to me time after time was the sense of appreciation for having been allowed to live.

In May 2010 I first visited my half sister at her home, and she helped me open up a whole new side to my life. She had worried about what type of person I might be. Her husband and eldest daughter had offered to be at the door with her just in case. She declined their offer. I equally was apprehensive over what I might find when I knocked on the door. In reality I discovered a wonderful and compassionate person, someone who you would be proud to call your sister.

On my mother's side I was the eldest child; on my father's side I was the youngest. I have continued regular contact with my sister and with her daughters and their families, and have also been introduced to more distant relatives. I am totally proud of my new family and am continuously amazed that I am still here on this planet. The two sides of my family are slowly coming together. My half brother and I have still to meet. He lives overseas and, to date, prefers not to revisit the past because of the bad memories it brings back and his apparent suspicion that I might be the cause. Hopefully, at some future date, we will meet.

Karen's father's passport and visas that allowed him reach Shanghai, China

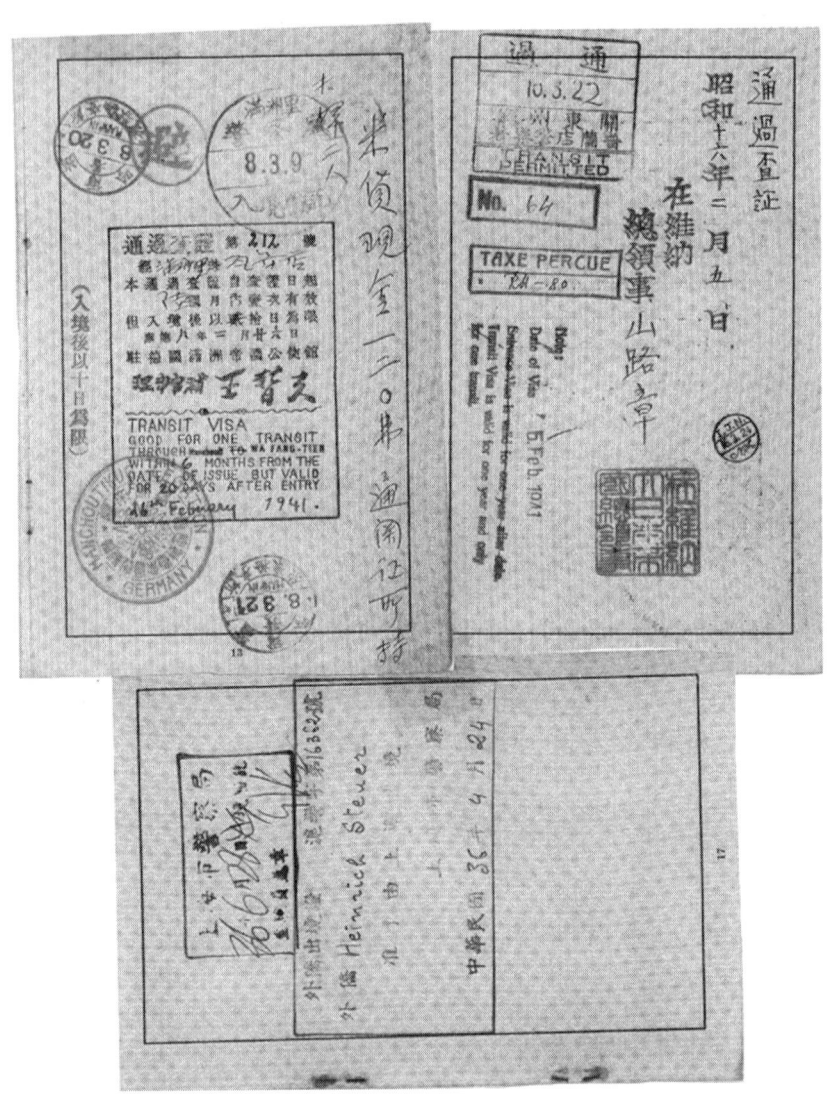

Karen's father's visas, including exit out of Shanghai